Legacy in Legend

Lost in Nowhere

Book Three

Barbara Pietron

Scribe Publishing Company
Pontiac, Michigan

Legacy in Legend
Lost in Nowhere
Book Three

Scribe Publishing Company
29488 Woodward, Ste. 426
Royal Oak, MI 48073

www.barbarapietron.com
Cover design by Hadrout Advertising + Technology
Interior design by Inanna Arthen
Interior illustrations by Allison Janicki

ISBN: 978-0-9916021-8-6

Library of Congress Control Number: 2020945218
Publisher's Cataloging-in-Publication data is available.

Printed in the U.S.

Also by Barbara Pietron

Legacy in Legend Series:
Heart of Ice
Thunderstone
Veiled Existence

Soulshifter

This one is for my sisters, Judy and Linda,
because they understand taking the road less traveled.

The Vrillier

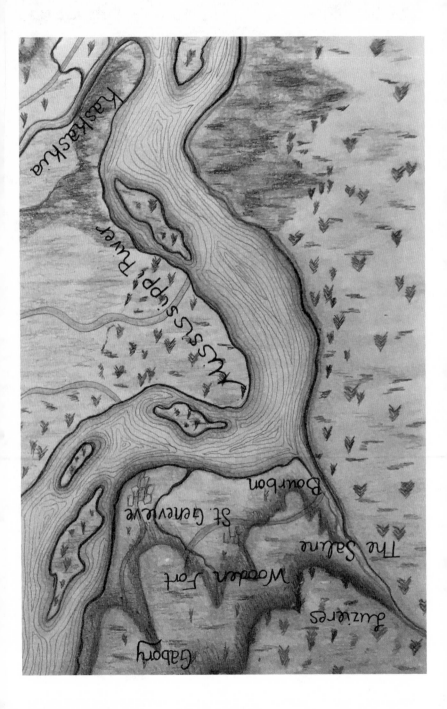

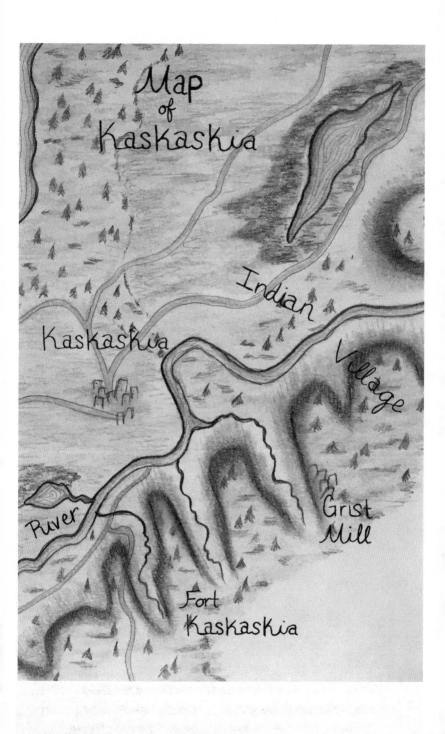

It isn't just cleverness you'll be needing now,
but discernment and good judgment too, and persuasiveness,
and perhaps even some courage.

The White Cat ~ Henri Pourrat

Chapter 1

*J*eni froze, her gaze fixed on a book title: *Myths and Legends of America's Heartland.* Her hesitation to pick the book up was unwarranted, and she knew it. She'd learned the hard way that she couldn't ignore what she was—what she'd started. After being burned twice by stories that shouldn't have been true, she'd be a fool not to learn if there were any threats in the immediate area.

She'd arrived with her parents last night to the row of cabins known as the River Aux Vases Resort just outside Ste. Genevieve, Missouri. The resort office was closed then—keys left in the cabin—and her mom had walked down to officially check in that morning. When she mentioned the office doubled as a gift shop, Jeni agreed they should go back together and take a look.

Daylight revealed that the office was actually a room attached to what Jeni assumed was the owner's residence. The dimly lit interior was rustic, but clean. Clothing filled the majority of the space—sweatshirts and T-shirts primarily, some hats and tank tops, even a few infant onesies. Aside from the rotating wire rack of books Jeni had been perusing, the remaining items were small, like beer cozies, keychains and bottle openers.

Filling her lungs with air, Jeni plucked the book from the rack and fanned the pages in search of a table of contents. Scanning the list of stories, the word "curse" nearly leapt off the page, making her heart stutter for a moment.

Not again, she thought. *Please, never again.*

Flipping to the correct page, Jeni found *The Curse of Kaskaskia* and began to read.

Marielle knew her love was forbidden.

Yet she could no more control her feelings than she could stem the flow of the mighty Mississippi River. So she held out hope.

She knew Papa loved her above all. And he was the only family Marielle had ever known. After her mother's death, Jean Bernard had taken his infant daughter from the cold, northern region of New France and settled much farther south, in the village of Kaskaskia.

Marielle's earliest memories were of animal fur. Sleek beaver pelts were by far the most sought after, but her father also traded the smaller soft furs of mink, marten, fox and otter. She grew up accustomed to rough men with long bushy beards and dirty clothes. The black-robed Jesuit missionaries and fierce-looking Indians she saw less regularly, although Papa had told her Kaskaskia was established by the missionaries to spread God's word to the Indians and they'd named the village after one of the local tribes.

As the town grew, so did her father's business; his trading post expanded to a general mercantile. Nearly a

Lost in Nowhere

woman by that time, Marielle was not sorry to leave behind the cleaning of animal hides for stocking shelves, helping customers and managing supplies that arrived by riverboat. But the highlight of her days became working with Amakapa, a young Indian man her father had hired to do menial work.

At first Marielle had hardly noticed the well-mannered, soft-spoken Indian. Then, one day, she asked Amakapa to move a crate for her. As she gazed into his gentle eyes—so deeply brown they were nearly black—Marielle became hopelessly smitten.

About the same time, her father came to recognize Amakapa's capabilities. Taught by the Jesuit priests, Amakapa spoke English and could read, write and do basic math. He was also baptized in the Christian church. Marielle realized Papa had grown fond of the young man when he gave Amakapa jobs he'd previously reserved for his white employees.

Observing this, Marielle allowed herself to hope that she might have a future with Amakapa. She knew an Indian man with a white woman was met with disapproval among the townsfolk—even though most accepted a white man with an Indian wife—but if papa gave his blessing, perhaps the town would accept their relationship.

With only rare, clandestine moments to spend together, Marielle and Amakapa awaited an opportune moment to make their plea to Jean Bernard.

Fate, however, never gave them that chance.

Arriving unexpectedly at the mercantile, Bernard discovered the lovers in a passionate embrace. Flying into a rage, he ignored Marielle's attempted explanation and immediately fired Amakapa, adding that he would spread *word about town making it impossible for the Indian man to find work. Then he threatened to kill Amakapa if he caught him with his daughter again.*

With no means of supporting himself, Amakapa was forced to leave Kaskaskia, but he managed to get a note to Marielle promising to return for her.

Marielle pretended to recover from her broken heart, while inside, she lived for the day she would see Amakapa again. When she had nearly given up hope, her love crept into town in disguise. That very night, Marielle and Amakapa fled.

Their freedom was short-lived. They were captured and taken back to Kaskaskia to face Jean Bernard's wrath. Marielle wailed in protest when Papa ordered his men to truss Amakapa to a log and set him adrift on the Mississippi River.

Although Marielle did not witness Amakapa's death, word spread. As the log swirled away from shore, Amakapa proclaimed that he and Marielle would be together forever in the afterlife and Jean Bernard would be dead within the coming year. Then he cursed all of Kaskaskia, saying the town would be destroyed, its churches and homes ruined and the dead would be disturbed from their graves.

The townsfolk gave Amakapa's words little thought until the foretold events began to take place. Heartsick at her father's cruelty, Marielle refused to eat. Although her father threatened and ultimately begged, she welcomed death so she could join Amakapa on the other side.

Incensed by his inability to prevent Marielle's self-imposed death, Bernard became crazed, turning his wrath on anyone and anything. Five months after burying his daughter, he accused a man of cheating him in a business deal. The man refused to concede, so Bernard challenged him to a duel. Jean Bernard lost the duel and died of the gunshot wound, fulfilling the second part of Amakapa's proclamation.

In time, the remainder of the curse came to pass. Though it had once been named the capital of the Illinois Territory, Kaskaskia lost the distinction as continual flooding battered the town. Eventually, the residents relocated Kaskaskia farther south. In the late 1800s, a great flood swept away all remnants of the original town, necessitating an emergency operation in which three thousand graves were exhumed and relocated atop a river bluff to the east.

The aftermath of the great flood left the relocated town of Kaskaskia severed from the state of Illinois. The Mississippi River, which once flowed west of the town, had shifted into the Kaskaskia River, to the east. Today, Kaskaskia is nearly a ghost town, with less than twenty residents and a mere scattering of buildings.

Jeni stared at the page for a moment. There was no monster or otherworldly creature to fear in this story, although it left her with a wistful sadness. She was lucky to live in a time where diverse couples weren't unusual.

"Are you interested in local lore?"

She fumbled the book, whirling to face the deep voice. "Uh, I…" She swallowed, her next words drying up on her tongue. A guy around her age regarded her; his raised eyebrows nearly eclipsed by the shock of straw-colored hair that fell across his forehead. His eyes were deep blue and a smile softened his square jaw. Broad shoulders and a narrow waist rounded out the stereotypical look of a high school football captain. "Yeah. I mean… it depends on the story, I guess," Jeni finally managed to say.

A blush heated her cheeks as she realized how stupid her answer sounded out loud, but he was gracious.

"I can understand that," he said, smile widening. "Some legends are just ridiculous."

"True." Jeni hitched her purse higher on her shoulder as she glanced across the room for her mom.

"Kaskaskia's close by if you're interested in seeing it."

When Jeni returned a blank look, he said, "The story you were just reading, wasn't it about Kaskaskia?"

"Oh… uh… right. Yes, it was." The blundering response lit Jeni's face aflame. "But… it said the town was in Illinois. I didn't expect it was around here."

"Sure is. Only about fifteen or twenty minutes away. I can give you directions. Or better, I'd be happy to take you out there."

His good looks were immediately negated by the creepiness of his overfriendly vibe. Spying her mom, Jeni took a step backward. "I should see if my mom is done."

He nodded, shifting on his feet. "Wow, sorry, that was awfully forward. It's just that I'm kind of a buff on this area's history—including the legends— and I can tend to get too enthusiastic about it." He sidestepped, putting more space between them. "You just let me know if you have any questions about the area. I can tell you what things are worth your time and what things are as pointless as a bucket under a bull. I'm Ansel, by the way. Me and my ma run the resort."

With a stiff bob of her head and no intention of sharing her name, Jeni stuffed the book back in the rack and then hustled toward her mom, perplexed by the warm feeling in the pit of her stomach. Had he been coming on to her? Or did he offer personal tours to everyone? And what was that comment about a bucket under a bull?

Her mom held up a shirt which had "Ste. Genevieve Est. 1735" printed on the front in distressed lettering. "Do you think this will fit Dad?"

Jeni sized up the shirt and then nodded. "Yeah. It looks like his style, too."

"You mean black with worn print?" Her mom chuckled. "That's what I thought, too." She draped the shirt over her arm and headed for the cash register.

To avoid further awkwardness, Jeni drifted to the rack of local attraction brochures near the door as her mom paid Ansel for the shirt. Although he'd been forward, Jeni blamed herself for the uncomfortable conversation. She'd never been great at talking to guys in the first place, but now that she was in a relationship—particularly a long-distance relationship—she wasn't sure of the proper protocol. At what point should she blurt out that she had a boyfriend? What if the guy was just being friendly and not coming on to her? Especially at school, she often felt like guys thought she was making up an excuse since they never saw her with a boyfriend.

Bright sun and warm air greeted them as they exited the store and Jeni pulled her sunglasses from her head to put them on. She noticed her mom had slowed while rummaging in her purse.

Recovering her phone, Jeni's mom read a text message. "It's Jessie," she reported. "She and Neil will be here in about ten minutes. Let's stop in and let the others know." She turned toward the first, and largest, log cabin in the row of four that made up the resort.

"Awkward" must've been the theme for Jeni's afternoon, because her cousin, Tyler—who had always treated Jeni like an annoying little sister—barely spared a glance at her as they entered the cabin. He was sitting on the couch with a pretty dark-haired girl snuggled under his arm.

Jeni's mom followed Tyler's mom into the kitchen area, while Jeni trailed behind since her cousin hadn't offered any introductions. She hadn't seen Tyler since the riverboat cruise last fall, which had left their relationship on a tenuous note. She had no idea what to say to him, especially since he had a girl with him.

"Hey, is that a *Second Star to the Right* shirt?" an unfamiliar feminine voice inquired.

Jeni jerked her chin up, turning toward the couple on the couch. She ignored her cousin's displeased glare. "Uh… yeah." She straightened, smoothing the wrinkles from her shirt. "They're my favorite band."

Eyes animated, the girl replied, "I love them, too." Her straight, shiny hair brushed along her jawline as she nodded. "I'm Mandy."

With the issue forced, Tyler spoke up. "This is my cousin, Jeni."

"Nice to meet you, Jeni." The corners of Mandy's

a derisive snort that only she could hear, Jeni cranked the window half-shut.

"Are you related to Mandy or Tyler?" Ansel asked.

The question took her by surprise until Jeni realized Ansel had checked them in at the resort office. He would know that a family group had booked the cabins. "Tyler is my cousin," she answered, giving him credit for not making an assumption based on Mandy's darker skin.

The mention of her cousin's name renewed her anger. Not only was it his fault she was in this car, it was also his fault she was in the front seat with Ansel. This might possibly be the first time she'd gone anywhere with Tyler where he willingly chose the back seat. Now, instead of chatting with Mandy, she was forced to make small talk with an unnervingly attractive guy.

She should just enjoy it, part of her brain argued. It wasn't as if she were doing anything wrong. She wasn't even touching him. (Unlike Ice, who *was* touching the girl in that picture.)

Immediately her thoughts retorted that she wasn't being fair; she'd noticed the tense set to Ice's face in the photo and how his pasted-on smile didn't reach his eyes. The close embrace had clearly taken him by surprise.

The mental diatribe went on and on, torturing Jeni with mixed emotions.

Ansel eased up on the accelerator as they entered a residential area. Mandy sat forward. "Are we in St. Mary?"

"Not yet, but we're close."

"Is it on the Mississippi River?" Jeni piped up suddenly, struck with a jolt of alarm. She should've asked that question *before* agreeing to the ride.

"Not anymore," Ansel said.

Mandy stretched so her head was over the seat back. "Did you say, 'not anymore'?"

Glancing in his rearview mirror, Ansel nodded. "Back before the floods, the town was established by August Sainte Marie. Folks called it Sainte Marie's Landing on account of it being right there on the river. 'Bout thirty years later another guy bought the land and laid out the lots and streets, thinking it would become a great river port."

Jeni looked out the window as she listened. They were passing a place called Bader's Garage; next to it was a bank, and then a bar—Bader's Place—and she wondered if the name Bader would enter into Ansel's account.

"Fast-forward forty years," he continued. "St. Mary was on its way to becoming a thriving port town, 'cept this area was heavily deforested to feed the steamboats. Erosion made the river wider and shallower and more likely to flood. Ste. Genevieve and many other towns around here were moved to higher ground. Then there was a huge flood in 1881 and when it was over, the Mississippi River had changed its course."

"Wait." Jeni turned in her seat to read a sign as they rolled past. "Did that sign say 'Kaskaskia'?"

"Yeah. Told you it was close by," Ansel confirmed. "That same flood is the one that wiped out most of Kaskaskia and cut it off from the rest of

Lost in Nowhere

Illinois. If you believe the legend, the devastation of Kaskaskia was a result of a Native American's curse." He shot Jeni a quick smile, then flicked his turn signal and made a right turn. A few minutes later he pointed through the windshield. "This is what brings most people to St. Mary these days: an antique mall."

Jeni contemplated the long, low building, wondering if it was on her mom's or any of her aunts' list of things to do while they were in the area. Two right turns later Ansel announced, "This is Eighth Street."

"My mom sent me a picture of an old photo of my Grandma's house." Mandy passed her phone to Jeni.

The black-and-white photo showed a small house with a dirt driveway and scrubby grass. Ansel rested his foot on the brake and Jeni handed him the phone. "No house numbers," he commented, returning the phone to Mandy. "Even though the town is no longer on the river, it still floods here on occasion. No telling what was damaged and then demolished."

Although none of the houses on Eighth Street resembled the photo, Ansel pulled to the side of the street so Mandy could get out and snap a few pictures for her mom. When Tyler followed his girlfriend, Jeni quickly exited the car so she wouldn't be alone with Ansel.

Tyler sidled up to her. "Legend? Curse?" The words were rife with sarcasm. "I hope you're not going to cause any trouble this time."

As much as Jeni wanted to retort that *she* hadn't been the cause of the misfortune on past trips, she knew it wasn't true. Sure, she hadn't asked for trouble, certainly hadn't sought it out, but she knew she ultimately was the reason why bad things kept happening. She was in the crosshairs of some kind of evil related to the Mississippi River and, unfortunately, the river was the backbone of these intermittent family gatherings. "The idea is to be proactive and avoid anything before it happens," she hissed.

Tyler snorted. "Well, keep me out of it."

"Gladly." Jeni stalked away and snapped a picture of something… anything.

On the way out of town, the sight of Bader's Place and Bader's Garage eased some of the tension between Jeni's shoulders. They would soon be back at the resort. She checked the time on her phone, wondering if Ice was finished showing Wenonah the campus. The initial surge of jealousy was now more of a dull irritation. She saw no point in sending a text. She wanted to talk to Ice.

Ansel made a right turn, breaking into Jeni's thoughts. They'd been on the River Road. It should have been a straight shot back. Her spine stiffened and she swiveled her head side to side as they crossed a bridge.

A sign was posted on the bridge rail and before she could speak up, Tyler's voice came from the back seat. "Illinois State Line?"

Ansel nodded. "This bridge crosses what used to be the Mississippi River. It's not much more than a creek nowadays. The bed even dries up sometimes after a long hot spell." He looked at Jeni. "I thought you might be interested to see Kaskaskia, since we're right here. It's nearly a ghost town; there's a church, a few houses and farms… oh, and the Liberty Bell of the West. You don't want to miss that!" He chuckled.

For a moment, Jeni felt as though the wind had been knocked out of her. She most definitely did not want to visit a cursed town. Heart hammering, she was unable to draw air into her lungs. Speech was impossible. Forcing tiny breaths while her mind raced, she searched for a viable reason why they needed to turn around and get back to the resort.

Then she breathed a little easier as she recalled Ansel's explanation that clearing trees from the forest had caused erosion and then flooding. The legend she'd read in that book was simply someone's fabricated explanation for why the town had perished. Her face twisted into a sour expression. Of course whoever made it up had blamed the Native American boy in the story. Wasn't it just as likely the French girl would curse the town and her father for killing her love?

Story or not, Jeni resolved not to leave the car when they arrived at the ill-fated town.

Seemingly endless brown and green fields flanked both sides of the road. Ahead, a sign stated: "Village of Kaskaskia. Pop. 18," and beyond it, Jeni spotted a figure out in the fields. It appeared to be a woman wearing a dress. "Hey, is that—"

Ansel cut her off, braking abruptly. His eyes darted between the road and the rearview mirror. "Is everything okay?" he asked as he pulled to the side of the road.

Jeni twisted in her seat to find Mandy frantically digging in her purse, movements jerky and eyelids fluttering.

Creases lined Tyler's forehead. "Hang on," he said. "I got it." One of his hands was on Mandy's shoulder trying to still her while the other burrowed into his pocket.

"What's going on?" Jeni asked, releasing her seatbelt so she could kneel on the seat.

Tyler produced a roll of Lifesavers and tore one from the package, popping it into Mandy's mouth. She crunched it up as he thumbed another from the roll, holding it out to Mandy until she finished the first and opened her mouth.

"Is she diabetic?" Jeni guessed, meeting Tyler's eyes.

He nodded.

Jeni braced herself as Ansel swung the car around. "Do you need more candy?" she asked. "I think I have some Mentos."

Mandy shook her head, looking visibly calmer, one hand clasped on Tyler's knee. "I'll be fine." She accepted a third Lifesaver and placed it on her tongue, this time letting it dissolve instead of chewing it.

Tyler put an arm around her shoulders, running his fingers along her cheek as he murmured something Jeni couldn't hear.

Obviously, he had the situation under control, so Jeni turned to face the front and buckled her belt, trying to come to grips with this new Tyler who carried a roll of Lifesavers for his diabetic girlfriend.

As they crossed the bridge over the old Mississippi, she sighed, hoping Mandy would be all right, and relieved that their trip to the "ghost town" had been interrupted.

I am the mortal enemy of your family, my pet.
All the world hates me and I hate all the world.
I shall follow you now for the rest of
your life, wherever you go.

The Little Grey Mouse ~ Comtesse de Ségur

Chapter 2

*H*is plane just landed," Jeni announced.

"Perfect," her mom replied. "I think we're only a couple miles from the airport exit."

Picking up her mom's phone, Jeni checked the ETA on the map program and sent a text to Ice with the information.

Helping her mom follow the arrows indicating the passenger pick-up zone, they maneuvered around cars, taxis and shuttle buses, finally making it to the curb. "Do you know if he's reached the baggage claim?" her mom asked.

"I'm not sure." Jeni started to type on her phone.

A security officer blowing a whistle and gesturing to cars was headed in their direction. "Loading or unloading only!" he shouted.

"Why don't you hop out and meet him at baggage claim? I'll make a loop."

Jeni opened her mouth to protest and then closed it.

The officer pointed at their car and the whistle shrilled loudly.

Jeni released her belt. "I'll let you know what's happening," she said, swinging the door open. Then she was surrounded by a bustling crowd and her mom's taillights merged with the traffic.

She should have jumped at the chance to go meet Ice. In a long-distance relationship, every minute was precious. But the prospect of confrontation was eating away at her.

A little while after they'd returned from the drive to St. Mary, Jeni had received a text from Ice letting her know that the tour was over and he was heading for the airport. She would've liked to call him then, but she'd been helping her Dad with dinner—dinner that was early because they had to pick up Ice from the airport—so she could hardly just walk off and make a phone call. So she'd simply responded with *"Looks like you guys had fun"*. She hadn't used an exclamation point, an emoji, a punctuation smile or even a period.

Ice knew her well. When he'd had a chance to respond to her text, he was in the airport. His text said: *"Fun isn't the word I'd use. Sorry about the picture Wenonah posted. I had no idea she did that. I untagged myself. They're getting ready to board but we might be able to talk for a few minutes."*

Jeni debated. Would a few minutes make a difference when they'd actually be together in a couple of hours? The flight from Minneapolis to St. Louis took nearly the same time as the drive from Ste. Genevieve to the airport, so Jeni and her mom were getting ready to leave, anyway. What really mattered was that Ice hadn't known the picture was out there. And he apologized. Jeni told him they could talk later. And she used a heart emoji.

Now nerves were edging out her excitement as she dodged people to make her way to the list of flights. Did she need to mention the drive to St. Mary? It really wasn't a big deal, after all.

Approaching the flat screen of ever-changing arrivals and departures, Jeni found Ice's flight and corresponding baggage carousel number. Passengers were gathered around it, although the conveyor was still. Her eyes scanned the crowd for Ice's black hair. A hand in the air drew her attention, and then she caught a glimpse of bright blue eyes and a wide smile.

Anxiety momentarily forgotten, she ran to him, circling her arms around his waist as he folded her into a tight hug. She raised her chin, meeting his gaze briefly before their lips met and her eyes closed. Steeling herself for the mental images caused by their skin-to-skin contact, she relaxed when her mind stayed clear. Anticipating their embrace, Ice had already adjusted his inner balance to prevent the visions.

"God, I missed you," he murmured into her hair. "I'm sorry I couldn't get here yesterday."

"Me too. But you're here now," Jeni whispered back.

Loosening his hold so he could look her in the eyes, Ice said, "Sorry again about the picture."

Jeni shrugged. "It's all right. The worst part was that Tyler saw it before I did."

"Oh." Ice grimaced. "Now I'm even more sorry."

Eager to shed her unsettled feelings, Jeni drew a breath to spill out the details of the drive with Ansel but a thud followed by a low electric hum interrupted her, and people surged past to the edge of the conveyor, which was now moving. Ice looked over his shoulder.

"Go ahead." Jeni unzipped her purse. "I'll let my mom know to look for us in a few minutes." She would definitely tell him as soon as she got the chance.

When she looked up from her phone, Ice was hauling a rolling duffel bag from the moving belt. Extending the handle, he strode in her direction. She fell into step beside him and he slipped his free arm behind her, his hand resting lightly at the small of her back.

A smile played on Jeni's lips as she reveled in asserting their relationship in public. More often than she'd like to admit, she'd watch enviously as couples strolled the school hallways joined at the hip.

As they stood on the curb watching oncoming traffic, the urgency to tell Ice about the drive simmered in the back of her mind. She regretted not blurting it out earlier when she had the chance. It wouldn't have hurt for Ice's duffel to ride the circuit one time. Now she didn't want to start telling him and have her mom arrive in the middle of her explanation.

Her decision proved sound as her mom's car appeared in the throng of vehicles.

"Nice timing," she said, sliding into the back seat. "We just walked out."

Lost in Nowhere

A moment later, the trunk lid thumped and then Ice joined her. "Hello, Mrs. Stonewall. Thanks for picking me up."

"Hi, Ice. Glad you could make it." Her eyes were on the rearview mirror as she inched ahead.

Jeni twisted in her seat, evaluating the mass of cars and shuttles. "You're clear." As her mom accelerated into traffic, Jeni turned to Ice. "Tyler brought a girl with him and, get this, he seems to actually be nice to her."

"Is it Mandy?" Ice asked, his eyes twinkling.

Jeni leaned forward and rotated to look Ice full in the face. "Just how good of friends are you guys online?" She didn't like feeling as if her cousin and boyfriend knew more about each other than Jeni did.

Ice chuckled. "It's not like we talk. He's been posting pictures of her for a few months now."

Months? Jeni narrowed her eyes thoughtfully. She hadn't connected with her cousin online because she didn't want him in her business or making stupid comments that all her friends could see.

"So?" Ice rested his hand on her leg. "What do you think of her?"

"I haven't had a chance to talk to her much." The last few words took on a bitter edge as Jeni remembered how she'd been forced to sit in the front seat with Ansel. Then she brightened. "But she is a fan of *Second Star to the Right* so she can't be all bad."

Ice laughed out loud and Jeni caught her mom's smile in the rearview mirror. "She's also diabetic. Did you know that, Mom?"

"Actually, yes. I guess she was diagnosed just a couple of months ago and is still getting used to regulating her blood glucose. Her parents weren't sure she should come on the trip, but apparently Tyler won them over."

"Well, he certainly is prepared." Jeni told them about Mandy's low blood sugar reaction and Tyler's quick response.

Her mom smiled. "Apparently he has an entire case of Lifesavers. His mom also told me that after Mandy's diagnosis, he stopped seeing other girls."

"That is so opposite of what I would have expected." Jeni scooted a little closer to Ice so she could rest her head on his shoulder.

Her mom asked Ice about his classes and final exams while Jeni half-dozed. A change in the car's motion roused her and she lifted her head, realizing they'd exited the highway. "Wait. Is this the Ste. Genevieve exit?"

"Yeah," her mom replied.

Jeni looked at Ice. "I fell asleep? I'm sorry."

"It's all right," Ice said. "I was beginning to nod off myself. I've been up since six."

The crunch of gravel under the tires seemed extra loud in the still of the night as the car climbed the hill to the resort. Jeni tried unsuccessfully to stifle a yawn as they rolled past the other cabins to the last one in the row. Once parked, Mrs. Stonewall popped the trunk open and then headed for the cabin. "I'll see if Dad left the door unlocked," she said over her shoulder.

Shivering, Jeni shouldered Ice's backpack and then rubbed her arms as she waited for him to get his duffel from the trunk. The floodlight on the cabin picked up the blue highlights in his black hair—one of Jeni's favorite features. Although as he bent down and hoisted the bag from the trunk, she couldn't help but appreciate the bulge of muscle in his shoulders and the way his T-shirt clung to his back and chest while hanging loosely over his flat stomach.

She'd noticed in the airport that the advent of summer was already darkening his copper skin to a bronze hue. A secret smile played on her lips as she mused over how she could identify with the French girl in the legend who fell for the Native American boy.

As he reached to pull the trunk shut, movement drew Jeni's attention down the road along the row of log structures. A figure stood near the biggest cabin, apparently having heard them come in. She couldn't tell who it was at this distance but guessed it might be Tyler's mom, wearing a nightgown. She lifted her hand in greeting.

"Are you waving?" Ice asked, fixing her with a perplexed stare.

"Yeah, I think it's Aunt Andrea, Tyler's mom. Or maybe Aunt Jessie." She giggled. "Unless one of the guys wears a nightshirt."

"I must've missed whoever it was," Ice said, peering down the road.

Jeni glanced at Ice to confirm he was looking in the right direction. When she turned back, the road was empty. "Well, she's gone now. Let's head inside." Her words were nonchalant, but cold fingers danced down her spine, spurring her on to the cabin door.

The resort was fairly new compared to the

history of the region, probably built in the seventies or eighties. The main entrance to the Stonewall's cabin led into the living room, which was open to the dining area on the left. An entryway beyond led to the kitchen. To the right were two bedrooms with a bathroom sandwiched between them. Across the room, a sliding glass door opened to a patio.

The walls, peaked ceiling and floor were all made of wood. Outside, the logs were rounded, but inside, the wood was flat and sanded smooth. Natural grain and knots completed the atmosphere of rustic charm.

A sofa bed partitioned the chunky wood dinette set from the living room and two puffy armchairs with a table between them populated the wall next to the front door. A wooden rocker with patterned cushions tied to the seat and back flanked the far end of the sofa bed, and a classic combination floor lamp/table stood next to it. The furniture was the sort often obtained at garage sales, or from someone who'd redecorated, but it was clean and in good condition

When Jeni and Ice walked in, the coffee table had been moved in front of the sliding glass door and the sofa bed—Ice's bed for the week—was unfolded, Mrs. Stonewall stretching a bottom sheet over the mattress. "I know you guys were falling asleep in the car, so I thought I'd get this underway," she explained.

Jeni told Ice he could put his duffel in her room and then grabbed a corner of the sheet and fitted it onto the mattress. When the bed was made, Jeni's mom left them alone.

Ice sat on the bed and gave a little bounce,

pushing his hand into the mattress. "It'll do," he said with a smile.

Jeni perched on the edge of one of the puffy chairs facing him. "Looks like we're not going to have any time to ourselves tonight," she muttered, feeling oddly uneasy. It had to be that stupid drive with Ansel. Her guilt was festering like a splinter under the skin. "Hey, listen—"

"Are you two ready to hit the hay?" Jeni's mom entered the room.

"I just need my shorts." Ice rose and headed for his bag in Jeni's room.

Jeni stood and her mom pecked her cheek. "Good night, honey. Sleep well."

"Night, Mom." Jeni watched as her mom went into the bathroom, leaving the door open while she brushed her teeth.

When Ice returned, she said in a low voice, "I have a feeling she's going to find things to do until we're both in bed."

"That's not going to stop me from kissing you good night," he whispered.

Jeni moved closer, resting her hands on his waist. "Good." She kept one ear tuned to the bathroom as they pulled off a fairly long goodnight kiss.

It wasn't until she was in bed that she realized more than just the drive was bothering her. The figure she'd seen in the road—the one she thought was one of her aunts—had her disconcerted. The sense of familiarity hadn't been like recognizing someone she knew; it had been more like déjà vu. Had she dreamed the experience before tonight?

The more she thought about it, the more it disturbed her. Then realization dawned, raising the hair on the back of her neck.

The figure on the road had looked an awful lot like the woman she'd seen standing in the field in Kaskaskia.

The mattress shifted and the bed frame creaked, disturbing Ice's deep slumber. A warm body pushed up next to him and then Jeni's fruity scent reached his nostrils, turning the corners of his mouth up. He opened his eyes lazily.

"Hey," Jeni said softly. Her sleepy expression complemented her mussed hair and lack of makeup.

"Morning." He strained his ears for other sounds of habitation in the small cabin. "Uh, not that I'm complaining, but I got the impression this kind of thing was strongly discouraged."

"My mom went down to the big cabin to help with breakfast. We're having a group breakfast since it's the first day everyone is here. My dad's in the bathroom, which gives us seven to twelve minutes of snuggle time."

Ice rolled to his side, reaching an arm out from under the covers to pull her closer.

When they were face to face, she said, "I have something to tell you."

"Okay." The tense set to her brow stirred an ember of unease in his gut. His concern quickly dissipated though, as she relayed the story of the countryside tour she'd taken with Tyler, Mandy and the resort owner's son, Ansel. When she was finished, Ice said, "That was worrying you?"

She nodded, looking down. "I feel guilty."

"About what? Did you leave something out?"

Her eyes met his. "The only reason I went with them was because of that photo Wenonah posted. I was so mad after Tyler showed it to me."

Ice began to get the picture. "So this guy, Ansel, was he hitting on you?"

Jeni scrunched her nose. "I don't know. He was friendly. But he was friendly to Tyler and Mandy, too." She huffed. "I'm never entirely sure about stuff like that."

Ice snorted, and then laughed outright at Jeni's surprised expression. "When you look like you do, you should always assume a guy is hitting on you." Then, more seriously, "This kind of stuff is going to happen. I mean, we're in a long-distance relationship. I can't be with you all the time. Or even most of the time." He brushed the hair away from her face, careful not to touch her skin. "We just have to trust each other."

"I do trust you, Ice. And I want to be trust-worthy. That's why I feel so bad. I shouldn't have let Tyler get under my skin."

"And I shouldn't have let Wenonah hang all over me in a picture." He held her gaze. "How about we call it even and move on?"

Jeni's first smile of the morning was like the sun breaking through clouds. "Yes." Her body relaxed, sinking a little deeper into the mattress.

Finally, Ice allowed himself to consider her soft curves, running his hand down her side and across her lower back to snug her firmly against him. When she emitted the tiniest of moans, it was enough to accelerate his base instincts and blot out the shaman link that caused her visions. With skin to skin contact a go, he stretched his neck and Jeni did the same, meeting his lips with hers.

They lingered there for a long moment and then Jeni tucked her head under his chin, hugging him close. "I love you," she whispered.

"I love you, too."

A metallic squeal sounded from the bathroom, the protesting faucet handle signaling the end of Mr. Stonewall's shower. With a wistful sigh, Jeni said, "I should probably go make coffee."

"I should probably think about baseball for a few minutes."

Jeni pulled away, giggling, and scooted to the edge of the bed. Before standing, she glanced over her shoulder with a wicked grin. "How about those Twins?"

For a long moment, Ice focused on the buzz of a razor coming from the bathroom and then reached for his track pants, pulling them on over his shorts. He was sliding the folded mattress back into the sofa when Mr. Stonewall emerged from the bathroom.

"Coffee's almost done," Jeni said, poking her head out of the kitchen.

"I could use some," her dad said. "But we'll have to take it with us. Your mom just texted and asked us to bring another dozen eggs."

Lost in Nowhere

Jeni looked at Ice. "I guess that means no showers for us before breakfast."

Five minutes later, Ice and Jeni trailed behind her dad on the way to the big cabin. The sun had yet to warm the coolness that settled in overnight, making the hot coffee Ice carried even more appealing.

"You didn't see anyone on the road last night?" Jeni asked, seemingly out of nowhere. Ice noticed she had both hands wrapped around her mug.

"What?" Shooting her a quick sidelong glance, Ice returned his attention to his coffee. He was trying not to slosh the hot liquid out of the mug as he walked. "Oh, when we got here? No."

She was quiet for a moment. "This is probably dumb, but I saw a woman or girl, or whatever, in a field yesterday. It struck me as odd because she was wearing a dress. I mean, I know maxi dresses are a thing, but that's not what it looked like."

Ice didn't comment, sensing Jeni wasn't finished.

"And then the person on the road," she continued. "At first I assumed it was someone in a nightgown, but the more I thought about it, the more it seemed similar to what I'd seen earlier. Now, I just don't know. It was probably my overtired imagination."

"Are you saying it looked like the same woman?" Ice asked.

"Yeah… no… I don't know." She uttered a dry laugh. "I think I'm just skittish because of the last trip."

Ice stopped walking, waiting until Jeni turned to face him. "After the last *two* trips, you would be

41

foolish not to be suspicious of anything out of the ordinary. If something makes you feel uncomfortable, it deserves a second look."

"I know." She nodded. "I know you're right. I just don't want to be paranoid all the time." She glanced to her dad—who'd nearly reached their destination—and they resumed walking. "I prodded my mom to book this resort because it wasn't close to the river. I'd love to believe we can actually have a vacation for a change."

"That would be nice." Although his statement was sincere, Ice's medicine man intuition was already on high alert and he could tell it would remain that way for the duration of the trip.

The kitchen, dining area and living room was a large open space in the big cabin, but chaos still reigned as people were assigned duties or got out of the way. As Ice attempted to help Jeni stack up plates, silverware and napkins at the end of the kitchen island, he was interrupted with greetings from various family members.

Mandy introduced herself while Tyler did little more than make eye contact and lift his chin in Ice's direction. Ice wasn't sure if Jeni noticed, but Tyler observed Jeni and Ice sitting at the large kitchen table and then herded Mandy to the table outside.

Jeni had told Ice that she wanted to start a conversation about their family history while everyone was together, yet it was Mrs. Stonewall who brought up the subject first. "If any of you have information on Dad's side of the family, be sure to let Jeni know."

"Are you getting into genealogy?" Tyler's mom

asked, spooning a minuscule amount of eggs onto her granddaughter's plate.

"Not exactly," Jeni answered carefully. "I heard that there could be a big family history project in my biology class next year, so I figured it made sense to ask questions while I'm here with everybody."

She went on to explain that the holes in her genealogy research were on her Grandpa Chris's side of the family. In truth, Ice knew that the other branches of her family tree had received only cursory investigation. After all, it had been her Grandpa Chris's ashes that were spread in the Mississippi Headwaters—the trip where Jeni had accidentally freed the underwater monster, met Ice and discovered her inherited link to the spirit world. Later that year, she found her grandpa's collection of newspaper articles about floods, drownings and rescues on the Mississippi River. Both Jeni and Ice were convinced that the source of her spiritual ability was buried somewhere in her maternal grandfather's ancestry.

And the only way for her to learn how to control and use her inherited gift was to discover its origins.

Jeni looked across the table. "By the way, Aunt Jessie, I've been through the genealogy folder we found in Grandpa's apartment and I brought it for you."

"Thanks. I did want to look at it," Jessie said. "When I did *my* genealogy report in high school—we won't talk about how many years ago that was," she shot her boyfriend, Neil, a warning glare, "information was limited for that side of the family.

Dad—Grandpa Chris—always said it was because of the records destroyed in the massive fires they had in New Orleans back in the day. Now, with all the information sharing on the Internet, I was curious if he'd gotten anywhere."

"I don't think so," Jeni replied. "At least, not according to the stuff he had in that folder."

"Have you talked to Grandma Marie?" Tyler's dad spoke up, referencing Grandpa Chris's mother. He looked at his wife. "Didn't she say something about her brother working on a family tree?"

Tyler's mom pursed her lips. "Uncle Georges? I don't remember. But she is our oldest living relative on that side of the family."

"Wouldn't Grandpa Chris have asked her first? Before looking on the Internet?" Jeni asked. "She's his mom."

"You'd think," Jeni's mom said. "But it still might be worth finding out if Uncle Georges was working on the family history. And if Grandpa Chris had that information."

The conversation fell off after that, turning to the various local attractions people were interested in seeing.

As Jeni and Ice headed back to their cabin, Ice asked, "Have you considered calling your great-grandma?"

She shrugged. "I thought about it. But I figured Grandpa Chris would've already done that. I assumed anything she knows would've been in that folder."

"I don't know," Ice said. "I wouldn't make that

assumption. Maybe your grandma never saw the alleged information her brother had."

"True. I suppose it couldn't hurt to ask."

They walked in silence for another minute and then Ice said, "It sounded like we don't have any plans for today. Do you want to get online and try some of the tips I got from Mr. Hilstrand?" When he'd registered for the upcoming fall semester, Ice discovered that one of the professors at the university specialized in genealogy. Before leaving school for the summer, he'd tracked the teacher down and mentioned that his girlfriend could use some help researching her ancestry.

"Definitely." Jeni got out her phone as they entered the cabin. "I took pictures of the family history stuff that was in the folder I gave to Aunt Jessie," she explained as she tapped the screen. Ice leaned close to look as she pointed. "Grandpa's information ends at Grandma Marie's parents."

She left her phone with him while she took a quick shower. Ice typed in the names of Jeni's great-grandma's grandparents using the information from the teacher. He was scrolling through the results of his inquiry when Jeni emerged from the bathroom with a towel on her head. She stopped to look over his shoulder bringing an alluring cloud of scents with her.

"Unfortunately," Ice said, "There are *pages* of the names you gave me. Mr. Hilstrand's tricks only went so far. We'll need more information to narrow it down."

"Figures." Jeni straightened. "You might as well

go ahead and shower while I finish getting ready."

"Okay," Ice responded absently as he had another thought. Turning back to the keyboard, he typed "New Orleans fire" into the search box. After perusing a couple of the articles that came up, he returned to the photographed pages on Jeni's phone. The hollow drone of her hair dryer faded into the background as he began to mentally add and subtract dates.

"Have you even moved yet?" Jeni asked from the doorway of her room.

"Uh… no." He shot her a perplexed glance and motioned her over.

"What?" Jeni peered at his computer screen.

"Grandma Marie's grandparents were born in the 1880s. Their parents would've probably been born in the 1850s or 1860s, right?" Ice said slowly.

"I guess." Jeni was skimming the article on his screen.

"The biggest fire in New Orleans happened in 1788. There was another in 1794."

He watched her face as confusion morphed into understanding.

"The records we're looking for wouldn't have been destroyed in either of those fires," Ice said.

Dressed in shorts and a tank top with a flannel shirt tied around her waist, Jeni entered the empty living room. As she gathered dirty glasses from the coffee table, voices floated in through the sliding screen door and Jeni glanced out to see her mom and Aunt Jessie on the patio. Curbing the impulse to stop and divulge what Ice had discovered about the dates of the New Orleans fires, she continued to the kitchen, assuming he'd like to be in on the conversation. The news could wait until he'd finished his shower.

It seemed crazy to think that no one had discovered the inconsistency before. Though perhaps her great-grandma's brother had. But wouldn't he have discussed it with his sister? Or maybe the question was *why* wouldn't he have discussed it with her? And what happened to the information if he did have it? Was it thrown away when he died? Or were the answers she needed packed away in a box in her great-grandma's attic?

Ice stepped out of the bathroom just as she re-entered the living room. Jeni paused, hands resting on her hips as she took in his wet hair, slicked away from his face. "You look so different." She reached behind his head, wrapping her fingers around his damp hair. "Do you ever wear it like this? Pulled back?"

He shook his head. "It's not really long enough. The short ponytail just looks dumb."

"Well you could definitely pull it off." Jeni raised an appreciative eyebrow.

Ice hid a lop-sided grin as he bent to tuck a roll of clothes into his bag.

"Aunt Jessie's on the patio with my mom. Let's tell them what you found."

Mrs. Stonewall looked up as Jeni stepped out the door, Ice behind her. "What're you two up to today?"

"We were looking into the genealogy stuff after the conversation at breakfast. Guess what Ice just figured out?"

"What?"

"The New Orleans fires aren't the reason for the gap in our family history."

Jessie frowned. "What do you mean?"

"There were two major fires," Ice explained. "The worst one happened in 1788. The other was in 1794. The family history falls off in the 1880s—nearly a hundred years *after* the fires."

"Seriously?" Mrs. Stonewall looked at her sister. "Why have we always been told that?"

"Beats me." Jessie shrugged. Then her eyes narrowed. "Although I did find it odd that even though Dad was researching the family history, he never really wanted to talk about it. He'd cut off conversations about certain relatives and always had excuses for not visiting certain places. I always felt like there was some kind of family secret he wanted to hide. Like an illicit affair." She wiggled her eyebrows mockingly.

"I figured there was some family feud he didn't want us kids to know about," Jeni's mom said blandly. "But you're right about the places. He loved to travel—I mean, he more or less went around the world after he retired. And when we were kids, we'd go on epic National Lampoon style road trips; east coast, west coast, Texas, Florida... but it was like he shunned the Midwest."

From the corner of her eye Jeni noticed Ice stiffen, but when she shifted her gaze to him, he shook his head subtly. "All I knew was that he never went to New Orleans to visit Grandma Marie," Jeni chimed in. "He always flew her to Michigan. I assumed it was too humid or just too loud there. He always liked things quiet."

Her mom smiled. "Grandpa was a unique individual with strong opinions about certain things." She looked at Jessie. "Remember the Ouija board?"

"How could I forget?" Aunt Jessie said. "He was so pissed." She turned to Jeni and Ice. "Not only did we get grounded, but he took the board and we never saw it again."

"And it wasn't even ours!" Jeni's mom exclaimed. "It was Trisha's!"

Eyebrows raised, Ice interjected. "Did you actually contact spirits?" He delivered the question with amusement, but Jeni knew he seriously wanted an answer as much as she did.

Jessie shrugged, meeting her sister's eyes. When Jeni's mom didn't speak up, she said, "I thought so at the time. But there's always the chance that someone was pushing the... that disc we put our fingers on. What was it called?"

Mrs. Stonewall wrinkled her brow in thought. "Was it a planette? Or planket? Something like that."

"Right," Jessie snapped her fingers. "Was that the sleepover where we fell asleep with the candle burning, too?"

As Jeni's mom started to reply, her phone rang. She turned it over and lifted it from the table, her eyebrows riding high as she read the display. "It's Grandma Marie," she muttered before answering. "Hi, Grandma."

When it had seemed like her mom and Aunt Jessie were about to launch into a "remember when" session, Jeni intended to excuse herself and Ice, but now she remained rooted to the spot, curious about the call. She exchanged a look with Ice, who seemed equally interested.

"We're in Missouri, Grandma." A pause. "Yes, all of us kids and our families." She locked eyes with her sister and shook her head. "I know you do, but everything's fine, I promise. There's nothing to worry about." After a few more seconds, she said, "Yes. We'll be careful." Then her eyes shifted to Jeni. "Hey, listen Grandma, Jeni's here and she has some questions for you."

Jeni gaped at her mom. She wanted to talk to her great-grandma, but not at this moment. Not without preparation.

"Yep. Okay, here she is."

"I don't know what to ask," Jeni whispered as the phone was extended in her direction.

"I needed to change the subject," her mom replied, keeping her voice low. "Just ask her about the family tree."

Curling her fingers around the device, Jeni drew in a breath, unsure why her heart stuttered for a moment. "Hi Grandma, how are you?"

Three pairs of eyes bore down on her so she turned her back.

"I'd be a lot betta if y'all would stop these river trips," Grandma Marie replied, her familiar Louisiana accent transmitting clearly over the phone. "I told your mamma and her sisters and brother. I been tellin' them all that the trips were a bad idea, but they think I'm a crazy old woman."

Jeni cocked her head, surprised to hear the warning about river trips. "Why, Grandma? Why are the trips a bad idea?"

"Do that be your question, child? Your mamma said y'all had a question for me."

"No. I mean, yes," Jeni floundered. "I have a question. It's about Uncle Georges. Someone said he worked on a family tree. Have you… um… do you know what happened to it?" Then she added quickly, "Or if it exists?"

Silence stretched out on the other end of the phone, then finally, "Now why would ya be askin' 'bout that?"

"For school," Jeni said, glad she actually had an answer. "A project on family history."

"Anythin' that should be known is already documented."

Jeni crinkled her brow. "What does that mean?"

She expected Grandma Marie to bring up the New Orleans fires, but instead the old woman said, "It means ya shouldn't go diggin', child. Best leave things be."

"Why?"

"Darlin', it's time for my shows. I gotta go. Stay away from the river now, ya hear?"

"What? Grandma?" Jeni took the phone from her ear and saw that the call had ended. Frowning, she said, "She's gone."

"What did she say?" her mom asked.

After a brief glance at Ice, Jeni focused on her mom. "I'm pretty sure she just told me to stop investigating the family history."

Aunt Jessie sighed. "I'm worried about her. I'm not sure she should be living alone anymore."

As her mom began to respond, Jeni lifted her chin at Ice and motioned with her head toward the gravel drive that ran in front of the cabins. "We're going to go for a walk," she said over her shoulder as she followed Ice from the patio.

After Jeni relayed the phone conversation, he said, "So she not only thinks your family shouldn't be doing these river trips, but she specifically told you to stay away from the river?"

"Yeah."

He drew his chin back. "Wow."

"I know," Jeni muttered, wondering if the river had anything to do with the reason her ancestry seemed to dead end. She just couldn't see how there might be a connection. "Hey, you looked like you thought of something when they were talking about vacations."

"Right. Your mom said something about your grandpa shunning the Midwest." Ice dug his phone from his pocket. "Check this out." He stopped walking and touched the screen a few times before passing the phone to Jeni. "This is the Mississippi River drainage basin."

Jeni peered at the topographical map of the United States. About two-thirds of the country was highlighted in yellow, the rivers within that area were shown in a contrasting bright blue.

"Look." Ice pointed. "As far west as Montana, and even a little into Canada, all of these rivers flow toward the Mississippi. And then here," he indicated the opposite side of the image. "All the way to New York, in the east. Everything drains into the

Mississippi River. Look what's not included."

"Michigan," Jeni responded immediately. "Where Grandpa Chris relocated and started a family."

"And when they traveled, he shunned the Midwest," Ice said, his finger circling the drainage basin.

"To keep them out of reach of the Mississippi River." She raised her eyes to meet his. "Which totally fits with the folder of news clippings Grandpa Chris collected. There were articles about people who saved lives on the river and then later articles about the same people dying on the river. My grandpa saved two lives. He must have believed he was in danger so he stayed out of the river's reach." She uttered a humorless laugh. "I have a hard time reconciling this with the man I knew as my grandpa. He was so logic-minded. I can't imagine him suspecting, let alone *believing*, that a river was out to get him."

"Yet it looks like that may be the truth."

Jeni nodded slowly, feeling like a rock had dropped in her gut. "All his life he tried to keep his family safe. Then I fell in the Mississippi River when we were at the headwaters. Worse, I *bled* in the river."

"He sent his family to the headwaters with his ashes." Ice pointed out, his voice soft.

Jeni stared into Ice's blue eyes, her thoughts reeling. "Maybe he thought it would end it," she whispered. "That if he gave his eternity to the river, his family would be safe." She tried to blink the sting from her eyes. "I think he tried, Ice. He tried to make it right in the end, but it wasn't good enough.

Because…" A lump had formed in her throat and she swallowed hard.

Ice's expression softened in understanding. He reached for her, fingers gentle as they settled at her waist. As he drew her forward, she shrunk in on herself, letting her forehead fall to his chest.

Wrapped firmly in his arms, Jeni murmured, her voice rough with emotion, "Because he was already dead."

The being, waxen white with gleaming eyes,
didn't seem to be of this world at all.

Fearless Jean ~ Henri Pourrat

Chapter 3

*A*pproximately equidistant from the Mississippi
River's headwaters in Minnesota to its mouth
at the Gulf of Mexico, the River Aux Vases Resort was
built atop a modest rise on the west side of the Great
River Road. The cabin's patios (and the deck on the
largest cabin) faced west, with a picturesque vista
including a good-sized pond at the base of the rise
backed by a patchwork pattern of farmland in various
hues of green and brown. Houses, barns, silos and
clusters of trees dotted the landscape. On the east side
of the resort, across from the gravel drive, a thick line
of trees concealed the row of cabins from the River
Road below.

A path led through the trees along the edge of a
rocky escarpment that flanked the road and Jeni and
Ice ambled slowly, enjoying the solitude. Held back
by the dense canopy of leaves above, the sun had yet
to drive away the coolness brought by night, so Jeni
untied her flannel shirt and put it on.

"Nice shirt," Ice said.

Jeni snorted. "It's just an old flannel shirt."

"Exactly." Ice turned his head slightly, taking in Jeni's drooped shoulders and the preoccupied flutter of fingers at the bottom of her shirt. "And I'm from the north woods. I appreciate a girl who can make flannel look good."

The comment elicited a genuine chuckle, dissipating the air of melancholy that had surrounded her. "Okay, I'll give you that." She shifted her eyes to his.

Smiling, Ice offered his open hand.

Jeni hesitated to take it, examining his face with a raised eyebrow.

When he was a boy, the tribe medicine man, Nik, had taken Ice's hand to test his link to the spirit world. The contact had caused Ice to see visions of his spiritual origins. Back then, Ice hadn't considered what might happen if he tried to hold hands with a girl who possessed a spiritual ability. That problem had only come to light when he met Jeni. By that time, Ice's spirituality had progressed so that when he touched Jeni, he caused *her* to see visions of her true self.

It became a real complication the first time he tried to kiss her.

When he sought his mentor's help, Nik reminded Ice of the tripartite—or three part—balance of body, ego soul and free soul. By letting his free soul have the edge over his ego soul, Ice could tip the balance of his inner self so that his instincts could override his spirituality and prevent the visions. It was no easy feat, but certainly worth it.

Now, as Jeni reached out, Ice reflected on the striking contrast of her golden hair against the wooded backdrop. He thought about the softness of her skin, letting instinct take the lead. The adjustment was less difficult when they were alone.

Jeni placed her hand in his and they linked fingers. The warmth between their palms radiated up Ice's arm, igniting his desire. This was the complication—he couldn't let his base animal instincts rule his actions. To keep his impulses in check, he returned to their earlier conversation. "It sounds to me like someone started the story about missing records to discourage anyone from looking further into your family history."

"Maybe even Grandma Marie," Jeni grumbled.

"But the good news is that the records are out there. We just need to track them down."

"True." She paused. "It makes the rumor that Uncle Georges had constructed a family tree more believable."

"Had?"

Jeni nodded. "Yeah, he passed away about, I don't know, seven or eight years ago."

Ice guessed he knew the answer, but asked anyway. "What happened to his things?"

"I don't really know. But he never married or had kids, so there's a good chance Grandma Marie got his stuff. Although she probably would've gotten rid of his genealogy research if she's trying to cover something up."

"Well, the information should be part of public records," Ice said. "Mr. Hilstrand said aside from city records we can also check cemetery archives, newspapers and historical societies." Squeezing her hand, he added, "Just get into your Nancy Drew mindset."

"I don't know," she muttered, but she was smiling at his reference to the online Nancy Drew games she liked to play. "I doubt there will be any cool puzzles to solve."

Ice chuckled, glad she was cheering up. "Want to check out the side path?" He pointed to a break in the trees.

It was narrower than the track they were on, so Ice reluctantly let go of Jeni's hand to push a tree branch out of the way and usher her forward. The wooded area thinned and then gave way to a ledge of rock. Jeni side-stepped, staying well away from the edge. Ice slipped behind her, wrapping her in his arms and taking in the scenery from over her shoulder.

Across the road, the earth-toned checkerboard of fields continued, although the terrain was flatter. Trees bordered the farmland, both in bunches and in rows, perhaps forming a wind barrier or designating a property line. The view from this side of the resort had a barren feel which Ice at first chalked up to the flatness, but then discerned what this view lacked: structures, signs of habitation. "It's a flood plain," he said out loud as the realization struck him.

"Yeah, the Mississippi is out there, about a mile or so away," Jeni confirmed with a shiver. "Actually, Ste. Genevieve used to be located right on the river, but it was flooded so many times they moved it to where it is now."

Ice rubbed her upper arms, unsure if she'd caught a chill or the creeps. "Was that part of your tour?" he asked.

Lost in Nowhere

Jeni nodded. "The town where we went to look for Mandy's grandma's house—St. Mary—was built right on the river, too. But they didn't have to move it, the river changed course."

"That sounds both good and bad." Ice spotted a nearby tree with a thick trunk. He headed for it, capturing Jeni's hand and pulling her with him. He settled on the ground, knees bent, and patted the space in front of him. "Do they know why the river changed course?"

Accepting the invitation, Jeni scooted backward until her back touched his chest. He looped his arms around her and she sighed, melting against him. "They do now. The forests were cut down to feed the riverboats. It allowed massive erosion. Although," she twisted her head so she could look up at him, "some people claimed it was a curse."

Ice smirked. "Sure. Because it couldn't have been their fault."

"Exactly." Sarcasm tinged her voice. "The legend is really a tragic love story about..." Again she looked up at Ice. "Are you ready for this?"

"Sure," he said.

"A French girl and a Native American boy."

He chuckled. "Do you know the entire legend?"

"I can give you the basics." Jeni recounted the story, ending with, "So Amakapa swore that he and Marielle would be together again in the afterlife and that—" She broke off, sitting up so fast she nearly smacked her head into his chin. "Ice. Please tell me you see her this time," she said in a low voice.

Ice searched the vista for a figure. "Where?"

"Across the road. Behind the fence, just to the left of where it's leaning forward." Her entire body was tense.

His eyes scoured the fence line, finding a spot where the wire bowed out as if something had pushed against it, or possibly fallen on top of it, but he saw no one.

"Do you see her?" Jeni's voice faltered.

"No. Is it the same girl you saw before?"

"Oh, God." With a strangled cry, Jeni clambered to her feet and dashed for the pathway.

Ice rushed after her. When she reached the trail, Jeni broke into a run, her face a white mask when she glanced over her shoulder. Ice swiveled his head to make his own cursory check, wondering if the figure Jeni saw had given chase. The path behind them appeared empty. He knew, however, something might be there. Something he couldn't see. When Jeni broke out of the shadows and into the sunshine, she finally slowed, breathing hard.

Ice approached, placing a protective hand on her back while she bent over, hands on thighs, drawing in air. "What happened?"

She shook her head and straightened, hands over her face. "She…" Jeni sucked in a shuddering breath. "It looked like she was trying to speak to me." She let her fingers trail down her cheeks, meeting his eyes with a haunted gaze.

"What did she say?"

"I couldn't hear anything," Jeni said. "But I didn't need to. I could read her lips clearly. She was saying 'help me.'" A tremor jerked through her. Ice steered her toward the cabins, his arm firmly around her shoulders.

The incident unnerved him, yet he felt unsurprised. Likewise, although Jeni was clearly frightened, Ice detected no sign of shock, or disbelief. They both had been waiting for something ominous to happen.

An angry determination seized him. *And so it begins.*

Jeni felt a bit better as she and Ice entered the cabin. It was an irrational sense of security, but her parents talking in the kitchen seemed so normal—so benign—that she no longer felt susceptible to a random spectral apparition.

Mrs. Stonewall spied them. "Hey, we got the sandwich stuff out if you two are hungry."

Her focus on Ice, Jeni said, "I feel like I'm still digesting breakfast. How about you?"

One corner of Ice's mouth lifted. "I could eat."

With a subtle shake of her head, Jeni followed Ice to the kitchen. Minutes later, her parents took their plates to the patio, leaving Ice and Jeni alone. While he layered turkey, ham and cheese on one piece of bread and then spread mayonnaise onto another, Jeni cut a single slice of bread in half and added one piece of ham and one slice of cheese. She still didn't feel hungry, but figured if she didn't eat now she'd just munch on a bunch of junk food later.

"Please tell me I'm not seeing a ghost," she muttered.

Ice paused to look at her, one hand holding a

knife while the other rested on top of his sandwich to keep it from falling over. "You think it's been the same woman every time?"

"Well, it was at a distance the first time, and the second time it was dark, but judging by the old-fashioned clothes, I'm going to say yes." She opened the refrigerator and pulled a can of flavored water from the door. "What do you want to drink?"

"You got Coke or Pepsi?"

"Pepsi. Caffeine free," she added.

"Any caffeinated choices?"

"Iced tea?"

"Sold." Ice transferred his cut sandwich to a paper plate and heaped some potato chips alongside it. Jeni added some chips to her plate, and they sat down at the table in the dining area.

Jeni regarded her plate as Ice bit into his sandwich. "Since you didn't tell me I'm not seeing a ghost, I'm guessing you think that's exactly what's happening. But I swear to God, Ice, I haven't been to a cemetery or purchased any souvenirs." She couldn't help the pique that crept into her voice. "And I haven't even visited Historic Ste. Genevieve yet. It's got to be some kind of trap."

Ice finished chewing and sipped his tea. "I felt the same way, at first. I think we need to step back, though, before we overreact. Ghosts happen." He wore a wry smile.

"Well, they don't happen to me." The retort sounded childish, but Jeni didn't care. Sure, she could communicate with spirits, but she didn't expect them to come looking for her.

Lost in Nowhere

Ice looked down at his plate, crunching up a few chips. "Did you feel any malevolence from her? Some sense of wrongness?"

Shooting him a contemptuous look, Jeni popped the pull-tab on her can of water. "A ghost tried to talk to me, Ice. Everything about it was wrong."

Ice let the chip he'd just picked up fall back to his plate. "Before I was kidnapped—when I simply *saw* that witch, Elletre, across the room—I had the worst feeling." He turned toward her, searching her face. "Remember me saying that? That's why I left the party. I asked you that question because you've been practicing meditation and learning to be in touch with your inner self. I think you can put some trust in your gut feelings."

She had no cause to be annoyed with Ice; he was just trying to help. And he had years of spiritual training backing him. Trying to shrug off her bad attitude, Jeni considered his question. "It scared the crap out of me when I realized she was trying to communicate." She took a small sip of her carbonated water as she considered what else she'd felt as she watched the ghost's lips move. "I can't say I felt threatened, per se." Plunking the can down, Jeni added, "But that doesn't mean we should give her the benefit of the doubt."

"I fully agree." He looked at her plate. "Aren't you going to eat?"

Jeni picked up her sandwich and took a bite, chewing stiffly. Her eyes remained fixed on Ice, conveying the message that she expected more of an explanation.

"You've seen her three times now," Ice said. "Let's see if we can figure out if there's a trigger for the appearances. That might help us identify who she is or why she shows up."

"The first time was on the drive," Jeni responded, on board with Ice's idea. "Ansel was going to take us out to see Kaskaskia." Reviewing the memory, her spine stiffened. "We had to cross over the old Mississippi River." She swore under her breath. "I didn't know he was doing that until it was too late."

Ice narrowed his eyes. "What do you mean, old Mississippi?"

"Remember how I said the river changed course? When it did, it diverted into the Kaskaskia River, which essentially cut Kaskaskia off from Illinois." Jeni took her phone from her pocket and touched the screen a few times. "Here, look." She slid the phone to him. While he viewed the map image, she ate a potato chip, the oily saltiness sparking her appetite.

"And you saw the figure in a field?" Ice passed the phone back.

Jeni nodded, having just popped another chip into her mouth. She remembered she'd been about to ask a question about the woman in the field when Mandy had her diabetic reaction. Before that, Jeni was pretty sure she'd been trying to come up with an excuse to stay in the car when they reached Kaskaskia. She hadn't wanted to go traipsing around because... "Ansel called it a ghost town," she said out loud. "Kaskaskia. Ansel said it was nearly a ghost town. So maybe ghosts were in the back of my mind and that's why I saw her?"

Lost in Nowhere

A crease appeared between Ice's eyebrows. "And what about last night? Were you thinking about ghosts when you saw that woman on the road?"

The image of Ice leaning into the trunk to lift out his duffel bag flashed in her mind. "No." She remembered exactly what she'd been thinking about, and it wasn't ghosts. "I was just waiting for you to get your duffel from the trunk."

While Ice ate the last of his sandwich, Jeni took another bite of hers, noticing the faraway look in his eyes as he thought things over. "Kaskaskia."

"What about it?" Jeni asked.

"Today. When you saw the ghost you were telling me the legend about the Kaskaskia curse."

Jeni nodded. "And?"

"And yesterday you had crossed over to the Kaskaskia island, so that's a common thread between two of the sightings."

Jeni sat back in her seat. "Ice, if you're suggesting I'm seeing the girl from the legend, that can't be right. Number one, the story is probably not even true. Number two, if it is true, it happened hundreds of years ago. Number three, I'm sure I wasn't thinking about Kaskaskia when we got here last night."

He raised an eyebrow. "How sure?"

She took a large bite of her sandwich, feeling her cheeks flush. Again, the image—Ice bent down, his T-shirt stretched across the contours of his back, his arm muscles straining against the sleeves—appeared in her head. She swallowed. "Sure."

When she didn't say anything else, he prodded, "Are you going to tell me what you were thinking?"

His expression was impassive, but Jeni guessed it was taking effort for him to appear that way.

"I was thinking about you." The admission made her blush furiously. But she didn't have to admit she'd been admiring his physique and his sun-kissed skin. That she'd been thinking about Marielle and Amakapa and how she could totally relate to the French girl who'd fallen in love with a Native American—she drew in a sharp breath when the realization struck her. "And it made me think about the legend."

Ice's eyebrows rose as he studied her.

"No." Jeni shook her head emphatically. "Ice, it's ridiculous to think I'm seeing the ghost of that girl. It's either my imagination working overtime or something out to get me that's using that form."

"I'm not convinced." Ice leaned back and crossed his arms. "Most legends include a small amount of truth. This girl would've definitely had some unfinished business that could have bound her spirit to the living world."

Jeni stared at the small piece of sandwich left on her plate and then shoved the dish aside, displeasure growing in her belly. "So I see ghosts now. Fabulous," she grumbled.

"Sounds to me like you see her when she's on your mind. You read the legend, what? Yesterday?"

Jeni nodded.

"So it's fresh in your mind. It'll fade. Something else will take its place."

"Sure, another ghost." That brought an even more alarming thought. "Do you think this is going to start happening all the time as my ability grows? Am I going to see George Washington in history class?"

Ice chuckled, shaking his head, and Jeni glowered at him. "Seriously," he said, losing the smile. "The more you develop your ability, the more control you'll have. And I can't say for sure, but I think this occurrence is a mix of circumstances." He began ticking things off on his fingers. "You sympathize with this girl—or identify with her, like you said. You have a spiritual connection. And she's looking for someone to help her."

Jeni scrunched her nose up like she'd tasted something bad. "Well, I can't help her, so what do I do about it? How do I get her to leave me alone?"

"Honestly, the best way to get her to move on would be to see if you can help her finish her unfinished business." Ice watched for her reaction.

Jeni's jaw dropped. Ice was the voice of reason, constantly warning her about spiritual dealings. "You're suggesting I talk to this ghost? This ghost that might have been sent to kill me?"

Ice reached for his iced tea. "Look, I'm just as suspicious as you are, but I was with you when you saw her the last two times, and I felt nothing. I've spent years honing my spiritual intuition. I think if you can do it safely, you may want to hear her out."

"Just to get her to go away?"

His eyes followed the dark amber drink as he swirled it in the bottle. "Sure, ultimately." Then he focused on her. "People who can connect with spirits are rare. As one of those people, I've always felt a responsibility to do things that others can't. I'm not telling you that you should have my philosophy. You should do what you feel is right. But I am asking you to consider it."

She should have realized that although Ice's warnings were all about keeping her safe, he was still altruistic at heart. "So how would I go about contacting her safely?"

His lips curled. "That's what we need to find out."

Jeni's eyes fluttered open. A quick glance at the nightstand informed her that it was nearly one o'clock in the morning. Her shoulders slumped. The pillows stacked for maximum comfort were supposed to encourage her to stay sleeping once she'd dozed off.

Her idea wasn't working.

She and Ice had hung around the resort the rest of the day, watching funny videos together and joining the family for a game of Taboo after dinner. They hadn't spoken further about the apparition. Ice was giving Jeni time to think it over, and Jeni was trying not to think about it at all, especially once the sun set and darkness blanketed the landscape.

Alone in her room, she was becoming more and more agitated; she was afraid to be awake because she might see the ghost again, but was worried that if she fell asleep it would haunt her dreams.

Groaning out loud, Jeni pushed the covers aside and retrieved her laptop from the neighboring bed. She chose a favorite show, replaying an episode she'd watched more than once. Staring at the screen, her stinging eyes begged her lids to close, but sleep seemed an impossible prospect.

When the episode ended, she stopped the next one from loading and got out of bed. The hinges of her bedroom door whined softly, but the cabin remained still, so she slipped into the hallway and padded into the living room. Moonlight streamed through the window blind, striping the blanket on Ice's sleeping form. She kneeled on the mattress next to him and put a hand on his shoulder, shaking him gently. "Ice," she whispered.

He grunted, cracked his eyelids, then scooted over, trying to lift the covers for her to climb in.

She jostled his shoulder again. "Ice. Wake up."

Rising to his elbows, he blinked, the moon's luminescence shading his irises deep blue. "Jeni? What is it? What's wrong?"

"I can't sleep."

He pushed himself up and tucked his pillow behind his back, motioning for Jeni to sit next to him. She poked her feet under the covers and snuggled up to his side. His arm circled her shoulders. "Did something happen?"

Jeni guessed he wanted to know if she'd seen the ghost girl again, but she was reluctant to bring it up. "No." She rested her head on his chest. "I'm afraid to be awake and afraid to fall asleep. My brain just won't shut down."

Ice squeezed her shoulder. "That sucks." He let his head loll against hers.

Jeni felt the tension leech out of her as the clock on the mantle ticked off the silence.

Next thing she knew, she was being prodded gently. "Jeni. Wake up."

Her eyelids batted in confusion and she turned her head toward the voice. "Mom?"

Her mom's robed form straightened, arms crossed over her chest. "Come on," she whispered. "Back in your room."

The last vestiges of sleep disappeared as Jeni slipped from under Ice's arm, swinging her feet to the floor. They were totally sitting up. Surely her mom didn't think they were messing around out here, did she?

The bed creaked as she stood. Jeni saw Ice's eyes open, and then widen. They exchanged a look before she turned away, following her mom to her room.

Jeni sat down on her bed as her mom closed the door. She took a seat on the extra bed, opposite Jeni. "There's a reason why we put Ice on the sofa bed."

Jeni pushed back against the pillows. "I know, Mom. Sorry. I just couldn't sleep. Every time I drifted off, I... I woke up again." She gestured to her computer which was still among the rumpled covers on her bed. "I tried watching YouTube videos, and then a show, but the same thing happened. So I woke Ice up instead of you." An apologetic smile backed her words.

"Are you having nightmares again?" She referred to the nightmares that had plagued Jeni last summer—after the trip to the Mississippi Headwaters.

Taking in the furrow of her mom's brow, Jeni answered carefully. "No. Nothing like that. It's probably just, you know, being in a strange place."

Lost in Nowhere

"Okay, well, remember that sleeping together wasn't part of the deal when we said you could invite Ice to join us."

A flush worked its way from her neck to her face. "We weren't sleeping together, Mom. We were sitting together... and... and accidentally fell asleep."

Jeni was pretty sure amusement caused the crinkles in her mom's brow and that her pressed lips suppressed a smile. "I believe you. And not just because you guys were sitting up, but because we have an understanding about trust. Am I right?"

"Yes." Jeni left it at that. The more she tried to justify her actions, the guiltier she'd sound. Besides, she'd been completely honest.

Her mom stood up and yawned. "I figured that's what happened, but it's my job to ask. Hopefully you'll fall back to sleep now." Striding to the door, she paused with her hand on the knob. "It's also my job to keep you on your toes."

As the door closed behind her mom, Jeni wondered if she should've spoken up and admitted outright that she and Ice weren't having sex.

Not yet, anyway.

Months ago, when Jeni was getting ready to spend a few days in Minnesota over Christmas break, her mom had brought up the subject of sex and birth control. Rather than a lecture about why Jeni shouldn't have sex, the focus of the conversation was about being safe and responsible when she was ready. "Your relationship and your life will become more complicated once sex enters the equation, so of course my advice is to wait as long as possible," her mom had said. "But if you're anything like I was as a teenager, the more I rally against it, the more you'll want to see what it's all about, so I'm not going to do that."

Jeni wasn't sure why her mom had thought it necessary to make that little speech when Ice's mom had already assured Jeni's parents via email that she was off work over the holidays so Ice and Jeni wouldn't be left alone. Besides that—and her mom had no way to know this—Jeni and Ice had agreed that their first time wouldn't be in a car or while parents were sleeping in the same house.

Although, Jeni had to admit that both of those options were starting to sound more attractive lately.

These feelings were particularly strong after Jeni had been shut down when she asked to visit Ice at the University of Minnesota this spring. She'd already stayed in his dorm room for a night during the river cruise the previous fall (albeit Tyler had been with her). Plus, Ice had a roommate. But her dad interjected and said it wasn't appropriate for a sixteen-year-old girl to stay with her boyfriend on a college campus.

It wasn't as if Jeni planned to have sex while she was there, but when her idea to visit Ice at school had been vetoed, she felt more determined to do whatever she wanted, anyway. Perhaps they'd been foolish to think they would find the perfect circumstances.

Her phone buzzed. *"Do you think your mom will mention it to your dad?"*

"Probably not," Jeni assured Ice. *"She didn't seem too concerned. It's not like she caught us in the act lol."*

"So you're not in trouble?"

Lost in Nowhere

The corners of Jeni's mouth lifted. *"No. She let me off with a warning :)"*

"Are you going back to sleep?"

Jeni had noticed light beginning to brighten the curtained window in her room. *"I doubt it,"* she responded. *"But you should."*

"I'm not sure if I can. That really got my blood pumping."

Jeni smiled. *"Sorry about that."*

"How about if I fold up the bed and we sit at the kitchen table?"

Jeni checked the time. 6:30. *"That should be okay. See you in a few minutes."*

The early morning chill raised goosebumps on Jeni's legs as her bare feet hit the floor. Since there'd be no snuggling under covers, she pulled on some fuzzy socks. The mirror above the dresser showed deep purple smudges under her eyes—a consequence of her short night of sleep. "Gonna need some coffee and makeup," she muttered, running her fingers through her hair.

Jeni heard the squeak of hinges as Ice folded his bed back into sofa form, so she deemed it safe to emerge from her bedroom. She didn't see Ice, but there was a slice of light under the bathroom door, so she padded into the kitchen, glad that dawn provided enough brightness to function without turning on the overhead lights. The better to hide her dark circles. She scooped coffee into the filter basket and was running water into the carafe when Ice entered the room.

"Morning," he murmured, lightly touching her back and kissing her cheek.

Jeni glanced sideways with a half-smile. "Very early morning."

Ice chuckled softly and got out a couple of mugs, then leaned against the counter with his legs crossed at the ankles.

They were alone and the hiss and gurgle of coffee brewing was a perfect cover for their conversation. "I want to figure out how to contact her."

Ice appraised her for a moment. "Yeah, you can't be afraid of both being awake and going to sleep."

"Exactly. So how do we do this?"

Crossing his arms over his chest, Ice mused, "As a medicine man, I contact spirits by going on a vision quest. Though in this case the spirit is already here, so you don't need to call it; just communicate."

Jeni picked up her phone. "Should I look up how to conduct a séance or something?" She shivered.

"I think that summons a spirit," Ice said.

In response to her pointed look, a lopsided grin spread across his face. "Busted. I did a little Googling last night. And, actually, I probably wouldn't have thought of this if not for your mom and aunt, but a Ouija board might be the best tool."

"Oh, yay." Her tone seethed with mockery. "Definitely not what I had in mind for a souvenir."

Curiosity has its lure,
But all the same
It's a paltry kind of pleasure
And a risky game.

Bluebeard ~ Charles Perrault

Chapter 4

*J*eni clutched Ice's arm and pointed to a stack of flyers on the information desk advertising Ste. Genevieve Ghost Tours. He curled his arm across her back. "Let's go watch the video," he murmured. She'd been skittish all morning about going into the historic town.

As the rest of the family group trickled through the door of the Ste. Genevieve Welcome Center, an attendant invited everyone to sit down and watch a video overview of things to see and do in town. A vaulted ceiling added to the spacious feel of the room. Display cabinets lined the walls, and in the center, couches, end tables and a few folding chairs for over-flow were grouped in front of a television screen.

Ice made brief eye contact with Tyler as he entered with Mandy. Jeni's cousin looked away, observing the furniture layout and Jeni and Ice's location on one end of a couch. He steered Mandy to a couple of folding chairs set up on the outside edge of the viewing area.

Barbara Pietron

The screen lit up as the last few people found seats.

After the video, the group agreed to meet at the Audubon's Bar & Grill for lunch at one o'clock, and then everyone dispersed into smaller clusters, looking at the maps provided by the welcome center and deciding where to start.

Jeni and Ice followed her parents to the Bauvais-Amoureux House where an impressive diorama depicted the village of Ste. Genevieve in 1832. Despite the warming temperatures, Jeni wore a sweater with pockets, inside of which she buried her hands. She was paranoid about accidentally touching the wrong thing, and although she might have been overly worried, Ice couldn't blame her. Until she understood her spiritual ability, it was better to be safe than sorry.

When her parents continued to an exhibit of the architectural history of Ste. Genevieve—featuring the rare *poteaux-en-terre* method of construction where upright cedar log walls are set directly in the earth—Jeni let her mom know that she and Ice were going to move on.

Jeni's shoulders sagged as she breathed a sigh of relief once they were outside. She was jittery about touring the centuries-old buildings. Instead, they'd decided to poke around in the couple of antique stores in town on the off chance they might find a Ouija board. Everything in the town was old—which meant antique stores housed in old buildings also had the propensity for paranormal activity—but Ice didn't point that out. He believed there was a reason why this spirit had contacted Jeni, and he didn't think she'd start seeing ghosts everywhere.

$\mathcal{L}$ost in $\mathcal{N}$owhere

Earlier, while Jeni was in the shower, Ice had called Nik to get the medicine man's opinion of his Ouija board idea. Like Ice, the medicine man had no personal experience with a board, but maintained that if they sold them in stores alongside other games, they couldn't be too dangerous. "Do your research and trust your instincts," Nik had said. "A Ouija board in your hands is probably safer than some kids messing around." Before they hung up, Nik added, "Let me know what happens." The curiosity in the medicine man's voice had made Ice smile. Their traditions and ways as medicine men had been passed down for generations; employing a method of spiritual contact outside their customs had piqued Ice's curiosity as well.

Jeni found a spot of shade to stand in as she unfurled the map of Ste. Genevieve. Ice looked over her shoulder. She pointed to a blue dot. "Three blocks up and then we make a left."

The first store was stocked primarily with truly old furniture, art and dishes. Ice's mom would've loved browsing through the place. She likely would've left empty-handed because of the steep prices, but that wouldn't have dulled her enjoyment of the beautiful antiques. It became apparent that a Ouija board would not be among the store's inventory.

"There's also a huge antique mall in St. Mary," Jeni said once they were back on the street. "Although a department store would probably be quicker and easier."

The next shop wasn't quite as upscale, but the selection of toys was limited. Consulting the map again, Jeni said, "I'm not sure if this one—Memories and Magic—is an antique store or a gift shop or what, but it is on the way to this." She tapped the paper.

Ice read the description next to her finger and laughed. "A coffee shop?"

"What?" Jeni replied with a grin. "I like coffee."

Peeking into the store window of the place Jeni had chosen didn't indicate which kind of shop it was. Some items on display were obviously new—like the souvenir Christmas ornaments—but others looked old, such as a clock from the '50s or '60s. "Look at that." Jeni pointed.

"The coffee mill?" It seemed obvious, given their recent conversation.

Jeni chuckled. "No, actually, beyond that."

Ice peered to the left, past the table in front of the window. "The toy phone on wheels?"

Jeni bobbed her head. "I used to have one. It has a pull-string and when it rolls, the eyes move. Come on, let's go in."

The heavy scent of incense enveloped them as soon as they opened the door. Once inside, Ice also detected an underlying earthy odor, distinctly different from the musty smell of the old building. Voices came from farther inside the store.

Jeni elbowed him. "Board games." Her hushed voice made it hard to discern if she was pleased, nervous or simply being discreet. He followed her as she made her way to a stack of faded cardboard game boxes. She tilted her head sideways to read the names.

Noticing another pile of boxes behind the first stack, Ice carefully twisted the cartons Jeni had already inspected to allow light to reach the hidden games.

"Check this one." Jeni poked a finger at a dark-colored box. Ice spun it away from the others so he could grab it. Wiggling it out from under four other games caused the front stack to teeter precariously and Jeni braced the pile with her leg as Ice extracted the dark box.

Jeni drew in a sharp breath as Ice balanced the box on his knees. Though made of cardboard, the graphic on the carton made it appear as an ancient, well-used wooden chest with cock-eyed metal hinges. Affixed to the chest was a black placard which read: *The Mystifying Oracle*. Large letters spelling out O-U-I-J-A seemed to float ominously above the box.

Ice admired the packaging—it was much cooler than he'd expected. Jeni could do worse than this as a souvenir. Before he could say so, Jeni lifted her head sharply, her eyes shifting to his as she tuned in to the conversation that was moving forward from the back of the store.

"...not exactly premonitions," chattered a girl's voice, "but I get a bad feeling about things sometimes or I'll hear the beginning of a news report and know what happened before they finish the story."

Ice met Jeni's gaze with raised eyebrows.

"It sounds like Mandy," she whispered.

A woman's voice responded with something Ice couldn't make out.

He stood, offering Jeni a hand as they continued to listen. "I thought about it," the girl said. "*He* doesn't think I should, but he also can't deny that whenever this happens, I'm always right."

"Or always lucky," a deep voice grumbled.

Ice and Jeni stared at each other, eyes widened in recognition. Her face split into a huge grin and she clamped a hand over her mouth. Ice pressed his lips together, suppressing a chuckle. Tyler. It wasn't only the timbre of his voice that gave him away, but the distinct attitude it relayed.

As the girl launched into a story about a bad feeling she had regarding a certain route home from work, it was obvious the group was coming their way. Ice was about to ask Jeni if he should put down the Ouija board when a woman perhaps fifteen years their senior came into view with Mandy and Tyler following.

Mandy spotted them instantly, giving a small wave as she finished her story. Ice lowered the game and turned it so the back faced outward.

The woman wore a jumpsuit of deep violet patterned with small white flowers. The full-length pants were loose and flowy while the long sleeves were fitted until they flared out at the wrists. "You may find that the crystal amplifies your ability," she was saying as she rounded the counter and set a necklace next to the register. She lifted her chin at Jeni and Ice. "I'll be with you folks in a minute."

Jeni's eyes darted to Ice and then down to the game still in his hands. She edged in front of him, but Mandy walked right up to them.

"Doesn't she have a great store?" Mandy gestured to the proprietor. "What did you guys find?" She leaned to peer around Jeni. The back of the box did nothing to conceal its contents, especially at close range. "A Ouija board! That looks like a cool old one."

Cat out of the bag, Ice lifted the box and flipped it over. "Yeah, I like how it looks like a wooden case."

As Mandy examined the game, Tyler glared openly at Ice and Jeni. Slowly, he shook his head. "I'll wait outside," he grumbled, and was out the door before Mandy could protest.

"He hates this kind of stuff," she apologized.

"I know." Jeni smiled sympathetically. "What are you buying?"

"A crystal." She took a step back toward the counter, beckoning Jeni and Ice to follow her. "This one encourages you to stay centered when life gets crazy. And my life has been pretty crazy lately."

"It's pretty," Jeni said as the store owner rolled the necklace in tissue and placed it in a bag. The crystal reminded Ice of the white rocks people used for landscaping, but he didn't say so.

"Okay, see you guys at lunch," Mandy said. "I'd better find Ty before he gets mad." She laughed, apparently not too concerned at the prospect.

Ice slid the game onto the counter and the woman's eyes touched his briefly and then appeared to analyze the space surrounding him. "Shaman?" she asked.

Ice nodded, impressed. "Medicine man."

She smiled. "I've been a practicing Medium since I was twenty. I'm rather attuned to the spirit world."

Jeni had drawn up beside him and Ice watched as the woman scrutinized her in the same manner. She narrowed her eyes, offering only a subtle shake of the head. "You, I'm not so sure, although the presence trailing you suggests you can communicate with the beyond."

"You can see her?" Jeni twisted her head to look over her shoulder.

"No," the medium replied. "It's more of a sensing, than seeing. I didn't know the entity was female in nature." She regarded the Ouija board. "Is she the reason for your purchase?"

"Yes." The relief in Jeni's voice was plain. "She keeps appearing to me. I want to find out what she wants."

"Is it a relative?" The woman paused with her hand hovering over the old-fashioned cash register.

Jeni shook her head. "No. This just started happening after we arrived."

The older woman looked unsurprised. "Too bad. Spirits usually use a personal, often beloved, possession to stay active in the human world. If she was a relative, I thought you might have access to the object. Then you wouldn't need the board to communicate."

"We'll need the board," Jeni confirmed.

Ice got out his wallet, but Jeni elbowed him saying, "No. I'm buying it. I'm the one who's going to take it home."

As Jeni paid the woman, Ice's attention was drawn to a painting hanging on the wall behind the counter. It was a portrait of a young woman standing under a tree with her arm looped through the handle of a basket of… apples, he surmised.

"I'm Phoebe, by the way," the store owner was saying as she slid the Ouija board into a bag. "That's one of my ancestors." Ice realized she was addressing him. "Rose Emerson. She established this business in Ste. Genevieve."

"This same store?" Jeni asked, brows arched.

"Oh no. Back when Ste. Genevieve was located on the Mississippi River, Rose's aunt lived on the outskirts of town, covertly dealing in herbal remedies. She'd learned her craft from a grandmother that fled to the Illinois Territory when the witch trials began in Salem."

"Were they witches?" Ice asked.

"No more than most of the women—and men— that were put to death. Mostly they were healers who believed that there were things that defied explanation. By Rose's time, she felt safe enough to offer her remedies openly in town. Her son and daughter were running the business during the flood of 1785. Reports say the water reached the rooftops of the village. Like many others, Rose's kids elected to relocate in this area, on higher ground. Ten years after that flood, only a few huts remained at the original site. I'd like to claim the relocated business was right here," Phoebe pointed down. "But I know the building isn't quite old enough."

"Has the business always stayed in your family?" Jeni asked.

"It has. And I have relatives in similar professions due to our inherited talent for supernatural dealings."

"Wow," Jeni said, catching Ice's eye. "It's pretty cool how much you know about your family history. I wish my ancestry was that cut-and-dried."

"Good luck with the board," Phoebe said as they

moved toward the door. "Let me know if you need anything."

Jeni and Ice were sitting at a long table at the Audubon Bar and Grill with her grandma, Aunt Jessie and Neil, waiting for the others to arrive. Tyler's older brother, Jake, and his wife, Josie, arrived next with Aunt Leila and the two toddlers, Molly and Nat. As they found seats and acquired boosters for the little ones, Jeni thought she spied Tyler's tousled hair and stretched her neck to confirm that it was indeed her cousin and his girlfriend.

As soon as Mandy spotted her, she grabbed Tyler's hand and dragged him to the table, pulling out the chair next to Jeni. "Did you guys buy the Ouija board?"

Jeni winced, glancing past Mandy to Tyler, re-lieved to find him talking to his brother. "Um… yeah, but can we keep that on the down-low?"

"No problem." Mandy leaned close to Jeni and spoke in a hushed voice. "But I'd love to join your session."

Jeni's mouth fell open and she snapped it shut, glancing quickly toward her cousin. "It's kind of just a novelty souvenir." Tyler would kill her—and prob-ably Ice, too—if they involved Mandy.

"Riiiight." Mandy lifted a dubious eyebrow.

Jeni turned to see that Ice had missed the ex-change while a waitress took his drink order. After ordering a cola, she immersed herself in the menu, making it a point to engage with others and ask what they'd decided to order.

ℒost in 𝒩owhere

Mandy, however, didn't bring up the Ouija board again, since she was busy talking about the new addition to her family—a puppy. Jeni's tension eased further when Mandy slid her phone in front of Jeni and Ice to show them pictures of the small ball of curls.

When her German wiener schnitzel plate arrived, Jeni forgot about the bag under Ice's seat. The breaded and fried thin pork medallions were delicious. Even the red cabbage, which she wasn't really into when her mom served it at home, was good, but it was more than she could finish. After stuffing the last bite of herbed spaetzle—the star of the dish, in her opinion—into her mouth, she nudged Ice and scooted her plate over. "Want the rest of my schnitzel and cabbage? I'm going to run to the restroom."

As she pushed back her chair, Mandy did the same, rising. "I'll go with you."

Jeni breathed an inward groan but waited courteously for the other girl. Once they'd cleared the dining room, Mandy asked, "Have you guys used a talking board before?"

"Talking board?" Jeni hedged.

"Yeah, like 'talking to spirits.' I've used one a few times."

Jeni stopped outside the door to the ladies' room. "You have? Does Tyler know?"

Mandy rolled her eyes. "That subject hasn't come up yet. But it shouldn't come as too much of a shock. He knows I was brought up Buddhist—my dad's from Sri Lanka and my mom's a yoga teacher. I work in the new age shop attached to my mom's yoga studio."

Taken by surprise, Jeni took a step back, bumping into the restroom door. She swung it open as if that's what she meant to do. Mandy chuckled, following Jeni into the bathroom. "I know, right? Tyler's such a skeptic. But that doesn't mean I am."

Jeni entered a stall, thinking it would halt the conversation—at least until they were done—but Mandy continued to chatter. "It's obvious that Tyler has been trying to keep me away from you guys. I wasn't sure why until we ran into you in that shop, Memories and Magic. That look he gave you before he stormed off led me to believe he thought you were going to use the Ouija board. I know from experience you need more than two people; that's why I offered to join. I wasn't trying to be pushy or butt into your business."

Thinking that over as she flushed the toilet, Jeni emerged from the stall to wash her hands and met Mandy's gaze in the mirror. "If we did that, Tyler would be really pissed at us—especially at me. Wouldn't he be mad at you, too?"

Mandy nodded, rinsing soap from her hands. "Oh, I'm sure he wouldn't be happy about it. But I'm not about to pretend to be something I'm not, so he'll have to get over it."

Jeni's admiration for the girl's attitude quickly soured to dismay as she realized that Tyler would probably drop her like a hot potato as soon as they got back home.

"You know not to use it in your cabin, right?" Mandy tore off a length of paper towel. "I mean, they say not to use them at home and that's your home for the rest of the week."

£ost in Nowhere

Jeni flattened her lips as she dried her hands. "No. I didn't know that. But it doesn't really matter since we'll probably never use it." Adding the word "probably" assuaged Jeni's guilt about lying outright to Mandy.

Seemingly unfazed, Mandy rummaged in her purse for a hairbrush. "So how many times have you seen *Second Star to the Right*?"

Jeni's lips stretched into a genuine smile. "Three times. Their tour came to Michigan in March."

"They were in Wisconsin in February. How cool was that pop-up stage?"

As they shared their concert experiences on the way back to the table, Jeni couldn't help feeling a bit wistful, wishing Tyler and Mandy's relationship would last. She could be friends with this girl.

The waitstaff was clearing the table while everyone discussed what they'd seen and what they planned to do next. Mrs. Stonewall approached. "I think we're going to the Ste. Genevieve museum, if you want to join us."

Jeni shook her head. "I don't think so. The smell of the old buildings is giving me a headache." Which was true, the musty odor in some of the buildings often hit her like a spike in the temple. She couldn't stop the corners of her mouth from lifting as she said, "I saw a coffee shop on the map. That's our next stop."

"I should've known." Her mom laughed. "Okay. Let's just keep in touch by text, then."

As the rest of the party rose from their seats and collected their things, Jeni and Ice lingered, waiting for the others to clear out before retrieving the bag with the Ouija board from under Ice's seat. As Mandy followed Tyler through the restaurant, she glanced over her shoulder, making eye contact with Jeni and bobbing her chin.

Stalling for time by rifling through her purse, Jeni leaned a little closer to Ice. "Mandy asked to join our Ouija session. I guess she's used a board before."

Ice's eyebrows rose. "What about Tyler?"

"Exactly what I asked. She claims she's a free agent and can do whatever she wants."

Reaching under his chair for the bag, Ice said, "Interesting. What did you tell her?"

"That we don't plan to use it." Jeni locked eyes with Ice. "I can't. Tyler would hate me."

"Except it's not like you asked." Ice pointed out. "Although I doubt the fine print would matter to him."

"It wouldn't." Jeni sighed, standing. "My very existence seems to annoy him."

The tables outside the coffee shop were in the sun, so Jeni and Ice walked down the block to a small park with plenty of shade. Setting his iced coffee off to the side of the cement table, Ice gave Jeni a hand as she wriggled out of her sweater. Then he opened the Ouija board box and found the instructions, again feeling that spark of curiosity along with the thrill of learning something new. He'd been trained to communicate with the spirit world in a much different way. Learning another method might make him a more well-rounded medicine man. He hoped so.

£ost in Nowhere

Unfolding the page, he smoothed it with his hands and then slid it between himself and Jeni so they both could read.

The directions were fairly simple: Participants should sit around the board with their knees or hands touching for "energy" flow. One person would be designated as the medium—the person responsible for asking the questions. Participants were to place their fingers lightly on the planchette, taking care not to force the movement. The medium should announce that only good spirits were welcome to guard against evil or unwanted spiritual entities. Having a non-participant who could write down the questions and answers was recommended, as spirits sometimes used an abbreviated code or spelled things out phonetically. The instructions also stressed the importance of closing the session by moving the planchette to the word *Goodbye* on the board.

"I can see why it would be nice to have at least three people," Jeni said. "If we do this alone, we don't have anyone to write stuff down."

"And more people generate more energy." Ice pointed to one of the tips listed on the sheet.

Jeni popped the top off of her frozen coffee drink and used the straw to transfer blobs of whipped cream to her mouth. "I'm not sure where we can do this, either." She gestured to the page. "This just says somewhere safe, but Mandy said you're not supposed to use the board in your home—and the cabin is our home for the next few days. Not that we'd ever be allowed to be there alone, anyway." She muttered the side thought.

Ice sipped his coffee, pondering the instruction

sheet. "This reads as if we're contacting any random spirit that answers the call, so to speak. I wonder if we need to do anything differently to reach a specific spirit." A breeze stirred, lifting the paper. Ice slapped his hand down, pinning the sheet to the table.

"Maybe I shouldn't have shut Mandy down." Jeni wore a pinched expression as she stirred her drink.

"She didn't say she was an expert, just that she'd used a board before." He stared across the table, eyes narrowed in thought, and then turned to Jeni. "You know, the woman at that shop—Phoebe—said to let her know if we needed help. Why don't we just go back and ask her some questions."

"Duh." The corners of Jeni's eyes crinkled. "That's exactly what we should do. I should have thought of it immediately." She snapped the lid on her cup and sipped, shifting in her seat. "Do you really think announcing we only want to talk to good spirits works? How will we know we've reached the ghost who asked me for help?"

"Both good questions for Phoebe," Ice said. "Remember, I know as much as you do at this point."

"True. Okay, let's assume we know we're talking to the right spirit. We mostly want to know what kind of help she wants, right?"

Ice drained his cup and then nodded. "We want to know how you can help her move on." He folded the instruction sheet and returned it to the box.

"And I'd like to know if there's a reason she's asking me, in particular." Jeni slid to the edge of the bench. "Come on. I'll finish this on the way."

Lost in Nowhere

Phoebe spied them as they entered Memories and Magic. "I expected to see you two again, just not so soon."

"After we read the Ouija board instructions, we had a ton of questions," Jeni said. "We hoped maybe you could help us if you have time."

Phoebe smoothed the hair from her face, though the curls promptly sprang back to her forehead. "It's not often that I use a talking board, but I do have some experience. What are your questions?"

Their first question—where to use the board—elicited not only an answer, but an offer. "You're correct. Don't use it in the cabins at the resort," she said. "Use it outside. Or, if you'd like, you can use my back room." She gestured toward a curtained doorway at the back of the store.

Ice glanced at Jeni, reading the eagerness on her face. "Could we use it… today?" he asked, drawing in a quick breath.

"You can use it right now, if you want," Phoebe said. "Although you may have to move some boxes off the table."

Jeni leaned toward Phoebe. "How do we reach a specific spirit?" The words rushed from her mouth.

"In your case, I don't think that'll be a problem." Her focus flicked over Jeni's shoulder and then back to Jeni. "Do you know the spirit's name?" When Jeni nodded, Phoebe said, "Call her by name. If you know something about her, ask a few questions to confirm her identity."

A metallic rattling came from the back room and, without conscious thought, Ice moved closer to Jeni.

Then a door slammed. Ice turned to the store proprietor and found her grinning. "That's Hannah. She comes by after school to help me out."

Seconds later, a girl whisked through the curtain. She had short, blue hair and extra-long eyelashes. "Hey, Phoebe," she said, then noticed Jeni and Ice. "Oops," She rolled her lips between her teeth. "Sorry."

"It's all right." Phoebe motioned her forward. "Your timing is perfect. These two bought a Ouija board earlier, and if you don't mind watching the shop for a few minutes, I'll get them started."

Ice exhaled as a small portion of his anxiety dissolved.

"That's cool," Hannah said. She joined Phoebe behind the counter, contemplating Jeni and Ice.

"I don't think we ever introduced ourselves," Ice said. "I'm Ice—short for Shattered Ice—and this is Jeni."

After hellos were exchanged, Phoebe led them to the back room. "Actually," she said as Ice lifted a box from the table, "since it's just the two of you, why don't you sit facing each other and balance the board on your laps?"

"You're not participating?" He'd hoped that since Phoebe was a medium, she'd take the lead and do the talking.

"No. Not while the store's open." She moved to the small desk in the corner of the room and rummaged through the papers lying on top, eventually producing a notepad and pen. "I can coach, though, and take notes."

Lost in Nowhere

Jeni sent him a questioning glance as they each grabbed a chair and turned them to face each other, probably picking up on the slightly higher pitch to his voice. She was surprised by his nervousness. They sat down, knees touching, and Jeni pulled the Ouija board from the table onto their laps.

The board was as intricate as its box. In contrast to the parchment-like tan background, black sun and moon images resided in the upper left and right corners, respectively, and stars decorated the sides of the board. Next to the sun was the word *Yes* and on the moon side, *No*. The letters of the alphabet filled the center, written in an old-fashioned script, with the numbers zero through nine immediately underneath. At the bottom of the board was the word *Goodbye*.

Anxiety crawled up the back of Ice's throat and he looked at Jeni, taking in her round eyes and pale cheeks. It seemed her enthusiasm also waned under the reality of what they were about to do. "Are you sure you want to do this?"

She filled her lungs and exhaled slowly. "Yes."

"Only one of you should ask questions. Who's it going to be?" Phoebe asked, making herself comfortable at the table.

Ice expected Jeni would want to direct the line of inquiry, but she appealed to him with wide, green eyes. "I—" Her voice broke and she cleared her throat. "I'd appreciate it if you would."

He raised an eyebrow, but her expression didn't change. "All right." The even tone of his words denied the pounding of his heart. *Pull it together*, he admonished himself. *It's not like I've never talked to a spirit before.*

He may not have been fooling anyone, though, because Phoebe said, "Remember, if you feel any negative energy, move the planchette to *Goodbye*. Then follow up by also speaking 'goodbye' out loud. Once the session is ended, the negative energy will dissipate." When they both nodded, she instructed, "Rest your first two fingers on the planchette."

Ice reached for the teardrop-shaped wooden piece. It was about the size of his palm and had a hole in the middle. When Jeni's fingers rested across from his, they stared at each other, waiting for something to happen.

"Since you haven't done this before, you might want to circle around the board allowing the momentum to take on a life of its own," Phoebe prompted. "Use a very light touch."

They followed her advice, gliding the wooden piece smoothly over the board.

A few moments later, Phoebe said, "Go ahead and ask if she's here."

Jeni closed her eyes, presumably thinking about the girl in the legend, since that was their theory on how and why the spirit appeared to her. After a minute or so, remembering the instruction sheet, Ice said, "We invite only good spirits to talk with us." Then he asked, "Is there a spirit here?"

The planchette moved immediately, nearly jerking from beneath their fingers, startling Ice when it moved to the alphabet.

Scraping sounds filled the small room as the wooden piece trundled across the heavy cardboard. *"H... E... L... P."*

Jeni's eyes had snapped open when the planchette began moving, and Ice could feel the weight of her stare.

"What is your name?" he asked.

Again, the disc glided over the alphabet. "M," Ice said. "A... R... I... E." It continued to move. "L... L... E."

"Marielle?" He exchanged a glance with Jeni as the planchette slid to *"Yes."* Then he asked, "Are you the girl from the Kaskaskia legend?"

The piece twitched, but remained on the *Yes.*

Checking on Jeni, Ice was glad to see she looked more fascinated than freaked out. He felt no animosity from the presence and his rapidly beating heart was beginning to calm. "What do you need help with?"

A long scrape brought the planchette back to the alphabet. *"S... A... V... E... M... Y... L... O... V... E."*

"Who is your love?" Ice asked.

"A... M... A... K... A... P... A."

Voices came from the front of the store. Ice shifted his focus to Phoebe, who listened for a moment and then gestured for him to go ahead.

Feeling confident that they knew who they were actually talking to, Ice asked, "Do you need help crossing to the other side?"

The planchette slid toward the moon on the right corner of the board and rested briefly on *"No."* Then it went back to the alphabet: *"H... E... I... S... N... O... W... H... E... R... E."*

Frowning, Ice looked first at Jeni, then at Phoebe. "He's not on the other side?"

The disc returned to *"No."*

"Is that why you haven't crossed over?"

Their fingers followed the shuffle of the wooden piece to *"Yes."*

Ice thought for a moment about his next question and came up with, "Why do you think we can help you?"

This time the planchette moved to the center of the board, between the *Yes* and *No*. It twisted under their fingers causing Ice and Jeni to hold their arms in a contorted position. When it stopped, the narrow end of the teardrop pointed at Jeni.

Her eyes widened. In the smallest voice, Jeni asked, "Is it pointing at me?"

Ice asked, "You think Jeni can help you?"

The indicator shifted left to *"Yes,"* then continued to spell out: *"S... H... E... K... N... O... W... S."*

Jeni flinched, deep creases forming on her brow. She drew her lips into a pucker.

Reading her confusion, Ice asked, "What does she know that will help you?"

"F... I... N... D... H... I... M."

The response didn't exactly answer his question, but as Ice opened his mouth to rephrase it, the rhythmic chime of a phone interrupted.

Jeni grimaced, muttering. "Frick, that's my mom's ringtone." Abandoning contact with the planchette, she fumbled the phone from her pocket.

"Goodbye," Phoebe announced emphatically, staring hard at both of them.

Ice uttered the parting word before lifting his fingers from the disc. He looked at Jeni expectantly.

Blinking, Jeni's round eyes darted to Phoebe

then back to Ice, her index finger poised over the still chirping phone. "Goodbye," she finally managed, poking the screen.

As she listened to her mom, Jeni pointed from the board to the box.

Message received, Ice collected the planchette and folded the board. But as he stuffed the box back into the bag, he paused, glancing at Jeni. She met his gaze, lines of worry etched on her forehead. She must be thinking what he was thinking.

The large bag would be impossible to hide as they approached the car.

But when she did appear, he found her beauty astounding.
Trembling a bit, he complimented her,
and she trembled a little, too.

The Pretty Spinning Girl ~ Henri Pourrat

Chapter 5

*J*eni's dad slowed the car and turned onto the road leading to the resort. After a bit of small talk with her mom, Jeni had fallen silent, trying to imagine how her parents would react to the Ouija board when she eventually showed it to them. Because her mom had admitted to using one in the past, Jeni was more concerned about her dad's response. He'd had an aversion to the subject of ghosts and spirits well before Jeni was born. This led her to believe he wouldn't like the prospect of his daughter owning a Ouija board and might possibly go as far as telling her she had to get rid of it immediately.

They were lucky to get it into the car without notice. Jeni and Ice had reached the parking lot first and when her dad spotted them standing there, he'd unlocked the doors. They were able to put the bag on the floor of the back seat and drape Jeni's sweater over it before her parents arrived and climbed inside.

Now, gazing out the windshield, all thoughts of the Ouija board were obliterated. From her position in the center of the bench seat, Jeni had a clear view of the vehicle heading their way, a cloud of dust rising behind it. There was no mistaking the chromed front end and hood scoop and the shiny Caribbean blue paint.

Her shoulders tensed involuntarily and Ice shot her a questioning glance. Then his attention was drawn to the rumble of the V-8 engine and he turned to the window to watch the GTO as it passed. "Wow, nice classic." He leaned forward and twisted in his seat.

When Jeni didn't comment, Ice studied her from the corner of his eye—he knew she was a car enthusiast. It didn't take more than a few seconds for the realization to dawn. "Don't tell me, it's Ansel's."

Jeni pressed her lips together and nodded.

"Of course it is." He didn't sound angry, just sort of begrudgingly tolerant.

Fortunately, their arrival at the cabin ended the awkward moment.

They'd stopped to purchase some vegetables to grill for dinner, so Jeni gathered her bag from the floor along with a grocery bag, trailing behind the others so she could make a quick detour to her room. Entering the kitchen, she plunked the bag of vegetables on the counter. "Should I unpack these?" she asked her mom. "Are we grilling them here or at the big cabin?"

"Let's take them down there," her mom replied. "They have a bigger grill. Actually, I was hoping you might grill them."

Jeni met her mom's inquisitive look with pleading eyes.

Lost in Nowhere

"Cooking crew doesn't have to do dishes," her mom said.

Jeni glanced at Ice. "I'll help you," he said. "It sounds better than dishes."

Deflating her chest with an inaudible sigh, Jeni nodded her head. They'd left Memories and Magic in a rush to meet her parents and she was dying to discuss the Ouija session. Perhaps they could talk as they grilled.

But as Jeni laid the first strips of zucchini across the grate, her dad appeared with a tray containing spices, utensils and packages of meat. He chose the table closest to the grill to prep the meat, which meant there'd be no Ouija talk. So she bided her time, hardly processing any of the dinner conversation, and as soon as the dishes were being cleared, Jeni and Ice escaped.

"How about the bench?" Ice pointed to the park-style bench at the edge of the pond. The sun was a red ball hanging low in the sky, staining the still surface of the water crimson.

The scene was beautiful, yet Jeni eyed the sunset warily. It wouldn't be long until full dark. "Mmm, let's just go partway down the hill and sit on the grass."

They sat side by side, knees tented, and Jeni pulled a folded paper from her back pocket. Phoebe had given her the notes from the Ouija session. "So the spirit claims to be Marielle, the girl from the legend. And she's uh…" Jeni refused to use the word *haunting*—even if it was technically the correct term—because it just sounded too creepy to admit out loud.

"She's stalking me because she wants me to find Amakapa, who is nowhere." She looked at Ice. "So if he died, and didn't make it to the other side, isn't he in limbo? Or purgatory? And if she died and didn't cross over, doesn't that put them on the same plane? The same limbo?"

"Apparently not." Ice crossed his arms and rested them on his knees. "She's still connected to the living world. Maybe that puts them in two different places."

Jeni stared at the pond. "If she hasn't crossed over, how does she know he's not there?"

"All good questions." He leaned toward her, until their shoulders touched, providing solidarity in lieu of answers. "Unfortunately, what happens after death is still a mystery."

The paper crinkled as Jeni scanned it again. "I just don't get it," she said. "What exactly does she think I know? What can this ghost possibly know about *me*?" She dropped the hand holding the notes with a heavy exhale. "I feel like we've uncovered more questions instead of getting answers."

"I know what you mean," Ice said. "How do you feel about it overall? Do you want to help if you actually can?"

Drawing her feet in closer, Jeni rested her chin on her knees. She studied the grass in front of her toes, nervous that Marielle's ghostly apparition would materialize since they were discussing her. "Well, considering that what she wants me to do sounds impossible, not to mention that I wouldn't have the faintest idea on where to start, I'm thinking no." Hugging her knees tightly, she turned to look at Ice. "I would help her cross over if I could, rather than just tell her to take a hike. But I don't know if that's even possible."

Ice leaned back on his hands, extending one arm behind Jeni's back, and she settled against him, resting her head on his shoulder. He kissed the top of her head, sending shivers over her scalp that tingled down her back. "Are you sure you don't want to transfer to the University of Michigan?" she asked. "Or Michigan State? Or any other college in Michigan?"

"Don't think I haven't considered it."

"What?" She lifted her chin to see if he was serious or humoring her.

"I have." He shrugged, his expression earnest. "I've looked into communications programs at some of the colleges in Michigan." Then the corners of his mouth twitched and he watched her with a gleam in his eyes. "Especially on those lonely nights when you're at some kind of school function without me."

"But I'm always just with Carolyn and other friends," Jeni protested.

"I know." The hand behind her moved up to her shoulder and he hugged her in closer. "But there's always going to be some Ansel with a flashy car who wants to take you for a ride."

"Just like there's always going to be some Wenonah putting her arm around you and taking a selfie," Jeni countered.

"Touché." His smile held a tinge of sadness. "I guess that's what we signed up for."

Jeni was quiet for a moment, not really wanting to voice the question on her mind. But it had to be asked. "Do you ever regret it?"

"No." His immediate response was reassuring. "But I sometimes wonder if it's a bigger deal for you, being in high school."

Jeni uttered a disparaging grunt. "You know what I've observed? A lot of times, the kids who constantly have a girlfriend or boyfriend are the ones who aren't really going anywhere. They're more concerned with their relationship status than their classes. And then the serious students who're part of a couple never have time to do things together—kind of like you and me." She chuckled. "So I'm not really missing out on anything. Especially since you came out to take me to Homecoming and the Winter Dance."

"Well it's one thing if guys look, but I can't have anyone else dancing with you."

His tone was playful, and Jeni tilted her head to catch the glimmer in Ice's eyes. He leaned in to kiss her so she twisted, extending her neck for full lip to lip contact. Ice's fingers softly stroked her cheek, then cupped her jaw.

She slipped her hand behind his neck, fingertips tracing the chain of the medal he wore—the one his mom had given him when he left for college, the one that had saved their lives on the last trip. Refusing to dwell on that memory, she combed her fingers into his hair instead, relishing the warmth and thick softness.

The sun was a slice of orange, sinking into the patchwork of fields beyond the pond. Worries about ghosts and long-distance relationships slipped from Jeni's mind as Ice became her sole focus. Each kiss became a little more insistent, a little more intense, and a slow burn began building inside her.

A loud scrape of metal on wood jarred her senses.

Someone was on the deck.

They broke apart. "Damn it." Jeni complained and Ice agreed with a soft snort. A few minutes later, they rose and headed back to the big cabin, finding a spot on the couch where they could snuggle up and watch the end of a Disney movie that was on while the kids played.

Jeni was exhausted by the time she crawled into bed and, refusing to be freaked out, pushed all other thoughts from her mind and channeled the memory of kissing Ice on the hill. Eyes closed, she relived the heady passion that warmed her middle with Ice's arm around her, his lips on hers and his fingers on her face.

Shaking the fantasy from her head, she hurried downstairs to the mercantile as she heard the third bellow of the steamboat's whistle. Surely, it was docking by now. Thank God in Heaven that the whistle's first blare had shaken her from her dream. Realizing she'd fallen back to sleep after her father had left for the riverfront, she hurriedly dressed and was lacing her shoes when the second bellow sounded.

Entering the store through the door in their kitchen, her heart stuttered when she turned and met Amakapa's eyes, dark as black walnut shells.

"Good day, Miss Bernard."

"And to you, Amakapa." Her cheeks flamed at the memory of her dream and she turned away, snatching her apron from behind the counter and tying it at the small of her back. "I do apologize, truly, as I slept overlong. What of the goods?"

"Two crates, as yet." He indicated a wooden box on the floor and another on the table in front of him that he'd already pried open. "I tallied eight and ten canteens in this one. O'course you'll want to reckon the count. You want I should move it to the counter?"

"There'd be no reason for it." Her mouth curled into a pleased smile.

"Ma'am?"

"Papa said." Marielle laughed at Amakapa's eyebrows, drawn tightly together. "You have garnered his trust."

He held her gaze. "A man that do trust another man with his worldly goods, mayhap one day deign to trust that same man with other things dear to him."

The heat returned to Marielle's cheeks and her breath caught in her throat. With fingers curled around the sides of her apron, they stared into each other's eyes and time seemed to stand still until there was a thump outside the door.

Amakapa turned, rushing to open the door to receive the next load of goods.

Francoise Poule, her father's right-hand man, entered and forced Amakapa to the side as he plunked another crate on top of the unopened one on the floor. Marielle moved behind the counter and pretended to study the territory map her father had tacked up next to the window as the men brought more boxes inside from the wagon.

"Ain't you a sight for sore eyes, Marielle."

$\mathcal{L}$ost in $\mathcal{N}$owhere

He'd spoken to her directly; she had no choice but to face him.

The chime of church bells came through the open door as Francoise tipped his misshapen hat and took a step in her direction.

"That's Miss Bernard, Mister Poule. I don't right think my papa would take kindly to you addressing me in such a familiar manner." She could smell the sour odor of wine and took a step backward, feeling the wooden shelves dig into her back.

His clothes were soiled with all manner of substances: sweat, dirt, drink, food and probably tobacco, too. Marielle held her expression carefully passive to hide her distaste.

"I'm none too shore 'bout that," Francoise said with a wink.

Marielle bent to straighten shelves that were in perfect order, swallowing her revulsion at his thinly veiled insinuation. Francoise was widowed, and though he wasn't a businessman, he was a landowner with a good job and money to spare. Some of the town folk might think those things constituted an eligible bachelor, but Marielle disagreed. He was an unkempt, sloppy drunkard, and the thought of being close enough to touch him turned her stomach.

Amakapa entered and Francoise stalked off, hollering over the church bells that he had to get the wagon back to the docks. Noticing Marielle's pale face, Amakapa asked, "Were he botherin' you?"

She forced a light laugh. "Mister Poule was simply himself. I remain unscathed." The last thing she wanted was for Amakapa to threaten the other man.

Even with the mixed ethnicities and inter-marriages in the town, an Indian could not go against a white man.

Amakapa looked unconvinced, but he bent to his work, prying open the next crate. He'd closed the door, but still the clang of bells sounded…

Jeni opened her eyes, the sight of her book on the mattress causing her to start in confusion. A quick sweep of the room reoriented her, though images from the dream remained sharp in her mind.

Okay. That was super weird. She'd never had a dream like that before. Sure, she'd dreamed she was other people—other characters, usually from shows or movies—but the inner thoughts were always hers. This dream felt as if she'd *become* Marielle, seeing what she saw, feeling what she felt.

A notification chimed on her phone, interrupting her thoughts. She realized at once it was the sound that her brain had attributed to church bells in the dream.

Sitting up, Jeni retrieved her phone from the nightstand. The messages were from Carolyn, who'd apparently had a fight with her boyfriend. For a few seconds Jeni was torn between her own conundrum and being a good best friend. No, she decided, setting the phone aside. She couldn't do this now. Becoming involved in a conversation with Carolyn would mean she'd lose the details of the dream, and it was important that she be able to relay as much as possible to Ice. She could text Carolyn in the morning. As far as her friend knew, Jeni had slept through the messages. Besides, it seemed as if Carolyn had a new fight—or a new boyfriend—every week.

Grateful she'd fallen asleep with the lamp on, Jeni scooted back under the covers, sorting out her feelings. The obvious assumption—that Marielle had somehow induced the dream—creeped her out. A ghost sending a dream was creepy. Yet the thought that Marielle hadn't sent the dream was worse. Jeni seriously doubted her mind had conjured a past scene in such detail. So if it hadn't been Marielle, was it some kind of trap like she'd suspected at first? A trap set by the next evil entity out to take her life?

Then she remembered Ice asking earlier if she'd felt any maliciousness coming from Marielle. Rerunning the dream, Jeni checked with her gut. There'd been no overtones of impending danger. She'd simply felt what Marielle felt.

Recalling the thrill of physical attraction and excitement at the energy flaring between Amakapa and Marielle, Jeni's pulse quickened. It had been the same for her when she'd first met Ice at Lake Itasca: the sparks that ignited whenever he'd come near, the rush of emotions when she first saw the hunger in his eyes and realized he felt the same allure that she felt, the fantasies of how his lips would feel on hers… Oh yes, she could empathize with Marielle.

She *knew* what that was like.

She knows.

Suddenly the dream made sense to Jeni. Talking through the Ouija board was a slow and awkward way to communicate. So Marielle had found another way to explain herself.

Marielle was right. Jeni did know.

God, it would've sucked so much if her dad had forbidden her to see Ice. Heck, Jeni was ticked off when she couldn't go visit him at school. She tried to imagine that feeling times ten. Or a hundred. Because Marielle's father had done far worse. And fate, it seemed, had dealt a final blow, separating the lovers eternally.

She flopped back onto her pillow, thoughts racing.

Perhaps she could find a way to help this spirit.

Jeni didn't think she'd be able to fall back to sleep after the dream, but her wakefulness the previous night caught up with her. The brightness that greeted her upon waking was more than just the bedside lamp. Soft morning light leaked from the sides of the window shade. As she blinked away the last vestiges of sleep, she remembered the dream and bolted out of bed, quickly pulling on a sweatshirt and socks.

Ice looked up from a magazine as she emerged from her room. "Morning." The admiration in his eyes stirred the embers started the night before—the same feelings that were reflected in the dream. His bed was already folded back into the sofa and he lounged against the arm, feet up. His long legs nearly reached the opposite end of the couch and he swung his feet to the floor to make room for Jeni. "Catching up on the latest in fishing lures," he explained, closing the magazine.

"Oh, really?" Jeni eyeballed him suspiciously. She knew the magazine was her dad's. "I thought you were just a social fisherman." The sharp aroma of coffee beckoned from the kitchen, but someone was clanking dishes and Jeni was impatient to talk to Ice. She snuggled up to his side, curling her legs next to her.

Ice snickered. "I am. But I still like to actually catch fish."

Jeni nodded absently, her mind elsewhere. "Hey, I think I figured out what Marielle meant by 'she knows.'"

Ice slid the magazine onto the coffee table and turned to her, an eyebrow peaked inquisitively. "Oh? It came to you in your sleep?"

"Kind of. I had a dream about her. Actually, it was more like I *was* her in the dream." Jeni burrowed closer, emotions flooding back as she recounted the dream. "I think she sensed my feelings for you. Maybe even the frustration of having to be apart."

"Mmm." The vibration transferred directly from Ice's rib cage to hers. "That does make more sense than her mistaking you for like, a medium, or something."

"Ice, I feel like I have to try and help her if I can." Craning her neck, Jeni searched Ice's face for a reaction to her statement.

His throat worked as he swallowed. When he shifted his focus to her, she read concern in his icy blue eyes.

"What?" Jeni asked. "I thought you wanted me to help her."

"Help her move on," he clarified, breaking eye contact by letting his head fall against the back of the couch. "You know, pass into the light or however you want to think of it."

"Wouldn't that be what I was ultimately doing? If I can resolve her unfinished business, she can move on." Jeni straightened, pulling away slightly, bewildered by Ice's change of heart.

"It's her unfinished business that bothers me."

"Why? Because of all those questions we don't know the answers to?" Jeni asked, referring to the previous night's conversation.

"No. Although that alone could be enough." He was staring into his lap. "Amakapa drowned in the Mississippi River. And we know whatever is seeking vengeance against you is tied to the river somehow. I'm afraid that if you get involved in this, it'll draw unnecessary attention to you."

Jeni wrinkled her nose. She hadn't thought about that. "But this doesn't really involve the river. I think she just wants me to find out where he is in the spirit world."

"The gravestone at the church didn't seem to involve the river, either, and look what happened during the river cruise."

Jeni didn't get a chance to respond because her mom entered the room. "Oh, Jeni, I didn't know you were up," she said. "I was just coming out to let Ice know the coffee is ready."

Jeni's dad joined them in the kitchen a few minutes later, the scents of spruce and mint giving away that he'd just come from the shower. "We're on our own for breakfast today," he said, opening the refrigerator. "Bacon?"

Lost in Nowhere

Jeni giggled. "That should be a statement, Dad, not a question." Before leaving the room, she filled another mug with coffee and moved it close to the stove where her dad was lining up strips of bacon in a large skillet.

Her mom sat at the dining table, thumbing through pictures on her phone. Jeni stopped to look over her shoulder. "Are those from yesterday?"

"Yeah," her mom replied. "I got some good ones. You guys want to see what you missed?"

Receiving a noncommittal shrug from Ice, Jeni said, "Sure," and sat down next to her mom.

Before Ice could grab another chair, Mrs. Stonewall stood. "Sit here, Ice, so you both can see. I'll narrate."

Most of the pictures were of the historic houses in Ste. Genevieve, both inside and out. "Where was this at?" Jeni asked. It was a picture of an old map of Kaskaskia, before the Mississippi River changed course.

"Those are from the museum," her mom said. "The place is tiny, but there were some interesting displays. I took a picture of one with you in mind. It's an exhibit of fashion items from back in the day."

"Will somebody get me a plate with paper towel on it?" Jeni's dad called from the kitchen.

"I'll get it. I'm up," her mom said. She was back a minute later with a stack of plates and silverware. "Did you find any good antique shops yesterday? There's talk of heading to the St. Mary Antique Mall today."

Jeni smiled. She saw that coming. "If you're

bargain hunting, you might be better off at the antique mall. The shops in town were pretty pricey."

Her mom distributed forks next to the plates she'd set out. "Are you two interested in checking it out?"

When Jeni turned to consult Ice, he'd scrunched his face and curled one side of his lip. "I think we're going to pass." She smothered a chuckle.

After breakfast and showers, Jeni's mom announced she was joining some of the others who were going to a nearby school. "Josie and Leila want to take the kids to the elementary school's playground, and the middle school across the street has a track we can walk." She peered out the window. "Since it seems to be clouding up, we figure we'll do the antique mall this afternoon."

About to ask if she and Ice could use the car, Jeni slumped in her seat when her mom swiped the keys from the table. "You're driving?"

"Yep." Her mom kissed her on the cheek. "See you in a little while." She whisked out the door.

Reading her downcast expression, Ice said, "Let me guess: you wanted to go to Memories and Magic?"

Jeni nodded. She hadn't had a chance to respond to his concerns earlier, and his point was valid, but if it was possible to help Marielle safely, she wanted to try. "I'd at least like to get some of our questions answered."

"Well, we've got all day." Ice shrugged. "We'll just go later."

"Yeah, I guess." Jeni finger-combed her hair from her face.

Lost in Nowhere

They wandered out to the patio where her dad was tying a lure to one of his fishing rods. "What're you two up to?"

"We're going to hang out here." Jeni glanced to Ice before lowering into a chair. "We might take a walk in a little while." She'd intentionally made it clear that they were not going to be inside the cabin alone. Ice seemed to catch her drift and sat on a chaise lounge, stretching his legs out. Then he took out his phone and began swiping the screen with his finger, appearing to be engrossed in whatever he was looking at.

Apparently satisfied with Jeni's answer, her dad gathered a few fishing rods in one hand and picked up his tackle box. "Well, you know where I'll be." He nodded toward the pond, where the water rippled as a breeze skimmed the surface.

Watching him stride down the hill, Jeni asked, "Do you think it would be okay to use the Ouija board out here? On the patio?"

Ice raised his head and shot her a quizzical look. "Seriously? Let's just wait. We should have someone to take notes, anyway."

Jeni sighed. "I'm going to go get my book, then." Standing, she caught sight of her dad stopped on the hill halfway to the pond. He was turned toward the cabins, apparently carrying on a conversation. She moved out onto the grass until the other cabins came into view. Tyler stood at the rail of the large cabin's deck, talking to her dad.

Her cousin disappeared inside while her dad waited. Tyler reappeared a minute later, trotting down the steps and accepting one of her dad's fishing rods.

Jeni glanced at Ice, who had apparently become genuinely absorbed in something on his phone. "Tyler is with my dad down at the pond," she announced, waiting until she had his attention. Then with deliberate emphasis she said, "This is a golden opportunity, Ice. I'm going to see if Mandy wants to help us." She struck off across the lawn before he could reply, telling herself he did not look dismayed when she blurted out her intention. He shouldn't have encouraged her to contact the ghost only to change his mind. It wasn't fair.

Approaching the screen door of the largest cabin, Jeni slowed, wondering if she should knock or walk right in. Whenever they came down for dinner, they just went inside. She paused, letting her eyes adjust to the darker interior as she peered through the screen. "Hello?" She realized she didn't even know if Mandy went with the others to the school.

A car door slammed and she jumped, backing from the door. Had someone returned from the school already? She wondered if one of the kids had gotten hurt, though it seemed like they'd just left.

"Hey, Jeni. Looking for someone?" Mandy was climbing the deck stairs, a towel over one arm and a magazine in her hand.

"You, as a matter of fact." Jeni stretched her mouth into a smile, shifting her feet.

"What's up?" Mandy dropped the magazine and her phone on a table and spread the towel over a lounge chair.

Lost in Nowhere

Jeni's hands found her pockets and slipped inside. "I… uh… wanted to take you up on your offer. You know," she glanced toward the cabin and lowered her voice. "With the Ouija board."

She had Mandy's full attention. "Right now?"

"If you don't mind. Most everyone is gone." She swept her arm out toward the pond. "Or occupied."

"I knew you guys wanted to use it." Mandy grinned, enthusiasm glittering in her brown eyes. "I'm in, but where are we gonna do this?"

"A patio?" At the look on Mandy's face, she amended, "Or the woods? There's a trail at the end of the road." She pointed.

Scooping up her phone, Mandy said, "Let's go."

On the way to her cabin, Jeni explained that they were trying to reach a particular spirit—one that had been appearing to her. They reached the patio before she'd finished recounting the legend of the curse of Kaskaskia.

Ice hadn't moved. His lips flattened as he contemplated the two girls and clicked his phone off. "You really can't wait?"

"Why should we?" Jeni fought the urge to cross her arms over her chest and kept her tone light. "We have the board, we have a third person and we know what to do." She looked from him to Mandy and then said, "I'll go grab the board."

Ice didn't say much as they crunched down the gravel drive toward the trail, lagging behind the girls while Jeni caught Mandy up.

"This is crazy, you guys," Mandy said. "But I'm glad I get to help."

"Tyler will probably kill me for this," Jeni muttered.

"Let me handle Tyler," Mandy said. "He doesn't dictate what I can and can't do."

Jeni rolled her lips over her teeth and pressed them tight. Her cousin was going to be pissed, regardless. "I think we'll have enough room at the end of this side trail." It was the path down which she'd fled after seeing Marielle materialize across the road.

When they reached the clearing at the end of the path, Ice let the girls set up the Ouija board. "I'll take notes." He claimed the pen and notepad.

A jolt of uncertainty warmed Jeni's chest. "I thought you and I would use the board. I won't make you ask the questions this time."

"Mandy wants to do this," he said. "Let her participate."

Jeni knew Ice wasn't simply being generous—he was clearly annoyed—but now wasn't the time to address it, so she let it drop. "Okay," she said to Mandy. "How about if we sit cross-legged, facing each other, with the board across our knees?"

"That should work." Mandy surveyed the ground for the best place to sit.

Once they were situated, Jeni began a quick review of the rules, and Mandy chimed in with the things she remembered from past experience. Ice perched atop a large boulder, watching them.

Jeni tried to shrug off her irritation at Ice's aloof manner and focused on Mandy. "Ready?" she asked. At Mandy's nod, she placed her fingers on the planchette, and Mandy did the same.

Lost in Nowhere

For a moment, Jeni did nothing. A flash of reality struck her as she stared at the board. What was she doing? The hair on the back of her neck stood on end and she struggled against chickening out. Why had this been so important?

She closed her eyes and thought of the dream, of the joy of newfound love, and then she recalled how it felt to have that ripped away—when she thought she'd never see Ice again—and her resolve solidified. "Are... are you here, Marielle?"

Jeni flinched as the planchette slid directly to *"Yes"* and then began spelling. *"I... C... A... N... H... E... L... P... Y... O... U."*

"Wait. What do you mean? How can you help me? I don't—" She stopped speaking as the wooden piece again traversed the alphabet. *"A... N... C... E... S... T... O... R... S."*

"Are you saying you know my ancestors? Can you help me find them?"

The planchette indicated *"Yes,"* and excitement swelled as Jeni considered the ramifications of Marielle's offer. Her eyes shifted to Ice. He raised a dubious eyebrow.

Jeni opened her mouth to make the next inquiry and then closed it, realizing she didn't know which question the spirit had answered. Drawing in a calming breath, she coached herself to slow down.

"Do you know my ancestors?"

The piece trundled across the board to *"No."*

So Marielle could help her *find* her ancestors. That could only happen after she crossed. Which meant Jeni would have to find Amakapa first.

Mandy's head was tilted and Jeni read the curiosity in her eyes. She would have to explain her family history search later. Right now, she had to figure out if there was a way to help this ghost. "Uh... Marielle, I'm not sure if I can help you or not. You said Amakapa is nowhere. What does that mean?"

"L... O... S... T... W... A... N... D... E... R... I... N... G."

The answer meant nothing to her and Jeni wanted to blurt out, "What's that supposed to mean?" but knew the only good that would do was blow off some of her frustration. Instead, she tried a different tack. "Why do you think I can find him from the living world?"

"C... O... N... N... E... C... T... E... D."

Assuming the ghost was referring to her connection to the spirit world, Jeni breathed an exasperated sigh. This disjointed form of communication was futile.

As if her heavy sigh were enough stimulus, the planchette moved again, spelling out, "R... I... N... G."

"I don't understand." Jeni imagined her own forehead was as wrinkled as Mandy's.

Starting over, the disc repeated, "R... I... N... G."

"She spelled 'connected' before 'ring,'" Ice offered in a hushed voice. "Maybe a ring is what connects her to the living world?"

Before Jeni could ask, the planchette indicated, "Yes."

According to Phoebe, a personal possession would allow them to communicate with the spirit without the Ouija board. But knowing a ring teth-ered Marielle among the living was only relevant if they could get their hands on it, which seemed highly doubtful.

"Do you know where the ring is?" Jeni asked.

"T... O... W... N... S... Q... U... A... R... E."

Jeni hadn't allowed herself to be hopeful, still, the answer was as disappointing as a "no." Surely the town square that existed in Kaskaskia during Marielle's time was lost to the floods.

"Do you mean the town square in Kaskaskia?" she asked anyway.

The planchette landed on *"No"* and then spelled: *"D... U... B... O... U... R... G."*

"Dubourg?" Jeni looked from Mandy to Ice, seeing no recognition on their faces. "Is that a city in Missouri?"

Whether meant for her or not, Marielle answered the question. *"No."* Before Jeni could think of what to ask next, the wooden piece began moving over the al-phabet. *"A... C... R... O... S..."*

Then, without warning, the planchette scraped straight down to *"Goodbye,"* momentum sending it off the board and onto the ground.

Jeni met Mandy's dumbfounded stare with one equally confused. "Why did she—"

"Goodbye." Ice cut her off, speaking the word emphatically.

First to recover, Mandy looked at Ice and repeat-ed the ending statement.

"Goodbye," Jeni echoed out loud, then closed the board and scooped the planchette from the dirt. "I wonder why—" she broke off as a car slowed on the road below them and turned onto the resort service drive.

"They're back from the school," Mandy said.

"Shoot." Jeni struggled in her rush to get the lid onto the box. "I've gotta get the board back into the cabin."

Ice typed "Dubourg Missouri" into the search engine on his phone, wondering why he felt so uneasy. At first he'd been annoyed that Jeni couldn't wait until they were at Phoebe's shop to use the Ouija board. The medium's presence had given him a measure of reassurance yesterday. Now, even though their recent session seemed to go just fine, Ice couldn't shake his unsettled feeling.

They'd managed to beat Mrs. Stonewall back to the cabin, spotting her car idling down the road while she dropped off passengers. Mandy and Ice went straight to the patio while Jeni had slipped inside to deposit the Ouija board into one of her dresser drawers. Seconds after he'd dropped into a chair, Ice had heard the car pull up followed by the squeak of the side door.

"My mom's getting in the shower," Jeni announced as she opened the sliding door and joined him and Mandy on the patio. "That was close," she added in a hushed voice, passing them each a bottle of water. "I panicked like a kid caught with my hand in the cookie jar when she walked in." She snorted, rolling her eyes. "So I grabbed water bottles as an excuse to be there, as if I needed a reason."

Mandy snickered, accepting the water. Ice just shook his head and put the bottle on the table next to him. Jeni would have to reveal the Ouija board eventually or leave it behind. He certainly wasn't going to try and pack it in his bag for the return trip to Minnesota.

A gust of wind rushed up the hill and a few dead leaves scraped the pavers as they danced across the surface. He scanned the search results on his phone. "I looked up 'Dubourg Missouri' and came up with a bunch of hits for Bishop DuBourg High School in St. Louis. There's also a Dubourg Hall and a Dubourg House."

Jeni leaned over the back of his chair to view the phone screen. "What's Dubourg Hall? That sounds like something that could be in a town square."

"It's part of a university. See?" Ice pointed.

Mandy joined Jeni behind Ice's chair. "Did you try 'Dubourg' with 'town square'?'"

Ice revised the search term. "Now I've got articles about Bishop Dubourg in Louisiana. Guess I'd better add 'Missouri' to this search, too."

"It's basically the same stuff," Mandy said when the results popped up. "Mostly about the High School."

"Take 'high school' out of the search," Jeni said.

That had been Ice's thought, too, and he was already changing the search text. The initial results seemed positive when the first hit read: Catholic Church of Ste. Genevieve—DuBourg Centre. He clicked on the article. The page described the restored historical building that was part of the Parish.

"That's not helpful," Jeni said as Ice continued to scroll down the page.

"Wait," Mandy said. "Look at the bottom. The address of the church is DuBourg Place. Let's search that."

Ice typed it in. The result was a list of articles about the DuBourg Centre. Setting the phone on his lap, he pulled the notes from the Ouija session from his pocket. The problem was they didn't have much to go on.

Mandy pulled up a chair and sat, pushing her hair behind her ears. "Maybe we should try 'Kaskaskia town square.'"

"But I asked Marielle if that's what she meant and she said 'no,'" Jeni said. "I suppose it can't hurt, though."

Ice retrieved his phone and shifted in his seat. "Kaskaskia town square" hit on "Kaskaskia" and "town" but showed nothing that included "town square." Silence reigned for a few minutes as he typed in other search terms. Jeni watched from over his shoulder while Mandy got out her own phone to double the effort.

Jeni breathed a resolute sigh. "We're not going to find anything. We need more information."

"Hey, look at this," Mandy said. Squatting next to Ice's chair, she pointed at an entry in what appeared to be some kind of guidebook. "This is in a book called: *Louis and Clark Road Trips.*"

The paragraph she indicated was about the Ste. Genevieve Museum.

Lost in Nowhere

Ice read aloud: "The Ste. Genevieve Museum is located on historic DuBourg Place. The town square in a French river town was called the 'Place de Armes' where the church, civil and military authorities were all located. The museum was built on the square—"

"DuBourg Place is Ste. Genevieve's town square!" Jeni interrupted.

"Okay," Mandy said. "But how would that be relevant? Marielle was from Kaskaskia."

"Right. But I read somewhere…" Jeni rounded the chair and looked at Ice. "Where did we see that? Remember? Many Kaskaskians fled to Ste. Genevieve after the floods. Because it was right across the river."

"That was in one of your mom's pictures," Ice responded. "With the map that showed Old Kaskaskia."

Mandy knit her brow. "Except by the time of the floods, Marielle was no longer living. She wouldn't have moved to Ste. Genevieve."

Jeni nodded. "Yes. But the ring might have been passed along to someone who did leave Kaskaskia at that time and settle in Ste. Genevieve. Hang on a second." She dashed inside the cabin.

Movement caught his eye and Ice saw that Mr. Stonewall and Tyler had finished fishing and were climbing the hill toward the cabins. Behind them, the surface of the pond was covered in ripples that changed direction at the whim of the wind. The sight seemed to reflect his feelings, shifting from interested, to impassive, to agitated.

Jeni returned holding a folded paper. "A map of Ste. Genevieve." She set it on the table and smoothed it out, plunking her phone down on one edge to keep the paper from blowing away while she tapped a location. "Here's the town square. This is the museum. Next to the museum is the courthouse and across the square from both of them is the church."

"A church and civil buildings, like the book said." Mandy stared down at the map. "So the ring could be in any of those places, if we assume Marielle was referring to this town square."

Ice reached for the sheet of Ouija notes. "The last thing she spelled on the board was 'across.' Maybe she was referring to a building across from the town square."

"We're talking about a ring, you guys," Jeni interjected. "Doesn't the museum make the most sense as a place to start?" She turned to Ice. "My mom took that picture of the case of old-fashioned accessories, wasn't there jewelry?"

"I didn't pay that much attention." He narrowed his eyes, studying Jeni. What was she thinking? Even if there was jewelry—or a ring—did Jeni really think she could somehow acquire it?

He didn't have a chance to comment, though, when Mrs. Stonewall appeared at the screen door. "Did I hear my name mentioned?"

Jeni blinked, hesitating before she answered. "Uh… yeah, actually. Can I see your museum pictures again? I wanted to show Mandy something."

"Sure, honey. I'll grab my phone. Are you guys hungry? Jake's putting hot dogs on the grill." She scrutinized the darkening sky. "It's a good thing they cook quickly."

"Count me in for one," Mandy responded immediately.

Ice held up two fingers. "Two for me."

"Yeah, I'll have one," Jeni said.

"Okay, I'll text our hot dog count and then send you the museum pictures."

Once Mrs. Stonewall's figure faded into the cabin's interior, Mandy asked, "Hey, what's up with the comment Marielle made about ancestors?"

Jeni sighed, folding the map. "I discovered I have some kind of spiritual ability." She glanced to Ice. "I need to know the origin of the ability so I know what to expect."

Mandy frowned. "I don't get it. How does Marielle figure into that?"

"Well, I've been researching my genealogy, but I've hit kind of a roadblock." Jeni shrugged. "Marielle is a ghost. I don't know—maybe she can find things out from the other side. It's another reason why it would be nice to talk to her without the board."

It looked as though Mandy was about to pose another question, but Jeni's phone chimed, interrupting the conversation. "Received twenty-seven images," Jeni reported. Pulling out a chair, she sank down while thumbing through the museum shots. "Bingo." She uttered the word quietly.

Jeni passed her phone to Ice. The case included shoes, gloves, hats, hat pins, hair combs... and there was the jewelry. He zoomed in on the picture, his heart sinking. She was right; the exhibit included rings. "There are four rings there," he said. "Even if one of these is Marielle's, how could we know which one?"

"Can I see?" Mandy reached for the phone and

Ice passed it to her, watching as she, too, enlarged the photo.

Ice slumped back into his chair, the cold roil in his stomach making him uncomfortable. A wind current brought the smell of charred meat, and he tried to tell himself he'd feel better after a hot dog.

Mrs. Stonewall returned, rounding them up to have lunch at the big cabin. As they arrived on the deck with Mandy, Tyler shot them a scathing look, his lips clamped together. Mandy immediately went to him, looping her arm through his and asking about fishing. True to her word, she didn't seem to be worried about what Tyler thought.

Apparently Jeni had noticed her cousin's expression, because she steered Ice into the cabin where the food was set out, cafeteria style. He let her decide where they should sit and was surprised when she led him back out to the deck, since most of the family had heeded the threat of rain. Then she set her phone between their plates to contemplate the rings further, and he finally understood why she'd sequestered them from the others.

"One has some kind of stones, and this one is obviously a pearl," she commented.

Ice popped a chip into his mouth, cupping his hand around the edge of his plate to keep the other chips from blowing away. He gave the photo a cursory glance. "It seems like a collection of different styles and time periods to me. And we have no idea what we're looking for."

Jeni groaned, finally letting the screen go black when she accepted the strong probability that her plate would flip if she didn't hold it down. Finishing her hot dog, she picked up her bottle of water and twisted the cap off. "You'd think she would have given us a clue if she really wanted us to find it." Jeni tipped her water bottle to her lips.

Ice drew in a deep breath. The food hadn't alleviated the knot in his gut. "Maybe it's better if we don't—"

He broke off as Jeni choked on her water. Ice took the bottle from her and thumped her on the back as she coughed and sputtered. "You okay?"

She drew the attention of the few others who'd braved eating on the deck and she held up her hand. "I'm okay," she managed to say, between small coughs. Then she dipped her chin, clearing her throat a few times to stave off more coughing. "Across," she said in a low, rough voice, raising her eyes to see if she was still the center of attention.

"What?" Ice drew his brows together, staring at Jeni.

She reached for her phone, bringing up the picture of the rings again. "A. Cross. Not across. Look, this gold ring looks like it has a cross stamped into the metal."

Ice leaned down to examine the round, flat top of the gold ring. He used his fingers to make the photo as large as possible. The surface was indented with a pattern. A cross. And something else.

An icy wave rolled from Ice's stomach to his chest, making him feel for a moment as if his hot dog and chips were going to come back up. He jerked his fingers from the screen and blinked, unnerved when the shape of the indentations seemed burned into his mind as if he'd stared at them too long.

Oblivious to Ice's reaction, Jeni had zoomed in on the picture again. "Is that what it looks like to you?"

"Yeah." Ice swallowed hard. The image stamped in his brain had nothing to do with how long he'd viewed the picture. It was a warning. His intuition raised an alert, and he wasn't sure why.

Worry lines appeared on Jeni's forehead, and she raised her gaze to his. "You sound unconvinced."

"I'm convinced about the cross." Rather than reveal his sudden, odd trepidation, Ice took another tack. "Let's just say for the sake of argument that this is Marielle's ring—the one that's keeping her here— how do you think you'd get your hands on it?"

Ice watched Jeni's face tense and then fall as she computed possible scenarios for obtaining the ring. "Maybe we can make up a story with a good reason to borrow it." Her voice faltered even as she voiced the suggestion.

Mrs. Stonewall slid the door to the deck open just enough to poke her head out. "We're taking off for the antique mall in about fifteen minutes in case you've changed your mind."

Jeni paused mid headshake, her eyes sliding to Ice's for a moment before returning to her mom. "Okay, I'll let you know."

"You want to go to the antique mall?" Ice asked.

"I saw the building, Ice. It's huge." Her eyes glittered. "It would be a great place to look for a ring that resembles the one in the picture."

Ice delivered a quizzical stare. "How would that help us?"

"We'd have a substitute," she said.

"Substitute? Jeni, the item needs to have once belonged to the spirit you're trying to contact."

The animation in Jeni's face disappeared. "I got that." Her voice was flat. "I'm talking about finding a ring that we can switch out for Marielle's ring."

Ice closed his eyes for a moment, feeling a knot forming under his right shoulder blade. "You want to steal the ring in the museum?"

"Exchange." She said it emphatically. "It's not for personal gain. I'm not going to sell it or anything. It's for a good cause."

"Regardless. You're talking about pulling off a heist." Ice stood, gathering his plate, fork and soda can. "Think about it."

He watched a muscle flex in Jeni's cheek as she clenched her jaw and stared up at him. "It can't hurt to look. If we don't find a suitable replacement, then it's a non-issue."

"And if we do?"

She looked away. "I'll cross that bridge when I come to it."

Here is your ring, which I put for safety into my purse.
Princess Rosette ~ Madame d'Aulnoy

Chapter 6

*T*hey'd barely made it to the car before the swollen clouds released their burden. Ice's sullen silence filled the backseat, crushing Jeni's earlier defiance. They needed to talk. The rain pounding on the roof might provide an opportunity to talk in relative privacy, but the potential that the conversation might get emotional gave her pause. The decision to wait until they were alone felt like a chasm between them. Jeni shifted a little closer to Ice, as if she could bridge the invisible gap.

She knew her idea was crazy—and perhaps impossible—but it was already Tuesday, and she was running out of time. In order to help Marielle—and get the ghost's help in return—she needed a more efficient way to communicate. Getting her hands on an object that had belonged to Marielle would provide a direct link. An advantage of that magnitude was worth pursuing.

Perhaps Ice didn't know how profoundly she'd been affected when he hadn't shown up for the river cruise last fall—when they'd realized he was missing.

The hole his absence left had been filled with guilt and despair. The memory of that feeling was what incited her deep-seated need to make sure Marielle and Amakapa could be together in eternity, since they'd been cruelly kept apart in life.

As soon as they were alone, Jeni pulled Ice off to the side and broached the subject. "Hey, what's up? You haven't been yourself today." She offered a small smile.

Ice's eyes slid to her and then away. "I'm not sure." He shook his head.

"You encouraged me to see if I could help Marielle and now you seem mad that I'm pursuing it."

"I'm not mad. I just have this weird feeling. A... a wrongness." He pushed a hand through his hair. "As if you're putting yourself in harm's way."

Jeni wanted to touch him, reach for his hand, his arm, but he wore short sleeves and there was no point. She'd see the visions and be unable to talk through them. "Did you change your mind? Do you think this is some kind of trap?"

He frowned. "I believe the spirit is Marielle, and that she wants your help finding Amakapa..." He shrugged. "It's my gut, my intuition. I'm on high alert. I just don't want anything to happen to you."

Jeni sighed. "I don't want anything to happen to *you*. I—" She swallowed over the lump that rose in her throat. "I know how that feels. To have someone you love taken from you." She blinked away the prickle of threatening tears. "I don't believe I can hide, Ice. I can be as careful as I want, but as soon as I leave home, as soon as I get close enough to the river... or cross a bridge... or... whatever, it knows I'm here. Whatever *it* is." A mirthless laugh sputtered from her lips.

He didn't respond and she searched his eyes, splintered into shades of blue.

"I refuse to hole up in fear. You know, it's like never going out in public because you're afraid of a terrorist attack. Then they win." She moved closer and put her hand on his chest, feeling the sun-shape of his St. Thomas Aquinas medal under her palm. "For the sake of everyone I care about, I need to get to the root of what's happening to me. Maybe Marielle can't help find my ancestors, but imagine if she can. She is a ghost, after all. It makes sense. Think of how much research it would save us." She closed her eyes for a second and shook her head. "But regardless of that, for once—for the first time, Ice—I have a chance to do something honorable with my spiritual ability. Something beyond chasing a monster. Something I feel passionate about."

His expression was so deadly serious, Jeni added, "Hey, she's a white girl in love with a Native American boy. I can't walk away from that." She allowed the corners of her mouth to lift, imploring him to understand.

The tense set to his face softened and his hands went to her waist, pulling her closer. "You're a courageous, hopeless romantic, Jeni Stonewall."

She rose up on her toes and kissed him lightly on the lips, aware of people meandering nearby. "Who knows? Maybe this experience will help me learn who I am and what I can do. What I'm meant to do."

"I still don't know how you think you'll get the ring from the museum, but I support you. Just promise me this: if things get dicey, you'll back off. Marielle's plight isn't your responsibility and we can figure out your ancestry on our own."

"Okay," Jeni said. "That's a deal."

The antique mall was the largest Jeni had ever been to. She imagined kids got lost in here all the time. The rows of stalls were almost labyrinthine; the myriad of furniture, tables and racks made the aisles appear misshapen and the thoroughfares unclear. Adding to the confusion were other shoppers who'd apparently decided the mall was an ideal place to spend some time on a rainy afternoon.

Her assumption had been correct; there was plenty of jewelry. They saw rings of all shapes and sizes: some with large gaudy stones, pretty gem-encrusted dinner rings, simple bands, class rings and tiny rings for children. The prices were as varied as the rings, and when Jeni saw some of the tags, she wondered how much this idea might end up costing her. Thank goodness she wasn't looking for a ring with gemstones.

They hadn't gotten too far from where they'd entered the mall when they came across a plain gold ring topped by a flat circle. Engraved on the front was the letter "A." All of the jewelry in this particular booth was in a glass case, and Jeni rose up on her toes, lifting her chin to catch the attention of the woman tending it.

"Did you want to see something?" the woman asked, dully businesslike.

£ost in Nowhere

"Yes." Jeni leaned over the case, tapping the glass top with a finger. "That gold one with the 'A' inscribed on it."

The woman slid open the door on the back of the case and reached inside, plucking the ring from the velveted holder. "Gold-plated," she said, handing it to Jeni, her eyes constantly darting to a couple of women inspecting a revolving rack of earrings. "They were popular in the seventies."

The price was certainly right at eight dollars. But as soon as it was in her hand, Jeni knew by the color and shininess that it wasn't an appropriate substitute and her enthusiasm faded. Though she shouldn't have expected to walk right up and find what she was looking for, she'd been excited by the prospect, none-theless. "It's not quite what I wanted." She handed the ring back to the woman. "Thanks for letting me see it, though."

"It looked too cheap... and new," Jeni muttered close to Ice's ear when they were in the next stall.

They found a couple other similar rings with an initial, including one with a three-letter monogram, but none could pass for such an old ring. Was she being excessively picky? She was really just looking for a placeholder.

Although she hadn't allowed herself to think too much about the logistics of the next step—exchanging one ring for another—her conscience dictated that she find the very best substitute for what she intended to take. It was the only way to assuage her guilt. And even then, if she somehow pulled this heist off, she knew she would never stop feeling bad about it.

Barbara Pietron

Many of the booths were unattended, and they quickly realized that these stalls rarely contained anything small enough to pocket. In the interest of time, they began to give the unattended spaces a cursory glance as they walked by. But Jeni was fortunate to have Ice with her, as he'd been trained for years to pay attention to detail.

"Jeni, wait."

She almost didn't hear him over the din and her eyes had already been sweeping the next booth. Pausing to look over her shoulder, she saw Ice step into the space she'd just passed. At the same time, a woman whose attention was somewhere across the aisle slammed into Jeni.

"Yeh can't jest stop in the aisle." She pronounced aisle as "ahll" and reproached Jeni as if it hadn't been the woman's fault for not paying attention to where she was going.

Jeni uttered a grunt of disbelief but pressed herself against the side of a dresser to let the woman pass. Slipping around the corner, she saw that Ice had spotted a cedar box with an open, hinged lid. Inside lay a jumble of jewelry. "There are some rings in here," he said. "And this stuff looks old."

The box sat atop a scratched and dented aluminum filing cabinet in a stall that was stuffed with an eclectic mix of items. Nothing was arranged to make it easy for customers to see what was there. It looked more like a storage space.

Jeni scooped up a handful of the jewelry and set it on the metal surface to sift through while Ice continued to rummage in the box. The flat top of the file cabinet allowed her to spread the pile out, causing the chunkier pieces to stand out from the bracelets and chains. None of the rings she found were suitable.

When Ice deemed his search unfruitful, Jeni returned all the jewelry to the box. "I don't know what's costume jewelry and what's actually worth money, but all of this stuff seems old, which makes me think it's worth something. I'm surprised the person who rents this space would leave this out in the open."

"It's so cluttered." Ice turned sideways and stepped over a wooden stool with a bucket of tools on top. "Most people probably don't stop."

Mimicking Ice's maneuver, Jeni paused with a foot in the air when she spotted a cat face. She'd collected cat statues (and all sorts of other cat-related items) since she was three or four. The incident at Lake Itasca had soured her inclination to purchase random old statues, but she still had to look.

Standing on tiptoe to see over a cardboard box, Jeni saw the cat was in a humped-back pose, its tail straight up. She had something similar at home. The cat's tail was extra-long to hold rings, and this one was doing its job. Leaning against the box, her arm was just long enough to pluck the cat from its shelf.

She held it up to Ice who waited at the edge of the booth, curious as to what she'd found. He stepped closer as she dumped the rings onto a desktop. Her eyes went instantly to a gold, flat-topped ring. Expecting another engraved initial, she picked it up, noticing right away that the ring felt different from the others they'd found—a little lighter, more delicate. The round gold surface was not shallowly etched;

rather, the shape of a sun appeared to be pressed into the metal.

Her reaction had given away that she'd found something, and Ice held out his open palm. She dropped the ring into his hand, waiting as he inspected it. "It's perfect," he said. "I wonder how much it is."

"Only one way to find out," Jeni replied, threading the other rings back onto the cat's tail. She returned the ring holder to the shelf and then made her way out of the stall. Glancing over her left shoulder, she said, "Didn't we pass a checkout counter back that way?"

"Yeah, I think you're right."

Because so many booths were unattended, signs were posted everywhere instructing customers to note the booth number and bring the item to the nearest checkout counter. They had to wait while a couple paid for an old wooden toy train, but with the amount of people milling about, Jeni didn't think that was too bad. When she set the ring down next to the cash register, the man behind the counter regarded it with wide eyes. "Someone wasn't minding the booth?" He eyeballed Jeni and Ice over the top of his glasses.

"No." Jeni shook her head. "It was booth number 102."

"It's right in the contract that jewelry should be here," he pointed down at the counter, which was the top of a glass fronted display case, "locked in a case, or in an attended booth." He shook his head and began paging through a notebook which sat next to the cash register. Running his finger down a row of numbers, he stopped, tapping the paper. A groan issued from the back of his throat. "Should've known. That's Henry Patokis' space. He treats it like an extension of his attic. Can't imagine it's cheaper than a storage unit, though," he muttered.

Then he picked up the ring, adjusted his glasses, and looked at it closely. "Looks old. Possibly nineteenth century or earlier. Solid gold, I'd bet."

Jeni's heart pounded as the man spewed out a list of attributes that she assumed would push the ring out of her price range.

The man raised his eyes and met Jeni's gaze over the rim of his glasses. It felt as though he was evaluating her, and she hoped he could read the desperation on her face. "Since the man dumps his items here with disregard, I'm going to assume he doesn't deem them too valuable. Plus, you were honest enough to bring the ring to me rather than pocketing it. How about forty dollars? It's worth at least double that, and possibly much more."

That amount of money was quite a few days of pet sitting, but it was doable. Jeni pulled her purse from her shoulder. "Deal." She exhaled, loosening the tight set to her shoulders.

But as the man handed her a small bag with the ring inside, Jeni's brief reprieve from tension ended. In the scheme of things, this had been the easy part of her plan.

Now she had to figure out how to access the ring in the museum and replace it with this one.

Barbara Pietron

They picked up four large pizzas on the way back from St. Mary and arrived back at the big cabin to a sizable green salad, plates and utensils waiting. The storm had cleared, and after they ate, Jeni's dad talked Ice into joining a game of horseshoes against Tyler and his dad. Since they were setting up down by the pond where the ground was level, Jeni pulled a chair up to the deck rail to keep an eye on the game. Her mind, however, was on the ring dilemma.

The sun had made an appearance in the wake of the rain, leaving the air warm and sticky. Jeni skimmed her hair away from her face and gathered it into a ponytail, fastening it with an elastic band from her wrist. At the scrape of the screen door, she twisted in her seat to see Mandy grab a chair to set next to her.

"Hey." Mandy dropped into the seat. "Did you guys figure out what the message meant?"

"I think so." Jeni looked over both shoulders, making sure they were alone on the deck. Then she caught Mandy up on everything that had happened since their conversation after the Ouija session that morning. First, Jeni explained how she'd noticed the cross on one of the rings in the picture. Then, dropping her voice further, she admitted her crazy idea and told Mandy about their trip to the antique mall.

Mandy's brown eyes widened. "But how are you going to swap out the rings?"

"I don't know," Jeni muttered. "That's what I was sitting here trying to figure out. I think I can pick the lock on the exhibit case. I mean, as long as it's the

142

same type of lock as the YouTube videos I watched." She'd scrutinized the picture her mom had taken at length, though only a portion of the lock was visible. Then she simply searched the Internet for museum-style display cases and looked at those locks before seeking out videos on how to pick them.

Mandy cocked her head. "Have you ever picked a lock before?"

Jeni watched as Ice threw a horseshoe. "Actually, yes, I have. It was a really simple one."

"You did?" Mandy's spine straightened. Then she leaned toward Jeni conspiratorially. "How come? Is there a juicy story there?"

Shifting in her seat, Jeni sent Tyler a reproachful look, even though he wasn't looking her way and certainly couldn't discern her expression from the bottom of the hill. "Let's just say I needed to read a diary."

Mandy nodded. "And…"

Jeni shook her head. "It's a long and complicated story."

"Was Tyler there?"

Obviously, Mandy was very perceptive. "Uh… yeah, but if he hasn't told you about it, it's not my place to tell you."

Mandy sighed. "All right," she relented. "I've felt like he's been hiding something for quite a while. Pretty much since we met. I'll have to keep working on him, I guess." She was quiet for a moment, staring at the horseshoe game. Then she combed her fingers through her hair, pushing the brunette locks behind her shoulders. "So… back to the ring. Are you going to try and sneak into the museum at night?"

"I don't think so. I mean, number one, there might be an alarm." Jeni ticked off the item on her index finger. "Number two, I'd have to sneak out of my cabin." She added a second finger. "And I'd need a car." Finger number three sprang up. "And, ugh, being in a museum at night? Too creepy." She touched her pinky finger to count the last reason.

"What about the docents that are there during the day?"

Jeni curled her top lip. "Did you guys go in there Monday?" She wished she and Ice had visited the museum so she could visualize what they'd be walking into.

"Yeah, we did."

"Are there security cameras?" Jeni asked.

Mandy shrugged. "I have no idea. It's not something I even thought about. Sorry."

The scuff of the sliding door interrupted their conversation, and Jeni's mom and Aunt Leila joined them on the deck.

"How's the game going?" her mom asked.

"It's hard to tell from here," Jeni responded. Mandy and Aunt Leila were talking, so she added, "I was thinking I'd wander down and sit on the grass. Want my chair?"

As she meandered down the hill, Jeni hoped she'd pulled that off without looking like she was dodging the company. Others may take offense, but her mom would understand her need to be alone. Being an only child, groups of people often got to be too much for Jeni and she'd disappear for a while to mentally recompose herself.

Lost in Nowhere

But that wasn't exactly what she was doing now. She needed some time to think through the plan and evaluate the feasibility of what she wanted to accomplish. The explanation she'd given Ice and the fervor behind her determination to find the ring weren't translating to pulling off the exchange in the museum.

What was she thinking? Ice was right, switching the rings was no less than stealing. She could be arrested. And what purpose would she give? That she was helping a ghost? Then she'd be committed instead of incarcerated.

By the time the horseshoe game ended, Jeni had worked herself into a state of turmoil. When Ice sat down beside her, she ended up spewing out all of her doubts.

"Well, you can stop worrying about that for tonight." Ice put an arm around her and kissed her forehead. "It sounds like we're going to St. Louis tomorrow."

Alarm and relief warred inside of her. Tomorrow was Wednesday. Her window to help Marielle had just gotten smaller. On the other hand, another day to work out the possibility of making an unsanctioned trade was welcome.

Jeni let the problem go and tried to enjoy the rest of the evening, knowing that a part of her brain would still be working out logistics. She climbed into bed, determined to get lost in her book and not stew over her dilemma. She needn't have worried, because when her head finally hit the pillow, she'd read barely half a page before her eyelids drooped and she drifted to sleep.

She sat at a wooden table, the aroma of meat and burning wax heavy in the air. The light outside the windows faded as Sally lit the candles, the orange glow burnishing her dark skin. Candelabras resembling mini chandeliers brightened the table with multiple flames that glinted off the glass and silver. Lifting a bowl of fresh lettuce, she passed it to her father. "'Tis the first lettuce from the garden, Papa," she said with pride.

Dutifully, he took the bowl. "Your garden does not want for vegetation this season."

"Indeed. We may yet see cucumbers, what with wholesome seed."

"I doubt not your abilities, daughter, as you have grown into a capable woman."

Her cheeks warmed at the compliment and she kept her eyes on her plate, lest she appear vain.

The room fell silent around the ting of silver on china. Papa cleared his throat.

A stab of trepidation coursed through her chest. She knew her father well; he always cleared his throat before saying something he thought the recipient would be unhappy to hear.

"'Twas proposed to me as to whether you might be suitable for marriage." His eyes remained on his plate as he stabbed a piece of meat.

Drawing a sharp breath, she hardly dared to look up, gazing through her lashes at him. Could this be good news? Had Amakapa approached Papa?

"A father willn't give his daughter lightly, yet I might gain a son, of sorts, to be part of the business."

She could hardly swallow the bite of mutton

she'd been chewing and reached for her wine.

Fork poised over his plate, her father was staring directly at her. "Will you be inquiring as to who made such a proposal?"

Lifting her chin, she took a sip of wine and swallowed. "I will." It was a tentative whisper.

"Francoise Poule."

Straightening in her chair, her face fell. "Land sakes." The words were out before she thought them and she lowered her eyes to her plate, rising panic pushing out the breath she'd been holding.

Her father, too, was surprised at the outburst, but he didn't comment, instead saying, "He does work hard and I have found no man to be more loyal to the company."

"His manners be crass," she countered. "Ogling me like a trollop whilst making rude discourse."

"Pah. 'Tis only the nature of a man." Her father raised the hand holding the fork. "A man taken in by a handsome woman."

Marielle's thoughts raced, reaching for anything that might dissuade her father. "He does stink of wine day and night," she blurted.

Her father snorted. "Find me a man who does not favor a flagon."

I have: Amakapa, is what she wanted to say, but knew it would be a mistake. "He be on in years, Papa. Would that I be widowed and me with youngins."

His forehead softened and sadness clouded his eyes as the argument met its mark. Papa had never remarried after the death of Marielle's mother and had raised her alone.

"Mayhap a man more suitable calls Kaskaskia home," she said quietly.

He sniffed. "This remains to be seen. Make no doubt that I shall make your situation known, so that other suitors might put their best foot forward." Papa's statement ended the conversation. He lifted his knife and sawed at his meat. "Sally," he called. "Bring the wine."

Jeni's eyes fluttered open, her brain taking stock of what she could see in front of her—she was in bed on her side, her book lying next to the pillow. The panic that held her muscles taut lessened with recognition of time and place, and the tightness in her chest eased.

Then confusion set in. If Marielle had sent the first dream to demonstrate that Jeni could empathize with her plight, then what was the purpose of this dream? She rolled to her back, exhaling, and then replayed the scene before it could fade from memory.

These dreams were unlike anything she'd experienced before. The sensory details were so vivid, Jeni felt as if she'd actually gone back in time.

As if she were experiencing the events firsthand.

The thought of having a husband forced on her made Jeni feel like she couldn't breathe. And her heart ached at the prospect of already being in love and then having that person deemed unsuitable.

Lifting her phone, she saw it was just after two. She had hours left to sleep. But Marielle's shifting emotions remained fresh in her mind, rekindling her earlier fervor. Her eyes refused to close.

This was an opportunity to prove to herself that

her spiritual ability was a gift, not an affliction. Past encounters had forced her to use her link to the otherworld defensively and uneasily. Finding Amakapa would allow her to employ her ability in a positive and purposeful way. But to do that, she needed to speak to Marielle directly.

She had to get her hands on that ring.

What got to me, you see, is that I had another dream.
Stop dreaming so much, it'll bring you bad luck.

The Devil's Three Golden Hairs ~ Henri Pourrat

Chapter 7

*T*he following morning dawned clear and sunny, the brightness of Jeni's room ensuring she stayed awake once her eyes opened. She didn't hear anyone in the bathroom, so she gathered her things and crept from her room. Ice was still a lump under his covers and she resisted the urge to climb onto the mattress next to him. It had been an astute decision, she realized, when she entered the bathroom and noticed the wet shower and the smell of her dad's deodorant and cologne.

As she showered, Jeni brooded over how to get her hands on the ring. The only plan she was able to hatch was to create a diversion—knock over a display or something like that—so that she could quickly pick the lock on the display case and exchange the rings. The drawback was that it required more than two people. She needed Ice nearby to keep watch while her attention was focused on the lock, and it would be best if the diversion happened far from where she was carrying out her task. Thus, she needed someone else to cause the ruckus.

Barbara Pietron

The only options, really, were Mandy and Tyler. After the scornful look from Tyler yesterday when Jeni, Ice and Mandy showed up for lunch together, Jeni thought it would probably be best to ask Tyler directly. She knew her cousin wasn't averse to controversial endeavors. He had helped her sneak into an old church in search of a diary, the glimmer in his eyes giving away how much he enjoyed the adrenaline rush of possibly getting caught. Days later, he'd provided a distraction when a policeman nearly discovered them in a restricted area. Tyler had voluntarily pretended to be lost and drew the cop away, allowing the rest of the party to continue their quest.

The key would be centering the conversation on the act of getting away with something while steering clear of all things supernatural. Jeni knew that Tyler had been blatantly avoiding her and Ice. She also understood that it wasn't so much their company that her cousin objected to, but rather the chance of being part of some otherworldly encounter. Tyler had already witnessed things on other family vacations that defied reason—things that he desperately tried to convince himself could be explained rationally.

Jeni's mouth twisted into a grim smirk as she recognized the irony. By going out of his way to avoid a possible brush with the supernatural, Tyler was really admitting that he knew the truth. If he actually believed past events had an ordinary explanation, he wouldn't have anything to worry about.

Digging her hairbrush out of her toiletry bag, Jeni attacked her wet, tangled hair, pondering when and how she might find a chance to talk to Tyler alone. She unwound the blow dryer cord and pushed the plug into the wall, surmising that the group trip to St. Louis made such an opportunity unlikely. She may have to wait until tonight.

Forty-five minutes later, that thought was proved wrong. Jeni's mom had asked her to run down to the big cabin to retrieve a map that she'd left behind, and the sight that greeted Jeni as she mounted the steps was Tyler sitting alone on the deck. Her heart leaped into overdrive as she realized this may be the opening she'd been looking for.

"My mom wants a map she left here." Jeni felt she should offer the brief explanation to Tyler before letting herself into the cabin.

"Just looking for my mom's map," she repeated to Tyler's dad, who seemed to be the only one ready and waiting. Her pulse pounded and her thoughts raced. She wished she'd given more consideration to what she might actually say to her cousin when the time came. The map was easy to find in a stack of travel information and brochures on the kitchen island. Still, she flipped through the pile slowly, giving herself a few extra minutes to think. If she asked Tyler and he refused, she could hardly approach Mandy later. Her one chance to get help with her crazy scheme was on the line.

Taking the map, she approached the sliding door, mouth dry. She half-hoped someone else was on the deck with her cousin. Then she'd have to wait to talk to him later.

But he was still alone.

She wasn't prepared for this.

Barbara Pietron

Jeni stepped onto the deck, swallowing hard. She stood awkwardly as her cousin ignored her, eyes fixed on his phone. "Hey, uh, Tyler." She moved closer and drew in a deep breath. "I wondered if you could help me out."

"Not interested in ghosts," he said without looking at her. Apparently, Mandy had told him about the Ouija session.

Digging her teeth into her bottom lip, Jeni tried again. "No, that's not it. I need a distraction so I can… borrow something."

That got his attention and he peered at her with narrowed eyes. "So you're going to steal something. And you want me to help you?"

She shifted her weight to the opposite foot. "It's not exactly stealing… it's… uh… trading?"

He sat forward, resting his forearms on his knees. "Trading," he stated, deadpan. His stare bored into her.

"Hey, it won't even look like we know one another. You and Mandy can go—" Jeni cut herself off. She knew she'd screwed up.

"Mandy?" Tyler shot her a venomous glare. "I really don't appreciate you dragging her into your nonsense."

Defensive anger flared and Jeni hissed, "I haven't *dragged* her into anything. She volunteered. And she said she can do what she wants."

"She can." Tyler retorted immediately. "It's just too bad she's around you guys since you're always getting up to something."

"Oh please, Tyler. You brought her here."

Lost in Nowhere

Jeni crossed her arms over her chest and huffed. "Apparently, without telling her anything. Here's a newsflash: she knows you're hiding something."

"It's not the kind of thing you blurt out on a first date," Tyler growled. "Not that it's any of your business. Why was she talking to you about this? What did you tell her?"

Jeni lowered her voice, hearing chatter from within the cabin. "I told her she needs to ask *you*."

"I planned to talk to her while we were here anyway," he muttered, his body slumping against the chair back. He looked away from her, toward the pond.

Jeni closed her mouth on the words that were ready to tumble out, her brain processing what Tyler had just said. The admission was not what she'd expected. She wasn't sure if she should say something or walk away.

Tyler swiveled his head back, not quite looking at her. "Isn't your mom expecting you?"

"Yeah." Jeni looked stupidly at the map in her hand. She'd forgotten it was there. Since the initial purpose of the conversation had been lost, she trotted down the deck steps, Tyler's statement about talking to Mandy repeating in her head.

Ice and her parents were waiting when she returned to the cabin and they all got into the car. Jeni and Ice had managed a brief conversation earlier and she'd relayed her idea, along with her intent to ask Tyler to be the one to create the diversion. Ice had looked dubious about both prospects.

Now, unable to bear that she had to wait over an

hour to talk to him, Jeni texted Ice as they sat in the backseat together, letting him know that she'd had a conversation with Tyler.

He raised his eyebrows in reply and she texted: *"I doubt he'll help us at the museum, but he admitted that he was going to talk to Mandy while they were here. I'm pretty sure he meant about the last two trips."*

They exchanged a meaningful glance and didn't discuss it again until they'd reached St. Louis and were strolling through the exhibit detailing the history and construction of the Gateway Arch. By the time they reached the tram ride that carried visitors to the top of the arch, Jeni had filled Ice in on the conversation completely.

Everything about the ride pushed Jeni's buttons. The tram was a string of small pods which seated four people each. Already uncomfortable in tight spaces, the fact that their destination was a towering height only ratcheted Jeni's anxiety up another notch. She stacked her purse on her lap, managing a wan smile for Ice when he squeezed her knee reassuringly. The tram engineers had had the courtesy to put windows in the pods' doors, which slightly alleviated the claustrophobic feeling. And thankfully, the only thing visible during the ride was the interior structure of the arch.

When the tram of pods stopped, Jeni disembarked with a grateful exhale. Then she hesitated, watching the other passengers climb the steps to the viewing platform. Ice offered a sympathetic smile and hung back with her. She mounted the stairs, clutching her purse tightly, and stopped at the top. Surprise and relief struck her at the same time as she took in the viewing ports—small rectangular windows set in the side of the steel structure—in lieu of large panes of glass that she would have stood well back from. She followed Ice to the left and stood just behind him.

The view was amazing. It always made Jeni feel as if she could take in the breadth of a new place by seeing so much at once. That's what pushed her beyond her fear of heights, and what she could see from the arch did not disappoint.

The sun caught the surface of the moving river, throwing sparks of light and rendering the usual muddy cast of the water to an attractive pewter. Across the river in East St. Louis, Jeni saw the Gateway Geyser that, according to what she'd read, spouted water into the air at the same height as the arch. The four smaller fountains surrounding the central geyser represented the four rivers that converged near the two cities.

Looking west, the city of St. Louis occupied the horizon. Jeni spotted the basilica that she'd learned was the oldest west of the Mississippi, and directly in front of the arch she saw the domed old courthouse building. Off to her left was the city's baseball stadium. The coolest part about this view was the shadow of the arch cast on the park below by the rising sun.

When they stepped safely from the tram at the bottom of the arch, Jeni breathed a sigh of relief. She was glad she went up, but was equally glad to be back on solid ground.

She noticed Tyler and Mandy holding hands as they joined the group at the prearranged meeting spot, and a thought struck her. Turning her head so her lips were close to Ice's ear, she said, "I was stumped about Tyler having a girlfriend—an obviously serious girlfriend—who believed in the supernatural. But I think I get it now. He's been carrying around this burden of the things that have happened, knowing most people would think he was crazy if he told them about it. Finally, he's found someone he can trust to take him seriously."

"Hmm." Ice pondered her observation. "Interesting point."

"I wonder if he waited to talk to Mandy here because he knows we can back him up."

Ice grunted. "I doubt it. That doesn't sound like Tyler."

Jeni cast another covert look at her cousin and his girlfriend. She'd only seen Tyler show open affection like that to Molly, his three-year-old niece. "I could offer to be around when he tries to tell her," she murmured, almost to herself. At Ice's sidelong glance, she added, "Whether he helps us at the museum or not. I know what it was like to try and explain what happened at Lake Itasca to my best friend."

"I suppose it can't hurt to offer," Ice said with a soft smile.

He was wrong, Jeni realized, thinking about it on the car ride back to the resort. They were talking about Tyler. Any offer from Jeni—no matter how well intended—could hurt. She was better off staying out of her cousin's business.

Lost in Nowhere

Marielle slipped through the barn doors silently, leaving one door ajar, and then stood still as the outlines of the interior structure took shape. Her pulse had been racing since she'd crept from the house, and now her heartbeat seemed thunderous in the serenity of midnight. Padding carefully to an empty stall, she side-stepped into the space, hand trailing the wall to guide her, and stopped where she was able to see around the thick support post. The dry smell of hay and musky odor of horses filled her nostrils, but she hardly noticed as her ears strained to hear the sound of footsteps over the hammering of her heart.

Without warning, the space between the doors widened. Pressing herself against the wall, she held her breath, panic sending a course of thoughts through her head. What would she say if it were her father? Or one of the servants? She should be in a stall with one of the horses so she could claim that she'd heard something and came out to check them. What reason could she offer for being in an empty stall? Dash it! Why didn't she think this through?

A silhouette moved through the doors and then paused. "Marielle?" The whisper came softly.

Her breath released in a rush as she poked her head around the post, confirming what her ears had already told her: the figure was Amakapa. Hurrying from the stall, she flung herself into his arms. For some reason, tears pooled at the corners of her eyes.

Amakapa kissed her, and then pulled back. "What be this?" His hands cupped her face, thumbs gently wiping her tears away.

She shook her head with a small laugh. "The courting. I cannot hardly bear it. This facade be wearing on my last nerve; my only reprieve being your own company."

"On the morrow shall I pay your father a visit," Amakapa promised.

Her heart skipped a beat. The moonlight streaming through the open doors must've allowed enough light for Amakapa to detect a shadow of doubt in her eyes. "This be not what you desire?" He frowned. "Do we not endeavor that our tryst be made proper?"

The ache of wanting something so bad but being unable to grasp it expanded in her chest like a black hole. "Should Papa protest," she said, her voice uneven, "our hope be lost." An exasperated sigh escaped her lips. "I deigned to demonstrate your worthiness against that of my ill-mannered suitors. Yet Papa does turn a blind eye in your direction." She felt the quiver of her chin and cursed herself for it. "Make no doubt that I beg to differ with his idea of a befitting match."

"Then ask I shall." Amakapa's firm tone was not reflected in his gentle touch as he smoothed the loose tendrils of hair from her face and tucked them behind her ears.

She dropped her gaze. "Mayhap we should take our leave under cover of night," she whispered.

"Trouble and hard times may befall us, but let it be as you wish." He kissed her forehead.

She lifted her chin, offering her lips, and he bent to kiss her.

Longing filled her soul as she desperately wished that she could somehow convey to her father the depth of emotion she felt for Amakapa, and his for her. Surely Papa couldn't deny them a future together. "Let us implore his favor together," she said when their lips parted.

Amakapa's dark brown eyes held hers. "On the morrow?"

The scuff of footsteps sounded outside the door.

"Hide," Marielle hissed, alarm streaking through her. She stood, frozen, as Amakapa disappeared into the barn. A shadow blotted out the moonlight and she shook free of the paralysis, dashing to the stall occupied by her horse, Fleur. Fumbling with the latch, she entered the stall as the barn doors swung open.

Her sudden movement caused the horse to shift uneasily on its feet and Marielle cooed softly, running her hands along its shoulder.

Her father's voice boomed in the quiet barn and her heartbeat stuttered. "Marielle?"

"Yes, Papa." Somehow she managed to keep her voice steady. She leaned over the gate so he could see her. "Fleur be distressed. Her whinny did reach my bedroom window. Upon entering the barn, a rat, or some such animal, did scuttle from the feed barrels." She gestured to his left, to keep him from peering into the back of the barn. She had no idea where Amakapa was hidden.

The light streaming through the open doors revealed the wrinkles on her father's brow and his narrowed eyes. "This must be a regular occurrence for a horse."

She pulled her head back into the stall, avoiding his scrutiny, while the scrape of footsteps let her know that he was headed her way. "Such an experience be the same for me. Yet still the situation be unsettling when taken by surprise."

His grunt in response came from just outside the stall. She glanced up to see him scanning the space—perhaps confirming she was alone although she'd never given him a reason to suspect some kind of clandestine meeting. Her guilty conscience must be supplying such thoughts. He continued past, inspecting the back of the building.

She moved to the stall gate nervously. "Fleur has settled," she said, wanting to draw her father out of the barn. "Mayhap Sally might warm milk that we, too, might settle." As she opened the gate and stepped out, a movement at the front of the barn caught her eye. Amakapa's upside down face peered from the loft.

Her eyes widened in alarm and she spun to see her father almost to the back wall of the barn. Swiveling her head, she drew in a sharp breath as Amakapa flipped from the loft to land soundlessly on the balls of his feet. Her eyes followed his form as he dropped to a crouch behind a wooden barrel.

"'Tis it that you are freeing the horse?"

She started at the sound of her father's voice, heart pounding wildly. Turning, she realized her hand was still on the open gate and Fleur had come to nose around the opening. "No, I..." She couldn't let her father pass until Amakapa exited the barn. "'Tis a problem with the latch," she blurted. It was a lame excuse; the fastener was a simple hinge mechanism.

Her father approached to look at the latch and Marielle positioned herself to block his view of the barn doors. He worked the apparatus back and forth smoothly, one bushy eyebrow arched as he met her eyes. "It does operate with ease."

She forced a laugh. "That always be the way of things."

"Come, daughter. The hour be late. You shall to bed."

She looped her arm through his until they were out of the barn and he turned to bar the door. She looked left and right, but saw no one.

The thick wooden slab thudded into place, securing the doors.

She hoped Amakapa had made it out.

Jeni woke, her elbow jutted out the same way Marielle's had been linked with her father's arm. A disconcerted feeling brought her fully awake, and her brow furrowed as she recalled what happened in the dream. When footsteps had sounded outside the barn, Jeni had thought, "Go to one of the horses," urging Marielle to move. Which she had. Then Jeni had thought, "Rats, the horse saw a rat," and that's exactly what Marielle said. Did she and Marielle really think that much alike? Or was Jeni interjecting her own version of the past into her dreams?

When she got the ring, she was going to ask.

*I didn't say just thief, I said master thief. You have
to be clever all over, sure-footed and sharp-eyed,
always quick and alert. You need sense and strength
and courage, and all sorts of things like that.*

The Master Thief ~ Henri Pourrat

Chapter 8

"Have you considered a funeral ceremony?" Nik's
deep voice rumbled.

"A death ceremony?" Ice shuffled his feet over
the gravel drive, phone pressed to his ear. "Don't we
need a body for that?"

"Sure, that's usually the way it's done," Ice's
mentor agreed. "But I looked into the beliefs of the
Kaskaskian tribe. They believed that on its journey
to the afterlife, the soul traveled to a blissful place
beyond a great river. To ensure the soul was able
to complete the journey, they performed a funeral
ceremony."

Raking a hand through his hair, Ice stared down
the road. Low-lying fog clung to the ground, congre-
gating thicker in the trees. "So you're thinking that
if Amakapa never had a funeral ceremony, his soul
never made it across the river."

"It's one theory."

"A good theory," Ice admitted. "I feel like I should have thought of it. I've just been distracted expecting an attack by some otherworldly creature—particularly since Jeni is contacting a spirit."

Nik sighed. "The entity seeking vengeance against Jeni used the Underwater Monster and failed. It tried again using a Korrigan and failed. You'd be wise to be on the lookout for a new approach. Jeni should use the utmost care in making contact with the other side. Spirits can be tricky."

"I fully agree." The bang of a screen door drew his attention to the cabin. Jeni spotted him and saw that he was still on the phone, so she pointed toward the patio and then rounded the corner. "Man, it would be great if you were right and we could just perform a ceremony."

"It may be worth a try. I'll see if I can find out what a Kaskaskian funeral would entail."

"Thanks, Nik. I appreciate it."

"Keep me in the loop." Then, as typical for the medicine man, he was off the line.

Ice pocketed his phone and was about to join Jeni when the rhythmic grind of footsteps on loose stone drew his attention. He turned back to the road. The mist swirled away from Tyler's feet as he strode purposefully down the drive, face set and eyes intent. Ice waited, feeling awkward as he watched the other boy approach. He was unsure if Jeni's cousin was seeking him out specifically or just headed in this direction. Finally, he asked, "Are you looking for me?"

"Yeah," Tyler replied. He didn't say anything else, though, until he was within a few feet of Ice.

Lost in Nowhere

Crossing his arms over his chest, he asked, "You guys still going to the museum in Ste. Genevieve?"

Ice nodded, observing Tyler's defensive posture. Jeni had told him about her latest dream. The attempt to switch the rings was imminent, even though it would have to be a two-person job.

"I'll drive you." Tyler spat out the words almost accusingly.

Blinking in surprise, Ice responded, "I… uh… I'll check with Jeni. I think she's on the patio." He motioned with his thumb. "Do you want to walk over there?"

"Not particularly." The stern lines etched in Tyler's brow when he'd arrived deepened. "Just let me know." He turned away. "Or text Mandy," he said over his shoulder as he strode off, hands burrowed in his pockets.

Ice raised an eyebrow, wondering if Mandy had convinced Tyler to help them, or if something else had happened. He hurried around the cabin and found Jeni in a lounge chair, flip-flops kicked off with her feet up.

"You're not going to believe this," he said as she looked up from her phone.

"What?" She bent her knees and motioned for him to join her on the chair, digging her bare toes under the edge of his leg after he sat.

"Tyler was just here. He said he'd drive us to the museum today."

Jeni's jaw dropped slightly. "Like… he'll help us?"

"That's not what he said. But why else would he drive us there?" He could feel Jeni's cold toes through his shorts and he drew her feet onto his lap, warming them with his hands.

She closed her eyes for a moment. "Good question."

"It was strange," Ice said. "He seemed... I don't know, agitated?"

Her eyes snapped open. "Like he was pissed off?"

Ice shook his head. "No. More... resigned might be the best way to describe it. Like he knew what he had to do even if he didn't like it."

"Wow." Jeni tapped her finger on her phone. "I was just thinking about asking my mom if we could borrow the car and do our own thing today." A conspiratorial smile played on her lips. "She'll like this plan better."

"I should shower then," Ice said, returning Jeni's feet to the chair.

"Thanks for warming up my toes." Jeni smiled as she swung her feet to the ground and wriggled into her flip-flops. "I think I'm gonna grab some socks and tennis shoes; it's chillier than I thought it would be. I'll check with my mom and then text Mandy to ask what time Tyler wants to leave."

Although nearly a half hour had passed before they struck off down the resort drive to meet Tyler and Mandy, the landscape remained blanketed in a white haze. The dense cloud cover seemed in no hurry to dissipate.

"Mandy said she didn't talk Tyler into this," Jeni reported. "He brought it up to her this morning. She's convinced something happened to change his mind, but he wouldn't admit anything."

Typical behavior for Tyler, Ice thought. While showering, he'd come up with two possibilities that might have swayed Jeni's cousin. The first—that Mandy had convinced him—had been ruled out by Jeni's conversation. Which left his second guess: that Tyler's change of heart was caused by something supernatural in nature. He was Jeni's cousin, and Ice had always wondered if Tyler shared any of her proclivity for the spiritual world. In his years as an apprentice medicine man, Ice had often observed that those who vehemently resisted the existence of otherworldly forces likely had experienced some kind of encounter with them. Perhaps the ghost had appeared to Tyler.

Mandy emerged from the cabin as they approached. "Ty will be out in a minute." She widened her eyes and held her arms out, palms up. "What can I say? He's a mystery."

No one commented as jangling keys warned of Tyler's arrival. The doors of his hatchback unlocked with a hollow click and they all climbed into the car. When the tires were rolling on the drive, Tyler finally spoke. "So, let's hear your grand plan." Though his tone conveyed mockery, the words were also tinged by the same angry resignation that Ice noticed earlier.

One look at Jeni confirmed they were thinking the same thing: it seemed Tyler's offer was for more than a ride; he intended to help.

Since Ice and Jeni had never been inside the museum, "the plan" was little more than an uninformed idea. So as Jeni outlined the basics, Ice interjected questions to try and nail down some details.

"I'm not sure there's anything we can knock down," Mandy said. "Not without damaging something."

"Yeah, no damage, preferably," Jeni said.

In the rearview mirror, Ice saw Tyler's focus shift to the backseat as if he wanted to say something, then he pressed his lips together, rolled his eyes and turned his attention back to the road.

Pulling into the lot at DuBourg Place, they found a row of parking spaces occupied by the bulky mass of a school bus situated perpendicular to the painted lines. Black letters that stood out starkly on the golden-yellow paint read: "De Soto Public Schools."

"Oh, no," Jeni groaned. "Field trip."

When Mandy pushed her hair behind her ear and looked over her shoulder with raised eyebrows, Ice said, "Jeni and I can go in and at least look around." He shrugged. "Who knows? Maybe the extra distraction will work in our favor. We'll text if it's a go, otherwise you'll see us in a few minutes."

Excited chatter reached their ears before they'd even stepped inside. The museum was one room, about the size of the community center on the reservation back home. Clusters of kids stood all around, most no taller than Ice's chest. Each group of three or four children included one adult. The docents were certainly distracted, but the visitors were everywhere, and kids in particular loved to ask questions.

Ice met Jeni's eyes with a small head shake. This was not a good time. Leaning in close to her, he quietly said, "Get a good look around."

"Can I help you folks?" A harried docent asked.

"I think we'll come back later," Jeni said.

"That's probably a wise decision," the woman replied, glancing left and right. "I expect the field trip should conclude in an hour or so."

"Okay. We'll see you later, then." Jeni turned toward Ice, focusing over his shoulder at the exhibit case containing the fashion accessories. Ice gave her a few moments to look before opening the door.

They climbed back into Tyler's car. "No go," Ice said. "There are kids everywhere."

Mandy twisted in her seat. "Now what?"

"We need to kill about an hour." Watching Jeni's brows lift and the corners of her mouth curve upward, Ice knew exactly what was on her mind before she said it. "Coffee?"

Tyler and Mandy decided to seek out something other than coffee, and the couples parted ways, agreeing to meet at a picnic table just behind the museum near the courthouse.

The sky had brightened, promising the sun would soon break through the clouds, but the air was still cool and they walked briskly, hands in pockets. Ice took the opportunity to fill Jeni in on his conversation with Nik.

"Mmm. I hadn't thought about that," Jeni said. "But they do hold funerals for people even when they don't have a body. It just seems so long ago that it shouldn't matter."

"Depending on Amakapa's beliefs, something like this could be holding his spirit back. We don't really know what happens after death." He held the door of the coffee shop for her.

"Guess that's something else I should ask Marielle about."

"When you do, also ask if there was more to his Native American name. That would be helpful for calling to his soul."

"Okay." Jeni said absently. Her brain felt like a sponge that was saturated with the task at hand, unable to absorb new thoughts.

They decided to get the kind of hot coffee that was made using a pour-over brewing process, which took a bit longer than an espresso machine. By the time they made it back to the town square, Mandy was down to the last couple bites of her doughnut and Tyler's soda was nearly half-empty.

Sliding onto the cold concrete bench, Ice felt the palpable tension between the couple at the table. He exchanged a quick glance with Jeni that said she'd noticed the same thing.

"Sorry it took us so long," Jeni said. "They make the coffee by putting this thing that looks like a ceramic filter over your cup and then slowly pouring hot water over the grounds."

"I've seen that before," Mandy said. Tyler remained silent, apparently studying the church spire, and ignored Mandy when she nudged him with her elbow. "Tell them."

Jeni sat with her side pressed against Ice; he felt her body go rigid as she fixed her attention on her cousin.

"Tell them," Mandy said again. "They need to know. Tell them, or I will."

Tyler shook his shaggy hair away from his face, attention shifting to Mandy for a moment. He exhaled audibly and then focused on the table in front of Jeni and Ice. "Molly saw your ghost."

For Ice, the statement wasn't entirely unexpected, but a gasp escaped Jeni's lips before her fingers covered her mouth. Scowling, Tyler raised his eyes to hers. "Kids see ghosts easier than adults. I don't want Molly to grow up freaked out. When you get this ring, I want you to tell that ghost to leave Molly the eff alone. Nat, too."

"I… wow… she did?" Jeni straightened her back and pulled her sweater closed. "Yeah, that's not cool. I had no idea. I'll tell her to stay away from the kids—to leave everyone alone." She'd read or heard somewhere that young children were more susceptible to seeing ghosts, yet it hadn't occurred to her that the three-year-olds might see Marielle if she was hanging around.

Mandy kissed Tyler's shoulder and rubbed a hand over his back. "Aside from not freaking the kids out," she said to Jeni, "I wanted you to know about this because we're not sure if Molly saw her incidentally or if Marielle actually approached her. I'm not sure how desperate this spirit might be."

Mandy's comment sent a warm rush of unease to Ice's gut.

"Ty also had a great idea for a distraction in the museum," she said.

"I don't know how great it is," Tyler muttered. "Or if it will work. When we were there a few days ago, I noticed the poster display track was coming away from the wall. I could maybe encourage it to come completely off, or at least make it loose enough that it requires attention."

"Poster track?" Jeni asked.

"I saw it," Ice said. "On the wall opposite the entrance?" He looked from Tyler to Mandy for confirmation.

Tyler nodded. "That's it. It would be better if it was on the opposite side of the museum from the case you're breaking into rather than right in the middle."

His deliberate choice of words made Jeni wince, but she didn't say anything, casting her eyes down to her phone and checking the time. "The place is pretty small; everything inside is close together," Ice said.

They volleyed different scenarios back and forth until the unmistakable roar of a diesel engine came from around the building. Not long after, children's voices carried from the museum parking lot. When the heave of the school bus's powertrain and the hiss of brakes faded, Tyler was first to rise from his seat.

"Showtime," he said.

Jeni wished she'd thought to ask for decaf. Nerves humming, she clenched her hands into fists inside her sweater pockets to keep them from shaking. Expanding her lungs to capacity while Ice paid their entrance fee, Jeni released the breath slowly, attempting to relax her neck and shoulders. As casually as possible, she surveyed the area for security cameras, finding none.

Exhibits lined the walls, enclosed in tall wood-paneled cabinets with glass doors. Freestanding display cases were arranged throughout the middle of the space, one of which held the collection of fashion accessories.

Lost in Nowhere

As Ice approached Jeni, he checked the timer on his phone that was counting down the ten minutes before Tyler and Mandy would enter. "Nine minutes," he whispered.

The exodus of the field trip had left the museum empty for the time being, and Jeni wasn't sure if she should be glad or bothered by the fact that they were the only visitors. It certainly left her feeling as if she were under scrutiny, and she didn't like that at all.

Stopping first at a diorama of a transfer boat—used to transport trains across the Mississippi River between Illinois and Missouri before there were train bridges—they then moved on to a shadowbox-style diorama depicting the Hindenburg crash.

Jeni was taking in very little from the displays as she fought the need to look toward the exhibit case with the fashion items. Inside her left sweater pocket, she fiddled with the replacement ring, confirming it was still there. The right pocket concealed her white knuckled fist which grasped two bobby pins, one partially straightened with a bent end—"the rake"—and the other straightened with a curled end—"the tensioner." Loosening her grip, she rubbed her thumb along the metal loop, wondering if she could really pull this off.

They shuffled on to the "poster track," as Tyler had called it, where poster frames were attached to a bracket, allowing the viewer to page through and look at both sides of the frames. Jeni had seen this setup many times, particularly in book and music stores that sold posters from movies, books, bands and other sources of pop culture. In this case, the museum utilized the system to display historic information.

"How long?" Jeni murmured.

"Six minutes."

"Let's go look at the exhibits on the outside walls near the case so I can check it out." Jeni stepped to her left, giving a cursory perusal of the items behind glass on the back wall, impatient to reach the front of the museum.

Continuing her circuit of the room, Jeni squatted in front of a display of weapons located on the side wall, rotating her body slightly sideways so she could view the freestanding cases. The structures were about six feet long, three feet wide and perhaps a foot deep. They stood on legs that placed them at roughly waist level for most adult visitors. Dark stained wood bordered the top and side glass panels. The long sides of the cases were divided into two panes of glass which, on one side, were access doors. As Jeni had noticed in her mom's photo, the doors were hinged at the bottom and she presumed they would articulate downward, coming to a stop parallel to the floor. The lock cylinders were centered at the top of each access door.

Her low vantage point allowed Jeni to inspect the locks. They appeared to be similar to one of the videos she'd watched numerous times, showing how to get into your desk or file cabinet with two bobby pins if you'd misplaced your key. Jeni wondered how many of the viewers were actually using the information to get into their own property, and her conscience prickled with shame. Trying to convince herself that she had the best of intentions was the only way to assuage her guilt. But the angel on her shoulder always finished that thought with "the road to hell is paved with good intentions."

"Three minutes," Ice said, his reminder making her jump.

They moved around the corner. The locks on the fashion display case were directly behind Jeni now. All she had to do was turn around. Nothing in the exhibit in front of her registered as she ran the lock-picking procedure through her head. The creak of one of the front doors swinging open brought her attention into sharp focus, and her heartbeat accelerated. Those three minutes had flown by.

Except it wasn't Tyler and Mandy. Instead, an older woman swept through the opening, followed by a man who had been holding the door for her.

Turning to the case of fashion accessories, Jeni watched the couple through her eyelashes, praying they would begin with the exhibits across the room. The man's attention, however, had already been drawn to the boat diorama, as it was the first thing visitors saw upon entering the museum.

The doors squawked again, and this time, Mandy and Tyler entered.

Panic squeezed Jeni's chest as she fought to draw in a breath. She looked at Ice, eyes wide. He raised his eyebrows and shrugged. "You don't have to do this," he said softly.

She huffed. That wasn't what she needed to hear. She wanted him to say, "You *can* do this."

Fueling her nervous energy into indignation, she composed her own pep talk, remembering Marielle's hopelessness in the face of her father's will. All Jeni wanted to do was find Amakapa and release his soul so the ill-fated couple could join each other on the other side. It was a noble goal. And she needed this ring for effective communication. Time was growing short.

Jeni scanned the exhibit, zeroing in on the cluster of rings. Leaning close, she scrutinized the gold ring that she'd seen only in her mom's photo. The ring she'd purchased to replace it wasn't as similar as she'd thought, a bit chunkier and the gold itself seemed slightly different in color. But it was close enough. It would take a long time—if ever—for someone to notice the substitution.

Provided she was correct in her assumption that there weren't hidden cameras.

Jeni glanced up, noting the older couple peering at the Hindenburg diorama while Tyler and Mandy had just finished paying admission. She made a mental note to offer to pay them back for the eight dollars they'd spent solely to help her, then returned her focus to the lock that was now opposite her belly button.

One last touch of the ring in her pocket, and then Jeni withdrew her left hand to accept the tensioner. The rake was gripped between her right thumb and index finger. The clatter of poster frames stiffened her spine as her shallow breath stuttered unevenly.

A quick look at Ice's expectant face told her to proceed. With a shaking hand, Jeni slipped the curled end of the tensioner into the lock and twisted it in the direction she assumed would open the case: left, because her dad had taught her "lefty loosie, righty tighty." When the cylinder stopped, she maintained pressure at that position. Preparing for Tyler's distraction, she stole a glance toward the counter where the docent had been when they entered. Unable to confirm the woman was there, Jeni forced air into her lungs, trusting that Ice was keeping watch. Then she inserted the rake into the keyhole.

Picturing the pins inside and how she needed to align each at the stopping point where the teeth of the key would place them, Jeni probed with the bobby pin.

Without warning, the door swung open and hit her in the abdomen. Instinctively, Jeni jumped backward, allowing the door to clunk loudly as it shuddered to a stop at a right angle to the cabinet. She jerked her head toward the rest of the room to find five pairs of eyes staring at her.

"Oh, my," the docent said, already on her feet and bustling over. "What an eventful day."

Jeni's face flushed and her eyes darted to Ice, who looked as much at a loss as she was. A light clink brought her attention to the floor where she saw one of her bent bobby pins and she realized she still held the other in her hand. She dropped the rake into her pocket and shifted her foot forward over the other, drawing it out from under the open door.

As she waited helplessly—caught red-handed— her thoughts raced. Imagining the local police coming in, she realized she should have dropped the rake on the floor and kicked it away. When they found the bent bobby pin in her pocket, it would cement her guilt.

The docent's hand wrapped around Jeni's arm and she flinched.

"Goodness!" The woman exclaimed. "Are you all right, dear?"

"I... uh... yeah," Jeni stammered, confused. "I'm fine."

Satisfied that Jeni was okay, the woman released her and bent to inspect the open door. Her brow furrowed in bewilderment. "I wonder if it was left unlocked or if it's broken." She again peered at Jeni. "You sure you're not hurt, dear?"

"No. It... uh... just surprised me."

The woman fingered the lock. "Let me just go get the key and see if I can lock it. Then I'll make a call to maintenance." She waddled away, leaving Jeni and Ice standing at the open case.

She'd get no better chance, Jeni suddenly realized, watching the woman's back as she crossed the room. Her attention shifted to the older couple. Both were still staring at the debacle, waiting to see what would happen next. Jeni fingered the ring in her pocket, willing the couple to turn around, move on. Nothing to see here.

Instead, Tyler inserted himself directly into their sight path and pinned her with a "what are you waiting for?" glare.

Without a further glance at the docent, Jeni snaked her arm into the case and dropped the ring next to the others. Then she snatched up the one with the cross stamped into it and nudged its replacement into position.

Heart beating wildly, the jingle of keys reached

her ears and she saw the docent making her way across the room. Mandy was talking to the older couple.

"Okay, then." The woman lifted the door of the display case and peered at the lock.

A streak of fear burned through Jeni as she wondered if she'd left scratch marks that the woman would notice.

"Should have brought my glasses," she muttered, then turned to Jeni. "Can you read the number on there for me?"

Jeni bent down and read the four-digit code on the lock, feeling the bile in her stomach rising up the back of her throat. It seemed to take an eternity for the woman to look through the fat ring of keys to find the right one. Finally, she poked a key into the lock and turned it, jiggling the door by its wooden frame to make sure it was held in place. "Seems okay now. I think I'll still make a note for maintenance. Don't want that to happen again, do we?" She peered at Jeni over her glasses. "Someone could get quite a bruise that way. Sure you're okay?"

Jeni nodded and then added, "Yes. Thank you. I'm fine. Please, don't worry about it."

"Okay, dear. Enjoy the rest of the museum, then."

Knowing she could hardly run out without wandering around the exhibits at least a little bit longer, Jeni swallowed hard. Unfortunately, enjoyment was out of the question. She'd settle for not throwing up.

*"Thank you for your kindness and your
trouble," replied the ghost,
and disappeared like a snuffed-out flame.*

Fearless Jean ~ Henri Pourrat

Chapter 9

Jeni heaved a huge sigh of relief as she stepped
out of the museum, bending over with her hands
braced on her thighs.

"You okay?" Ice asked, resting a hand on her
back. His voice sounded strained. "Come on, there's a
bench across the street."

Sucking in a breath, Jeni straightened, blinking
against the sunshine that had finally blazed its way
through the clouds. She trailed Ice as he crossed the
street, and then plunked down on the wooden slat-
ted seat, drained. "God, that was excruciatingly
stressful."

"Agreed," Ice said. "I hope it's worth it."

"It will be." Jeni injected more confidence than
she felt. "If I can find out who my ancestors are and
the nature of my ability, I might actually have a
chance to control this link, or whatever it is, to the
spirit world. Avoiding any more *accidents* would definitely make all of this worthwhile."

Ice didn't respond, slumping against the back of
the bench.

Feeling as if her hands were steady enough, Jeni took the ring from her pocket to examine it up close. "I couldn't tell in my mom's picture what else was on here besides the cross. It looks like another cross, except it's long and skinny." She held the ring in front of Ice.

After a moment, he said, "I bet it's a sword."

"A sword?" Jeni frowned.

"Sure. People have been going to war over religion for centuries."

"Oh, yeah, I see your point. It seems odd that this belonged to a woman." Wearing the ring seemed like the best way to not lose it, so Jeni attempted to slip it onto her ring finger. The gold band stopped at her knuckle. "Wow, it's really small." The metal felt oddly cool, despite handling it, and she shivered as she pushed the ring onto her pinky finger.

"Everything was smaller three hundred years ago," Ice said, eyeballing the ring.

"I'd like to go over to Phoebe's shop and ask her about using this," Jeni said. "I hope Tyler won't make a fuss about waiting."

"I doubt it," Ice said. "He was pretty ticked about his niece seeing Marielle—ticked enough to run interference for you—so I imagine he'll want you to talk to her ASAP."

"True." Jeni pulled her phone from her purse. "I'll text Mandy and tell them to meet us there. That'll be less time they'll have to wait for us."

Jeni and Ice were already on their feet when Mandy responded with an "OK."

The strip of sleigh bells on the door jingled merrily as they entered Memories and Magic. The store appeared empty, but seconds later, Phoebe swept through the curtains of the back room. "Hey, Jeni. Hey, Ice. How are things with your ghost?"

"Hopefully better," Jeni said. "She told us where to find the ring that tethers her here." She lifted her hand and wiggled her pinky.

Phoebe's brows arched and a hint of suspicion shone in her eyes as she met Jeni's gaze. Apparently deciding not to ask any questions, she caught the end of Jeni's fingers, twisting her hand slightly to see the ring. "By the sword and the cross," she murmured.

Jeni exchanged a glance with Ice. "Is that some kind of slogan?"

"It's a saying from Charlemagne, ruler of the Holy Roman Empire. At least in my reference. But that would've been a thousand years before your ghost's time."

Jeni peered at the gold band. After looking at so many similar rings at the antique mall, she was able to pick out the subtle differences—the deep color of the metal, the slightly imperfect shape, the simple symbols pressed into the center—that spoke of this piece of jewelry's age. Although, without the benefit of an expert, it was impossible to know from which century it might have originated.

"Well, I'm pretty sure it's the one Marielle wanted us to find," Jeni said. "But there's only one way to find out. I was hoping you could give me some pointers on using it."

Her fingers still wrapped around Jeni's, Phoebe raised her eyes and looked beyond Jeni. "Has your contact increased to two spirits?"

"No." Jeni knit her brow. "Why?"

"The presence is… more. Perhaps it's merely stronger because of your possession of the object," she said almost to herself. Releasing Jeni's fingers, she continued, "The ring will facilitate communication with your spirit, but know that it also serves as a link to the otherworld. You'll have to be careful not to cross over." Phoebe's voice had taken on a hard, serious tone. She locked eyes with Jeni. "I highly recommend you have a mooring point, or a foothold, in the living world."

"Like what?" Jeni asked.

The woman's lips curved and she glanced at Ice. "I believe your boyfriend knows how to remain rooted here while he speaks with spirits. Yes?"

As Ice nodded, tinkling bells announced Mandy's entrance. "Ty's going to wait outside." Her eyes gleamed as she strode forward. "Can I see the ring?"

Like a newly engaged fiancé, Jeni extended her hand. "We're pretty sure it's a sword and a cross."

Mandy looked up. "Are you going to use it?"

Turning toward the medium, Jeni said, "I'd like to."

Nodding, Phoebe motioned with her arm. "Weekday mornings are always slow. Let's go to the back."

Much like the Ouija session, two chairs were pulled away from the round table to face each other. "Okay, you two. Sit." Phoebe pointed at Ice and Jeni.

Once seated, they were instructed to hold hands. Jeni hesitated, attention fixed on Ice.

Lost in Nowhere

He closed his eyes and inhaled, pausing with his lungs filled. A moment later, the air rushed out as his eyes opened and he extended his open hands to Jeni with a slight nod. Jeni placed her hands in his, once again admiring how adept he'd become at adjusting his three-part balance.

The skin around Ice's eyes tightened, and he shifted his fingers away from her pinky.

"What is it?" she asked.

He shrugged, brow furrowed. "I don't know. The ring didn't feel right to me. But things can get weird when you're out of balance."

Phoebe had watched their interplay with interest. "Are your spiritualities at odds?"

"Too alike," Ice said.

The medium lowered her chin in understanding. Without further questions, she said, "When you're ready, speak the spirit's name."

"Out loud?" Jeni asked.

"It doesn't matter. Although we'll only hear your side of the conversation."

Feeling awkward, Jeni closed her eyes. *Marielle? Marielle Bernard.* She called the name in her head.

'Tis I, truly. An indistinct image appeared in Jeni's thoughts; Marielle's visage, blurred at the edges. *It must be that you found my ring.*

Yes. It was in the museum, Jeni said. *Thank you for telling us how to find it. I have so many questions and this will help us communicate.*

An odd smile appeared on Marielle's face, tense, or perhaps wistful. *I shall answer as best I can.*

Okay. Jeni paused, wishing she'd taken a moment

to run through the list of questions with Ice. She began with one of the first things that had her perplexed. *Excuse me if this sounds dumb, but if you haven't crossed over, how do you know Amakapa isn't already on the other side?*

I did travel to the bright light, but found his promise null. He was not there waiting, as he said. So I did retreat.

Jeni figured she had to take that answer on faith. In life, the natural response would be, "maybe he got held up," or "maybe he was waiting somewhere else," but since she knew virtually nothing about death, or life after death, she had to assume Marielle just *knew*. It seemed unlikely a soul would back away from the light without a reason.

Her next thought was of her recent conversation with Ice. *Do you know what happened to Amakapa's body? Was it ever recovered?*

Marielle's ghostly face fell. *I know not.*

Was there a funeral service at the church, or a ceremony with his tribe?

Of the townsfolk, few would mourn his death on account of the vicious lies my father did spread. And the prospect of a native man with a white woman was nigh forbidden, though the Christian priest did readily bless the marriages of a white man and a native woman. Marielle's voice held a justified bitter edge.

What about his tribe? Jeni reiterated.

Marielle shook her head. *They knew not of his return to Kaskaskia.*

Would they have had a ceremony anyway?

That, I do not know.

We might try having both a Native American and

Christian funeral. *Do you know if there was more to Amakapa's name when he lived with his tribe?*

He did not speak of it.

Another thought struck Jeni. *What about a Christian name? Was he baptized with a European name?*

Oh yes. Aloysius Pierre. Father Pierre did give Amakapa his own surname and chose the first name of a man of his order canonized a saint in recent years. Jeni wasn't sure, but thought she saw Marielle's ghostly lips curl up at the corners. *He was not fond of that name, and did swear me to secrecy, lest the dock workers learn of it.*

Aloysius Pierre, Jeni repeated, committing the name to memory. *We'll use that name for the Christian ceremony.*

Marielle's expression showed not even a flicker of hope. *I wish that it be so simple.*

Me too, Jeni said.

Holding Jeni's attention with an earnest regard, Marielle said, *Should you find him, should I cross to the otherworld, I would seek out your ancestors.*

I would really appreciate that. Jeni paused, considering if she had any other questions. Then she remembered. *Oh, do me a favor, would you? Stay away from the little kids. They can see you.*

The girl lowered her chin in assent. *Often do the young look upon spirits as equal to the living. No matter, I shall honor your request.*

Thanks, Jeni said. *I'll contact you after we try the ceremonies. If we're lucky, I won't reach you, because you'll have moved on.*

Come what may, know that I be grateful. A deep

sadness filled Marielle's eyes. Then her face demateri-
alized, leaving Jeni alone with only her thoughts.

For good measure, Jeni said, "Goodbye."

When she opened her eyes to Ice's rigid features and clamped lips, she smiled reassuringly and
squeezed his hands. "Now that was an actual conversation." She let go, noticing he rubbed his palms
on his shorts. "Sounds like Amakapa's body was
never recovered. There wasn't a Christian funeral,
and she seemed doubtful about a Native American
ceremony."

"Performing the rituals seems too easy to work,"
Ice said. "But it's also too easy not to try. Did you ask
about his name?"

Jeni nodded. "Amakapa is the only Native
American name Marielle knew of, but I did get his
Christian name, it's Aloysius Pierre." Her eyes crinkled at the corners. "According to Marielle, he tried to
keep it a secret from his co-workers."

Ice shrugged. "I've heard worse."

"If his body was recovered, and buried in
Kaskaskia, it would most likely now be at the Fort
Kaskaskia historic site in Illinois," Phoebe offered.
"During the flood of 1881 they moved as many graves
as they could, reburying the remains on the bluff."

"Do you mean the bluff on the other side of
the river?" Jeni asked, though she already knew the
answer.

Phoebe nodded. "There's a little bridge at
Chester that crosses the river; that's your best route."

As a barrage of questions ran through her head,
Jeni looked at Ice and saw the same uncertainty on

his face. Could they stage a funeral? A death ceremony? Was it worth a trip across the river to try something unlikely to work? Or was their time better spent elsewhere?

With no other ideas, it was a place to start.

After returning to the resort, Jeni and Ice collected some snacks and took them out to the patio. Exhausted by the stressful morning, Jeni collapsed onto a lounge chair and opened a bag of cheese puffs. She'd recounted her conversation once they were all in the car, so she wouldn't have to repeat herself. And she wanted Tyler to know she hadn't forgotten his request.

"I imagine it won't be a problem to come up with some Bible readings," she said now as she took her sunglasses from her head and slipped them on. "But what about a Native American funeral ceremony?"

"Nik is looking into that." Ice set down his soda and checked his phone. "Maybe I'll give him a call."

"Okay. I'll look for some readings." Jeni stretched her legs out, relishing the heat her black leggings collected from the sun. Toeing her tennis shoes off, she let them drop to the ground.

It sounded as though someone at the tribal offices had to track down the medicine man, but eventually Jeni heard Nik's baritone voice answer the call. Ice rose from his chair and walked out on the lawn to ensure his conversation wouldn't be overheard by anyone inside the cabin.

She watched him for a few moments as he

exchanged ideas with his mentor. It still surprised her to think she'd somehow attracted the attention of someone so unique, so interesting. His dedication to his heritage and his tribe was admirable.

She dragged her attention back to finding funeral Bible readings on her phone. As she scanned the screen, her eyes drooped.

She hustled down the stairs, her skirt held high so she wouldn't trip. Entering the dining room, she released a breath at the sight of her father's empty chair, and then plopped into her seat in a swish of fabric. Seconds later, her father entered the room from the mercantile.

"Good morning, Papa," she greeted him.

"And to you," he grumbled. "How is it that my coffee cup is empty? Sally!"

"Would you like that I go to the kitchen and fetch her?"

Her father straightened in his chair, gazing out the window. "No. I see she does hasten this way."

Moments later, Sally entered, a steaming pot in her hand. "Beggin' your pardon." She hurried to pour Mr. Bernard's coffee. "I declare, the wind done blowed the cover offa the woodstack. I dug to the bottom, I did, to find dry kindlin'."

Papa only grunted in response. Sally poured some coffee for Marielle before setting the pot in the warming stand on the sideboard and leaving the room.

"And how was your rest, Papa?" she asked, smoothing a napkin on her lap.

"Unfortunate, what with the rats in the barn," he said blandly.

Lost in Nowhere

Nervous, she studied his countenance, breathing an inaudible sigh when she noted the wrinkles at the corners of his eyes. He was teasing her.

She smiled as Sally returned with a platter and a covered dish, setting them on the table before hustling back outdoors to the kitchen.

Marielle pushed the platter closer to her father, letting him choose from the ham steaks first. Then she removed the lid from the shallow dish and transferred two fried eggs onto her father's plate before pushing the last onto her own plate. Silver clanked on the china as they both started on their food.

"Me again, with an empty cup." her father said. "What has that girl got up to?"

Marielle's chin jerked up, as if startled, and then she was on her feet. "I'll fetch it, Papa," burst from her mouth even as she raised a hand to cover her lips. Her fingers were curled around the handle of the carafe before she could absorb the irregularity of her actions.

She turned to see her father's round eyes and parted lips. "That be not your place, daughter. What causes you to act out of turn?"

"Cannot a daughter dote on her father?" The words rolled out of her mouth as she approached the table. "'Tis nothing, Papa, what with the coffee right here." She filled his cup to the rim.

Her father glowered, unconvinced, and she turned her back on him, replacing the pot on the warmer.

"I be not over fond of this cheeky behavior. I trust that you may act demurely when receiving gentleman callers lest you find yourself a spinster."

"Begging your pardon, Papa. I must repent the airs brought by growing into womanhood. Worldliness may serve in business, yet not so much in the home."

"Certainly not. Any man worth his salt does not want for a brazen woman."

"Forgive me, Papa," she said again, her cheeks blooming with heat.

"Promise to be gracious and humble with your gentleman caller this evening and I can forgive this wonton conduct."

"Tonight?" She looked up sharply, anxiety wending its way through her chest.

"Indeed. I did…" the rest of his sentence dissolved as Jeni awoke when a hand touched her shoulder.

"Sorry." Lines appeared on Ice's forehead. "You were actually sleeping?"

Jeni pushed against the lounge chair to sit up straight. "Yeah, I guess I passed out." She blinked, calling to mind what had been happening when she dozed off. "What did Nik say?"

One corner of Ice's mouth curved upward as he sat on the chair opposite Jeni. "The traditional funeral ceremony of the Kaskaskian natives was a 'Discovery Dance,' which was performed by a shaman, a drummer and warriors. Obviously, that's not something we're going to be able to execute. Nik, however, has those resources." He stopped for a breath, a glimmer of amusement in his eyes. "I don't think this has ever been done before—at least to my knowledge—but we're going to transmit it live though the miracle of technology." Ice held up his phone.

"Wait a minute, are you saying Nik's going to get some people together to do this dance in Minnesota? And you're going to play it on your phone?"

Ice rubbed the back of his neck. "Yeah."

"I think that's a brilliant plan." Jeni grinned. "I've got to get back to finding Bible readings. I didn't get very far before I passed out." She caught his gaze and held it. "I had another dream about Marielle."

Ice stared. "Just now?"

"Yeah, a short one." Jeni tilted her head, remembering how oddly the events of the dream had transpired.

Reading her posture, Ice asked, "What happened?"

Jeni drew in a deep breath. "It was Marielle and her father having breakfast, and…" She swung her legs off the side of the chair so she could sit facing Ice directly. "This is gonna sound weird, I know, but the last dream I had, it seemed like my thoughts were transmitting to Marielle. I figured it had to be just coincidence. During this dream though, I actually tried to get her to act out of character so I'd know if that's what was happening or not. And Ice," Jeni leaned forward, "I swear it worked."

Creases formed as Ice drew his brow low. "What?"

"They had slaves, Ice, which I find offensive." She wrinkled her nose. "Anyway, like I said, they were having breakfast. The coffee pot was sitting on a cabinet in the dining room right where they were eating. Marielle's father was complaining that his cup was empty and the slave wasn't there to fetch it. So I made Marielle get up and pour him some coffee."

Ice's eyes tightened, his expression dubious.

"Seriously." Jeni straightened her spine. "I could feel Marielle's surprise when she did it and her father was shocked. It's not something she'd ever done before. I had to feed her some BS explanations to calm her father down."

"But you can't actually change the past."

"Maybe it just alters the dream, then." Jeni splayed her hands out, palms up. "But it truly seemed like I was in the driver's seat."

Ice stared into the distance. "I know it's possible to change your dreams as they happen. Heck, I've been there and done that." His words took on a dark tone.

"I'd wanted to ask Marielle about the dreams, but I forgot. It seems obvious, though, that she's sending me the story in case it might help me to help her. I bet I'll have another dream tonight. I guess I'll see what happens then." She yawned, and then rolled her head, stretching her neck. "Unless, of course, one of these funeral ceremonies works and it's all over."

"We should be so lucky." Ice's forehead smoothed and he reclined in the chair, stretching his legs out. "Were you thinking about asking Tyler and Mandy if they wanted to go to Fort Kaskaskia?"

"No, we don't need them. I'd prefer to tick Tyler off as little as possible. I figured I could just ask my mom if we can use the car and go to the movies."

At first, she had considered inviting Tyler and Mandy. The thought of roaming around an historic cemetery at night became less creepy with more people involved. Safety in numbers and all that. There always was a slight possibility they'd want to go, just out of curiosity. Or more accurately, Mandy might want to go.

Jeni turned to Ice just as he slid his hands behind his head and closed his eyes. She exhaled and swallowed the words she'd been about to say. She didn't need to bother him with her paranoid thoughts. Tyler and Mandy had already ended up helping them despite Tyler's firm intention not to get involved. And when it came to her cousin, it was better not to push it.

Plus, if she'd learned anything during the last two ordeals that occurred on their family trips, it was that dealing with the supernatural was unpredictable.

Intuition urged her to keep Mandy and Tyler on the back burner for now. She had a feeling she'd need them later.

*The traces left by love were so powerfully inscribed
in his memory that they could never be erased.*

Donkeyskin ~ Charles Perrault

Chapter 10

*A*s they approached the car, Jeni held out her
hand, keys sitting on her palm. "You drive, I'll
navigate?"

Ice reached for the keys. "Your parents won't
mind?"

Jeni shrugged. "You've driven me around plenty
of times." She rounded to the passenger door and Ice
followed. "Even in Lake Itasca when we first met."

"But not in their car." Ice pressed the fob to un-
lock the doors.

"It's fine," Jeni said as he opened her door so she
could climb inside.

When they were on the road, Ice asked, "So what
movie are we supposed to be seeing?"

"*Fires at Dusk*," Jeni said. "I know you saw it, so
that's helpful, and it's a pretty long movie so it should
give us plenty of time."

Ice nodded without looking at her, intent on
driving.

The sun hovered above the horizon, casting
long shadows across the road. As they drove, the

intermittent light had a strobe-like effect so Jeni swung her sun visor to the side window.

"Thanks," Ice said. He really wasn't worried about driving Mrs. Stonewall's car—the rural Missouri roads were similar to home—but the flashing light in his peripheral vision had been distracting.

Jeni consulted her phone. "We stay on this until Highway 51, which will take us across the river into Illinois." She leaned forward, rooting around in one of the cubbyholes in the dash. "Music?" She asked, pulling out a cord.

"Sure." Ice had once preferred rock with a more classic, metal sound than Jeni's usual selections, which favored both the punk and pop sides of rock. Now, it wasn't unusual for him to realize the song that had been repeating in his head was one of her favorites. Occasionally, he'd even choose to listen to her music when they weren't together.

Jeni sang out loud and Ice smiled, relaxing his grip on the steering wheel. The Ouija board had made him nervous, but for some reason, the ring stressed him out even more. Tonight, however, he was entirely comfortable with what they intended to do. He hoped against hope that one of the ceremonies would send Amakapa to the light so they could leave this business behind them.

By the time they reached Highway 51, Ice was glad to make a left turn and put the sunset behind him. The sky was a beautiful riot of purples, blues and reds in the rearview mirror; a deep royal blue in front of them. As the road curved through the flat farmland, Jeni straightened in her seat. He glanced her way, noticing her attention was out the passenger window. Then he spotted the bridge.

The low, truss-style bridge was painted white. It looked quaint across the fields, standing out against the dark tree-covered bluff on the other side of the river. Judging by the crease in Jeni's forehead, quaint wasn't the word she had in mind. Ice extended his hand to her knee and she cast him a grateful look.

The next curve brought the end of the bridge into full view and Ice slowed, taking in the details of the crossing. Jeni stopped the music and sat forward in her seat. "Thank God." She exhaled. "It's not nearly as close to the water as it looked from a distance."

Taking that as a go-ahead, Ice continued at a steady pace. Although Jeni had passed over the Mississippi River before—just days ago, in fact—an Interstate bridge was a much bigger affair than this rural highway crossing. For the first several feet, a two-slat fence was the only barrier between them and a drop to the muddy waters. Then the trusses surrounded them, constantly interrupting the view of the broad, powerful river.

"It looks so peaceful." An air of wistfulness marked Jeni's soft words.

"It does," Ice said.

Seconds later, they left the bridge and entered Illinois. Heading north, they followed a rather desolate stretch of road that paralleled the river. A sense of unease permeated Ice's chest and he inhaled deeply through his nose, unsure of the reason for the feeling. Perhaps it was the distinct lack of other cars or signs of life. Or maybe the gathering shadows cast by the setting sun, though things of that nature tended not to bother him. Then he saw the sign: Prison Area Do Not Pick Up Hitchhikers.

Before he could ask Jeni if she'd noticed the sign, a large stone complex loomed into view on the right. A guard tower stood on the periphery of the facility, flanked by a tall chain-link fence topped with curls of barbed wire. Inside the fence, an imposing stone edifice stared at them blankly.

"Wow, that was unexpected," Jeni commented when the roadside returned to rock and tangled brush.

Ice merely nodded, attempting to shrug off his unwarranted discomfort.

But Jeni must have felt the same way because after instructing him to turn away from the river, she said, "It looks like there's a different route we can take back to the bridge."

"Sounds good to me," Ice said.

The park entry road snaked upward through the forest for about a half mile, and then the view opened on their left to a hilly, trimmed lawn peppered with grave markers. "Here's the cemetery," Ice said, slowing. "I don't see anything that says where to park." He guided the car to the edge of the road and stopped.

Jeni surveyed the stone crosses, tablet-style headstones and other grave markers in various shapes and sizes. "The readings are going to have to work from here or you're going out there to read them. Because the last time I got near an old cemetery, all hell broke loose."

"It's not as if you've remained incognito on this

trip." Ice tried to keep his voice neutral. "But you're right, better if you don't go traipsing around out there. This is a long shot effort at best."

Jeni brought her focus to Ice. "Do you think we're wasting our time?"

"No. It can't hurt to try." Then he smirked at her. "Besides, we got ourselves some alone time."

"Some kind of warped date." Jeni raised an eyebrow and then chuckled.

Ice checked to make sure he had cell service and then texted Nik to let him know they'd arrived. "He said it'll be about twenty minutes until they're ready. Is that enough time to read the Bible verses you found?"

"Yeah, I think so." Jeni reached into a bag and handed him a candle and a lighter.

The candle had been Phoebe's idea. She carried a variety of them for many purposes. The beeswax candles were popular for religious rites, such as the Christian anointing of the sick. She also mentioned remembrance candles. Most Catholic churches had a bank of candles that parishioners could light in memory of a deceased loved one. Jeni and Ice decided to purchase a beeswax candle to take with them.

Ice strode into the cemetery and then positioned the candle in the grass. It was breezy atop the river bluff, and he had to cup a hand over the wick to light it. As he rose to his feet, the flame guttered out. Sighing, he moved the candle to the lee of one of the tombstones and repeated the process. Hands stuffed in his pockets, he watched for a moment to be sure the candle would stay lit.

Returning to the car, he rolled the window down to allow Jeni's invocations to carry across the burial ground. The earthy aroma of decaying leaves and cut grass drifted into the vehicle.

He turned to Jeni. She nodded, and then said, "We're here today to remember Aloysius Pierre and to send his soul home to God, the Father." She'd raised her voice to an authoritative level, which sounded loud inside the car. Her eyes darted to Ice and then lowered to her phone. Drawing in a breath, she began to read. Ice was familiar with the verse she'd chosen because it had been used in an old song: a time to be born, a time to die… He appreciated her choice. Last, she intoned, "Eternal rest, grant unto Aloysius Pierre, and let perpetual light shine upon him. May his soul through the mercy of God rest in peace. Amen."

They let her words settle into the soft rustle of leaves and occasional sharp call of a bird. The candle flame flickered and danced. Ice touched Jeni's knee, squeezing gently. "That was nice."

"Thanks," she said.

They both jumped when Ice's phone rang. "Hey, Nik."

"We're ready here," Nik said over the murmur of voices in the background. "I've got Kal to help with the technical side of things."

Ice exhaled. He'd anticipated having to guide his mentor through the video meeting process. "Great, put him on."

"Hey, Ice. I've got my webcam set up," Kal said. "We're ready when you are."

"Okay." Ice eyed the cemetery. "Give us a few

minutes to get to a good location. Should I send the invitation to your email or Nik's?"

Kal snickered. "Definitely mine."

"You got it," Ice said. "And thanks, Kal."

After Ice ended the call, Jeni said, "Hopefully we can find an open space where I don't have to worry about walking around."

"Exactly." Ice retrieved the candle, and then they continued up the park road. Spotting a large sign near a short flight of cement steps set into a moderate rise, he slowed and then stopped.

"Site of Fort Kaskaskia," Jeni read the sign out loud. "Do you think they're stone ruins?"

"I'll go check it out." Ice understood her hesitation. Jeni had an affinity for stone that often worked as a conduit of sorts to the spirit world. Until she had a handle on her ability, she was right to keep her distance from stone remnants of old structures.

The sign included images, so he paused, thinking his query might be answered immediately. The picture, however, was not of the fort, but of its outline, although the description below told him what he needed to know. After a quick trot up the steps, he returned to the car. "The fort was built of earthworks and wood and the entire site is now covered with grass." He grinned. "It's a perfect location."

After the briefest hesitation, Jeni said, "Okay. I trust your assessment." She twisted to extract a plastic grocery bag from the backseat. Knowing that many Native Americans sent the deceased into the afterlife with food for the journey, they'd decided it couldn't hurt to include provisions along with the ceremonial dance.

From the top of the cement stairs, a large expanse of green lawn extended toward the edge of the river bluff. The area appeared as a vague depression in a rough rectangular shape. They walked to the center of the space and unloaded the few produce items from the bag.

"That's it." Jeni placed the last ear of corn.

Ice got out his phone and sent an invitation to Kal to join a meeting. Then he tipped his phone to a landscape view. A few seconds later, Kal's face appeared on the screen. "You got me?" he asked.

Behind Kal, a group of tribe members in ceremonial dress milled around in front of a blazing bonfire. "Looks good on our end," Ice confirmed.

Kal's face disappeared. The group spread out, ringing the fire. A drum initiated the tempo and soon chanting joined the rhythmic beat. The warriors moved in tandem with the pounding cadence, feet striking the dirt as they circled the leaping flames. The drumming ramped up, knees lifted higher and the voices rose, increasing the intensity of the ceremonial dance. Ice had seen and participated in many such dances so he mostly stole glances at Jeni, enjoying her apparent fascination.

When it was over, both Nik and Kal appeared in the frame. The medicine man's chest rose and fell as he caught his breath, but he was grinning. "This was highly irregular, but it is good for us to keep in practice."

"We appreciate it," Ice said. "Let's hope it worked."

Jeni leaned in so Nik could see her. "Yes. Thank you, Nik."

Lost in Nowhere

A sparkle shone in the medicine man's eyes and the corners of his mouth lifted. "I could see this combination of tradition and technology becoming the norm someday."

Ice shrugged, pleased at the comment. "It's my intention to guide us successfully into the future. I'll let you know if anything we did here tonight made a difference."

"Okay. Good luck."

Ice shut his screen down and turned to Jeni. "Well, that was relatively painless."

"It was. Unfortunately, I feel like anything that easy can't possibly be successful. But we couldn't really rule it out without trying." She shrugged and then looked around. "Do you want to see what else is here?"

They arrived at a picnic area with a scenic overlook and got out to wander around. The high bluff afforded a sweeping view of the river and the fields of Kaskaskia. Most of the brilliant color had leached from the sky and only half of the red sun was visible on the horizon. Nearby, stamped metal panels described the early history of Kaskaskia Village and its eventual destruction by the Mississippi River. They scanned the story, although the details had become familiar.

When Jeni crossed her arms over her chest, Ice moved behind her and gathered her close. "Cold?"

"A little." She snuggled against him. "It's also getting too dark to read these plaques."

They returned to the car and Jeni checked the time. "*Fires at Dusk* started at 8:35 and it's not even

9:30 yet. We've got some time to kill."

"Mmm." Ice gave her a sidelong look, lifting an eyebrow. "I can think of a good way to put that time to use."

"Oh yeah? And what might that be?" Jeni asked with mock innocence.

Chuckling, Ice leaned across the console. "Why don't you come over here and find out?" Already, he was making the necessary inner adjustment to prevent Jeni from seeing visions.

She didn't take much coaxing, and seconds later her soft lips were against his. His fingers dove into her silky fine hair and he felt her shiver. "You're right," she murmured between kisses. "This is a good way to kill time."

As their kisses became prolonged and more intense, the console became an annoying obstacle. Ice put up with it digging into his ribs because the kissing easily overrode the discomfort, but apparently, Jeni had had enough. She pulled her lips from his with an exasperated sigh. "Remember when cars used to have bench seats?"

Ice's chuckle trailed off as she moved away and slipped out of her sandals. Then, shooting him a wicked grin, she crawled over the console into the back seat. "Coming?" she taunted.

For a second, he considered the storage compartment between the seats that had been keeping him in check. But the part of him driven by instinct already had him toeing off his shoes. A moment later, he'd propelled himself over the seatback and Jeni pulled him down beside her.

Lost in Nowhere

Her warm curves along the length of his body triggered a slow burn in his gut. An entirely pleasant, carnal burn. Brushing her hair away from her face, he cradled the back of her head and kissed her thoroughly, eliciting a low moan from the back of her throat.

Jeni's fingernails grazed the back of his neck and moved across his shoulders leaving shivers in their wake. Ice came up for breath, pressing his lips to her temple, her jaw, her neck, and then pushed her top and bra strap aside to continue from her collar bone to her shoulder. Her heart thrummed under his fingertips and each heavy breath pushed her breasts amazingly, maddeningly, against his chest.

His mouth returned to hers as his hand journeyed along her side and down to her waist. Finding the edge of her shirt, he slipped his hand underneath and snaked it around her back, searching for the clasp of her bra. Nervous, yet determined, he fumbled with it, having done enough laundry at home to know the basic operation. Seconds later, he felt it give way and spring apart.

Jeni had pushed his T-shirt up to his shoulder blades and was working her way around the front, so he rose up on his elbow and pulled it over his head with his free hand. Meanwhile, she'd performed some kind of magic that extracted her bra from her shirt. She looked sexy as hell stretched out on the seat, her hair a golden halo of disarray. As she reached out, fanning her fingers over his bare chest, Ice dropped into her waiting embrace.

His heart beat wildly, a cognizant thought rising occasionally to wonder if this was it. *Is this really going to happen?* His hand had already made its way back under Jeni's shirt as if it had a mind of its own. She uttered a small gasp as his fingers skimmed over her stomach.

Her hands were at his waist, fumbling with the button on his shorts. "Ice?"

"Umm," was all he managed, completely lost in the feel of her skin.

"Ice?" Jeni moved her head so he couldn't kiss her again and cupped his jaw until he focused on her. "You have protection, right?" she asked, slightly out of breath.

His passion-swamped brain struggled to comprehend the question. He blinked once, twice. Then his chin dropped as he slowly shook his head. "No." Unable to bear the disappointment creeping across Jeni's face, he closed his eyes and collapsed like a balloon leaking air. Sure, he'd tucked some condoms into his duffel, but it hadn't occurred to him to make the transfer to his wallet before leaving for the park. What an epic fail.

Jeni sighed, her warm breath ruffling his hair.

"I'm sorry," he whispered. "I just didn't think…"

"Why would you have?" She brushed the hair off of his forehead, waiting until he met her eyes. "We agreed we weren't going to do this… you know… in a car."

She shifted and he moved with her so they were lying on their sides. His heart still thumped at a heightened pace and he pressed Jeni against him with his free arm, feeling her heartbeat echoing his own. He exhaled, closing his eyes, wondering at his own stupidity. Jeni was right, they had made that agreement, but as a guy, shouldn't he always be prepared? Did she feel as let down as he did?

When their heartbeats slowed, Jeni finally spoke. "What a stupid agreement." Her inflection was both bitter and mocking.

Ice emitted a dry chuckle, pushing himself up. "Yeah, what were we thinking?"

Wriggling to a sit, Jeni bent her knees and Ice scooted onto the seat next to her. She fished their clothes from the floor and handed him his shirt. He pulled it over his head in resignation and then climbed back into the front seat.

Jeni followed a minute later. As he started the car, she put a hand on his arm. "I make a motion that we strike that agreement."

Ice pressed his lips into a rueful smile. "I second the motion."

You must go tomorrow morning and leave me to the mercy of heaven. Heaven may still have pity on me.

Beauty and the Beast ~ Jeanne-Marie LePrince de Beaumont

Chapter 11

On the way back to the resort, Ice filled Jeni in on the details of *Fires at Dawn* just in case anyone asked about the movie they'd allegedly seen. The cabin was quiet when they entered, although Jeni heard the television in her parents' room on her way to the bathroom. She texted her mom to let her know they were back.

Ice had the couch pulled out into a bed when she returned, and she helped him straighten the covers and fix the pillows. Then he put his arms around her and kissed her goodnight. A long, slow kiss full of apology and promise. He drew away, leaving his fingertips on her cheeks. "I'm s—"

Jeni cut him off with two fingers on his lips. "Equal responsibility. You weren't the only one unprepared."

He smiled. "I love you," he said softly.

Staring into his eyes, stormy gray in the dim light of the table lamp, Jeni wondered how she'd gotten so lucky. "I love you, too." She squeezed him tightly and then reluctantly let him go.

In a partial daze of memory, she put on her pajamas and slid under the covers. She felt different, a little worldlier, perhaps. Although she hadn't lost her virginity tonight, the intention had been there. She'd crossed a mental line. Made a choice. Now it was only a matter of time and opportunity.

Her lips curved as she flexed her limbs under the covers, remembering the feel of Ice's fingers on her skin, the hot firmness of his body under her hands and the untamed certainty that something mind-blowing was yet to come.

She didn't even pick up her book, instead conjuring images of what would've happened next had they been prepared.

The sensations were so convincing, Jeni opened her eyes. But it wasn't Ice's blue eyes that met hers; these eyes were brown. Yet the same adoration and hunger filled his gaze.

They were in the mercantile. It was early morning, judging by the titter of birds outside. Amakapa's arms were around her waist, holding her gently, like a china doll. Her hands rested on his chest.

He dipped his head, bringing his lips down to hers, and she responded readily. Amakapa had been tentative and seemed to be momentarily caught off-guard by her fervor.

The door banged open and they both jumped, instantly putting space between them. Marielle's father stood in the doorway, his face red with rage. He glared daggers at Amakapa. "You dare to lay your hands on my daughter!" He advanced on the young man.

Lost in Nowhere

Marielle propelled herself between the two men. "Stop, Papa! Amakapa acts not against my wishes. Make no doubt about it. It be our intent to beseech your permission to court."

"Step aside, daughter," her father bellowed, shoving her out of his path with the back of his arm. "Never would I allow a heathen to court my daughter."

Amakapa had shrunk against the wall, but at Jean Bernard's words, he stood straight, his chin high. "I be no heathen. I practice the Christian way."

"A sow in a frock still be a sow," said Marielle's father. "This affront shall be exercised from your hide."

Again she inserted herself between her father and Amakapa. "Leave, Amakapa," Marielle said without taking her eyes from her father. "Be it that I talk to Papa alone."

"You'll not show your face here again, ungrateful savage," her father called after Amakapa's retreating form. "You are most certainly sacked and I endeavor you to find any work in this town when word spreads of your indiscretion. Return upriver to the heathens that bore you." He thrust his daughter aside and followed Amakapa, who'd fled through the house to the back door. Pausing in the doorway, her father shouted, "If ever you show your face in my daughter's company, I most certainly will kill you!"

Tears had won their way past her anger and she tugged on her father's arm, pleading. "Do not say it, Papa. I love him." He slammed the door as she crumpled into a chair, her breath hitching between sobs.

"Bah, you speak of love yet you are a child. You require a mature man to teach you about life." He stalked past her. "Best you compose yourself as customers soon be arriving."

She stood abruptly and said, "Attend them yourself!"

Then she heaved a shocked gasp, fear gripping her. That she should say such a thing was unthinkable. Already her father's footsteps pounded the wooden floor. "Insolent girl!" His voice boomed from the next room.

She ran, bounding up the stairs to her bedroom and slamming the door. There was no lock on her door so she cowered on the bed as the sound of her father's footsteps echoed up the stairwell. But her door didn't fly open. Instead, she heard Papa's carefully controlled voice as he stood outside. "Needs be that you attend the store as I be required at the docks." The statement was somewhere between a request and a threat.

Jeni opened her eyes and felt the wet trail of tears on her temples. She scrubbed her hands over her face, wiping away the dampness. *God, that had been horrible.*

Already thumping with emotion, her heartbeat ratcheted up a notch as she remembered Marielle shouting, "Attend them yourself." That had been Jeni. It was Marielle's mouth and Marielle's voice, but the words and the action of speaking them aloud had been controlled by Jeni.

It was much more than making a suggestion. She had become Marielle in that moment. Was that new? Or had she had that ability all along?

Jeni rose to her elbows. The bigger question

was, could she use this ability to help Amakapa? Having this dream led her to believe that the funeral ceremonies had done nothing.

She wanted to talk to Marielle, but she wasn't allowed to go out and sit with Ice. And she certainly couldn't ask him to come in here. There was no way she could fall back asleep, even if it was only one o'clock.

Jeni fingered the ring on her pinky while devising a plan. The problem with her idea was that it involved trial and error and time that she just didn't have.

Her breath hitched in fright as a figure materialized at the end of her bed. She scrambled backward until her shoulder blades ground against the wooden headboard.

Air escaped from between her lips as Marielle's features sharpened. "Marielle. I'm sorry," she whispered out loud, realizing what the ghost's presence meant. "I'm sorry the funeral ceremonies didn't work."

The ghostly apparition turned her palms facing out. *You did try.* The hollow voice was inside Jeni's head, as it had been at Phoebe's store.

Since Marielle was already here, Jeni wondered if it would be dangerous to talk to her. Was conjuring a spirit the risky part? Or was it the communication? Or maybe both?

Jeni didn't know, but her mind formed questions even as she debated whether to ask them. She considered asking Marielle if she was sending the dreams, but the answer seemed obvious, a waste of time. What she needed to know was if she could, indeed, change events while dreaming. So she thought, *I'm sorry to ask, but what happened after your father caught you and Amakapa together? Did he return to his tribe?*

Marielle's expression tensed. *He could not. The Indian village was located not far upstream on the Kaskaskia River. The risk was too great. Never had I witnessed such anger from Papa. He did assure that Amakapa would not find work. Moreover, he instructed his men to shoot Amakapa on sight. Both measures necessitated that he leave the area. In secret, he promised to return.*

Did your father ever suspect you were waiting for him? It was odd, carrying out a conversation as the room remained silent. Odder still was observing an apparition, right in her bedroom. Marielle's image was grainy with a two-dimensional flatness.

I gave him no reason to do so. I endured the gentleman callers Papa arranged, at long last finding someone I could trust. We became betrothed.

Jeni's eyebrows rose. *Wow, you got engaged? Now that's convincing.*

Every other suitor I received only once. But Claude was a friend. A true friend. The sorrow and wistfulness of Marielle's words tightened like a band around Jeni's chest.

How did it happen? was Jeni's next thought. There was no telling what her next dream might be about, but it couldn't hurt to collect some details that she might be able to change.

Having had my fill of boastful young men and old men with foul breath, I did design to find a man with redeeming qualities. 'Twas an afternoon walk when I found

*L*ost in *N*owhere

Claude, a tall, blond man tending a competing mercantile. Judging his age akin to mine, curiosity rose as to the reason he hadn't approached Papa. Or if he had, why I had not seen him as I made no doubt I had been courted by every eligible man in Kaskaskia. He spoke as if I were any person, not fumbling or boasting. When I admitted I was Jean Bernard's daughter, he confessed to be the son of Thibault Valle, the mercantile owner and my father's rival. Continuing my walk, it did occur to me that Papa would be truly vexed should I be courted by the son of Thibault Valle. And here was a man I could stomach.

I did make it routine to pass by the Valle Mercantile, and in time, Claude inquired that he might call on me. Previously, I'd required each suitor approach my father. With Claude, the choice was mine alone. I boldly announced the coming of a gentleman caller and then went off to ready myself.

Papa's face, as I accepted the daisies from Claude and directed him to the parlor, told of his recognition of Valle's son. His sour countenance did make me the happiest I'd been since Amakapa's leaving. Each visit Claude did bring daisies—remembering I favored them—so I chose their placement on the windowsill near to the territory map in the mercantile where Papa would no doubt see them.

Jeni smiled. She and this girl from the 1700's had so much in common. *But didn't it break Claude's heart when you ran away with Amakapa?*

No. He knew my heart was taken.

And he still proposed?

Marielle pursed her lips. *Had he had his way, Claude's heart would belong to the miller's son. Though we never spoke of it, he knew I was aware. His proposal took place at the inn, where he claimed a special meal could be had that night. This was part of his ruse. As we drank ale in wait of stew and biscuits, he did present the ring.*

This ring? Jeni glanced down at her hand.

Yes. He said that we matched perfectly as each of us could not be with the one we truly loved. I did promise that, in the fall, had Amakapa not come for me, I would marry Claude.

But Amakapa did come back? Jeni asked.

Yes.

The anguish in Marielle's face broke Jeni's heart. *Listen, Marielle, I have another idea to try. But I should go now so I can work out the details. Don't give up.*

Marielle tipped her chin down. *Goodbye.*

Goodbye. Jeni couldn't deny the creepiness left after the apparition winked out of sight.

She snuggled into her covers and reviewed the things Marielle had told her, banking on having another dream. But her mind spun with ideas and the ramifications of what she thought she could do... the possibilities. Simply closing her eyes was not going to be enough to get her to sleep.

Rolling to her back, Jeni arranged her limbs in Shavasana, or Corpse Pose, like they did at the end of every yoga class. Filling her lungs to maximum capacity, she then breathed out, open-mouthed, expelling all the air inside her. It worked, melting much of the tension in her muscles. She performed the breathing exercise again, trying her best to clear her mind.

Finally, after lying still and letting thoughts run through her brain without dwelling on any one thing, Jeni set the image of the mercantile in her head.

Lost in Nowhere

She opened the door to the street, sweeping the pile of debris from the floor onto the top stair. Then, swinging the broom sideways, she cleared the dirt from the step.

"Marielle!"

Recognizing the voice, she smiled as she turned toward the young man hurrying her way. The wind lifted his mop of blond hair, leaving it charmingly disheveled. She backed inside, giving him room to bound up the steps into the mercantile while pushing the hair from his eyes. When the door was closed behind him, she accepted his warm embrace.

Papa entered the room, eyeing the two of them as if he'd just bitten into a lemon.

Making no move to extract herself from the arm circled around her waist, she smiled up at the man. "I had not thought to see you. To what do I owe this afternoon's visit?"

"An inquiry. That you might accompany me to dinner this evening. If it pleases you, we might walk to the inn." There was an air of excitement about him.

Clearing his throat loudly, her father interjected. "Might I inquire as to the occasion?"

"The ship at dock has come from New Orleans," the young man said. "I wager the fare will be out of the ordinary."

"Indeed, Claude." Marielle rose on her toes to kiss his cheek. "I accept your invitation."

"Excellent. I shall return near seven." He leaned to return her kiss and then relinquished his hold. "I am now to the docks to attend our shipments."

The door closed behind him and she regarded

her father coolly. "And you? Are you to the docks as well?"

"Indeed," he said. "Of Kaskaskia's many men, my daughter chooses my rival's son? 'Tis not proper."

"'Tis an excellent business proposition, favoring the future of our store," she returned. Then, softening her voice, "He does make me happy, Papa."

He grunted, huffing out the door and slamming it behind him.

Once Papa was gone, she sighed heavily and slumped against the counter. Unable to help herself, her eyes drifted to the calendar. "Three weeks beyond one year. Yet where be my love?" she whispered wistfully to the empty room. "The nights be cool, and the fields yielding their harvest."

After stocking and straightening the shelves, Marielle went up to her room to prepare for dinner. As she chose a bracelet, her eyes fell to a small vial in the bottom of her jewelry box. Fishing it out, she held it in her palm, sending a prayer to Almighty God as she always did. She'd had to burn the note Amakapa left, promising his return, but she'd gathered the ashes into this vial and saved them, needing something concrete to hold on to.

A knock sounded at the front door. She called out that she was coming and slid a barrette into her auburn hair. With one last look in the mirror, she turned and went to greet Claude.

She opened the door to a bouquet of daisies, her favorite. "Claude, I assure you, this be most unnecessary." But the corners of her mouth lifted in genuine pleasure as she found an empty pickle jar and filled it with water. Breathing in the green scent of fresh cut flowers, she approached the windowsill and paused, then turned and placed the flowers on the counter, above the cash box on the shelf below.

Claude offered his hand to help her down the steps, and she looped her arm through his as they proceeded down the street in amicable silence. A blast of warm air carrying the aroma of alcohol, food, perfumed women and sweaty men swirled around them as they entered the inn. The tinkling of piano keys accompanied the loud chatter near the bar, so he escorted Marielle to a somewhat quieter table in the corner. The barmaid brought them tankards of ale and Claude inquired about that night's fare.

"Ain't nothing changed," the woman said. "Roast pork and taters, stewed beef or chicken."

Claude looked apologetically across the table. "Sadly, it seems I was mistaken."

"The stew appeals to me," Marielle told the barmaid. "And biscuits, should there be some."

"Aye." The woman looked at Claude.

"Same as the lady," he said.

As the woman turned, Marielle asked, seemingly despite herself, "Is there wine?" Covering her mouth with a hand, she looked from Claude to the serving woman, who gaped at her as if she were daft.

"'Course," the woman said.

"I'd prefer it." Marielle slid the tankard of ale away.

Swiping the mug from the table, the woman retreated.

Claude regarded her with lifted eyebrows, the

corners of his mouth curled into a slight smirk. "Who be this lady about town?"

Feeling her cheeks warm, she raised her chin. "Special meal, indeed."

"Truly," he said, eyes twinkling, "I confess I knew not what that boat held aside from goods for the store."

"I did not need coaxing," she said, chuckling.

"I should know better, yet your coming was most warranted." Claude reached into the watch pocket of his vest. He withdrew a ring and extended it across the table. "I would be most happy should you be my wife."

She swallowed, unable to speak, eyes fixed on the gold ring bearing an incuse cross and sword. The surrounding din faded and a flush crept up her neck.

"'Tis not a pretty thing, yet my family has kept this ring for more years than one could count." When she didn't respond, he lowered his voice to a whisper. "I feel closer to no one else, Marielle. I ask for no more than your companionship."

Tears filled her eyes. "Claude, I…"

"Accept the ring, will you? Afore the barmaid does return."

She took the ring and held it awkwardly between her fingers, averting her eyes. The smell of roasting chicken turned her stomach.

"It makes no matter that you are not in love with me," he said evenly. "That your heart belongs to another. I love you as a sister, not as a lover. We are happy together. Could we let that be enough?"

Inhaling deeply to steady herself, Marielle raised

her eyes. "Yes," she whispered. Clearing her throat, she tried again. "Yes, indeed. It is and shall be enough. However," she leaned forward, "I would give my true love just a little longer."

Comprehension dawned and Claude sat back in his chair. "Be it your belief he might still honor his promise?"

Her throat ached and, not trusting her voice, she nodded.

"Fair enough." Claude exhaled, smiling. "Might you wear the ring? Our engagement could be long. We may tell of our desire to wed in winter, after the harvest, at the first snowfall."

She managed a wan smile, wriggling the ring onto her finger. "A winter ceremony would be lovely. Should I be here, I shall marry you."

*I know you are not a prince, but you please
me just as much as if you were,
and we shall flee away together into some corner of the world.*

Princess Mayblossom ~ Madame d'Aulnoy

Chapter 12

*I*ce frowned as he watched Mrs. Stonewall go into her daughter's room for the second time. A moment later she appeared in the doorway. "You want to give it a try, Ice? I think she's ignoring me." She made light of the situation, but the crease between her eyebrows told a different story.

He nodded and stood, forcing himself not to rush, but the ominous feeling that had been building over the last hour and a half crescendoed as he crossed the room.

"You two didn't get in that late last night," Jeni's mom commented. "She must've been up late reading or something."

Ice went straight into Jeni's room.

She was on her side, facing away from him as he moved between the beds. Her right hand lay on the pillow next to her face and Ice stared at the gold ring on her finger, the expanding panic in his chest making it hard to breathe. Acutely aware of Mrs. Stonewall behind him, Ice said, "Hey, sleepy head, wake up."

His voice sounded weak. "I've been up for hours," he said, forcing a more normal tone.

He shook her shoulder, both alarmed at the sluggish feel to her body and relieved by the heat emanating from under the covers.

"Did she eat anything weird last night?" Jeni's mom asked, concern raising her voice an octave.

"Uh... not that I recall." Then, remembering they were supposed to be at a movie, Ice said, "She didn't have anything that I didn't eat, too." He couldn't bring himself to say that they'd shared popcorn when they hadn't even been at a movie theater.

Knowing Jeni had been having dreams of the past, Ice wondered if he might be able to contact her spiritual self through skin to skin contact. He reached as if to brush the hair from her face, skimming his palm against her cheek as he channeled his own spirituality.

Jeni's eyelids fluttered and she rolled to her back, confusion clouding her eyes for a few seconds.

"Holy smokes, kiddo," Mrs. Stonewall said. "You had me worried for a minute there."

Ice stepped back, allowing room for Jeni's mom.

"Do you feel all right?" she asked, pressing her wrist to Jeni's forehead.

Jeni pushed up to her elbows. "I'm fine, Mom. Can't a person sleep in on vacation?" She glanced to the bright light behind the window shade and reached for her phone. "What time is—holy crap, it's ten thirty?"

"Yes, and you were darn near impossible to wake up. I had to bring in reinforcements." Mrs. Stonewall gestured to Ice.

Lost in Nowhere

When Jeni met his gaze, Ice stretched his eyes wide, raising his hands in a "what's up" gesture.

Seemingly unruffled, Jeni sat up. "Well, I'm awake now. I'll be out in a minute."

Ice returned to the couch and picked up his laptop, staring vacantly at the screen. Mrs. Stonewall thanked him as she passed by on her way to the kitchen.

"Sure, no problem." He hoped he at least managed to sound neutral.

The bedroom door swung open. Jeni walked over and sank down into the couch next to him. "Sorry. I don't know why I slept so late."

"Did you have another dream?" Ice moved the laptop to the table and turned to face her.

"Two, actually." Her initial look of excitement was edged out by something else. She hesitated but then began recounting the first dream. Ice could sense a bomb was about to drop.

"...I really wanted to know if I had actually changed anything, but I knew I wasn't supposed to contact Marielle alone..." Jeni looked down. "Turns out, she contacted me."

"Wait." Ice shook his head, incredulous. "Let me get this straight. You talked to Marielle last night by yourself? Phoebe warned against it."

"Well, Marielle was there. I mean, I knew it was her because she appeared, so I figured, why not ask my questions." Jeni dropped her voice to just above a whisper. "I'm running out of time to solve this, you know."

Ice fixed her with a stern stare, breathing out his irritation. "So what happened?" He managed to sound more calm than he felt.

"I asked Marielle a bunch of questions about what happened after she and Amakapa got caught by her father, and then I tried to change up some things in the next dream. I need to talk to her now and see what she remembers, to see if I impacted anything."

"So you *are* trying to alter history." He didn't phrase it as a question, because it wasn't a question. That is exactly what she was trying to do and he needed her to comprehend it.

Her attention had been everywhere as she spoke and now her eyes finally came to rest on him. "Tweak," she corrected. "I'm only tweaking history."

Ice shook his head. "But you can't change history. And if you could, there would be too many ramifications. Dire ramifications."

"How can you say that? Who really knows? Maybe as long as nothing major changes—like stopping a war or saving someone's life—then it's okay. I'm just trying to save Amakapa's soul. He'll still die. History doesn't really change just because his soul ends up somewhere else." Her wide eyes were filled with exasperation. "Besides, if I can't change history, like you said, why does it matter if I try?"

Not an expert on time travel or the possible complications caused by altering the past, Ice had to let the argument go. Anything he might say was theoretical at best. Although he remained unconvinced, it was possible that Jeni was right. Besides, that's not what really bothered him. "The thing is," he said gently, "you don't know the nature of your ability yet. There's too much we don't know about the situation, yet you're forging ahead blind." He swiped a hand over his face. "Something is not right here. I feel it in my bones and in my gut."

After a moment, Jeni nodded, her lips pressed into a sheepish line. "You're right, Ice. I need to be cautious. I just… " She closed her eyes. "I just can't imagine the agony of spending eternity separated from the person you love the most."

Ice looked into her green eyes, loving her empathy and fearing her knee-jerk reactions to sentiment. "I can't imagine it either," he said, his voice husky with emotion. "But a few minutes ago, I thought I was going to find out exactly what that was like."

Jeni pulled her head back, dropping her chin. "Was it really that hard to wake me up?"

"Jeni." He locked eyes with her. "Your mom tried twice to wake you, and when she couldn't, she asked me to try. She tried to hide it, but I could tell she was concerned—you're not normally hard to wake. Her reaction alone had me nervous."

She shook her head, frowning. "But I did wake up."

"Not when I shook you. Or talked to you. Then I saw you were wearing the ring." Ice swallowed. His throat felt dry and scratchy. "I… it… that's when I was really scared."

Jeni stiffened. "I'm sorry, Ice. I didn't mean to scare you. I guess I was just sleeping really soundly."

He shook his head. "No. It was more than that." He reached out and put a hand on her knee, waiting for her attention to be fully on him. "I had to use our spiritual link to reach you. To break you out of whatever state you were in."

"State?" she asked, blinking rapidly. "Like I might have been too deep in the dream world?"

"Or in the past." Ice rubbed the back of his neck. "I don't know. This is so far out of my comfort zone, I can't even guess."

Jeni bit her lower lip, hands fidgeting with the bottom of her shirt. "Maybe we can go into town and talk this over with Phoebe," she suggested. "I don't think there's anything special happening today."

"All right." Ice let some of the tension ease from his shoulders, glad that Jeni finally seemed to grasp the significance of what had happened. "Yeah, I'd love to get her take on this."

"I'll go check in with my mom." Jeni stood. "And get coffee if there's any left." She bent down and gave him a quick kiss on the forehead. "I'm sorry I made you worry."

Ice watched her go with conflicted emotions. He hoped Phoebe would back him up, or, even better, advise Jeni to give up her quest to alter past events.

He was certain his worries weren't over.

Jeni drew the musky incense deep into her lungs as she entered Memories and Magic. The smell had a calming effect and she made a mental note to ask Phoebe about it. Ever since her life had been knocked off its mundane tracks, anxiety had settled into her psyche, ready to flare up in unpredictable circumstances. Anything that could alleviate that feeling of unease was worth noting.

The store owner lifted her chin in greeting without interrupting her conversation with a customer. Then she ushered the older woman into an aisle, explaining the significance of candle colors. "I'll let you look," she said. "Let me know if you have further questions."

Jeni twisted the ring on her finger and scanned the shelf of bottled essential oils, not reading the labels. She hoped the medium would support her cause and put Ice at ease. It felt like there was already a tiny rift between them—really just a difference of opinion—and the last thing Jeni wanted was for that space to grow.

"So what's the news with your ghost?" Phoebe asked when she was close enough to speak softly. Her outfit had a serious seventies vibe going on; paisley wide-bottom pants, a loose blouse and a long, knit vest with six-inch fringe on the bottom. "Any luck with the funerals?"

Jeni shook her head. "No, unfortunately. But I have another idea I'd like to run by you."

Phoebe tilted her head toward the curtained doorway in the back of the store. "Come on back." She swept the fabric aside, looping it behind a large hook mounted next to the doorframe. Then she positioned herself so that she could see the front door from her post. "Tell me about your idea."

As Jeni explained how she was able to affect Marielle's actions in the dreams, Phoebe's eyes narrowed, but she didn't comment. Although Ice was quiet, Jeni noticed he watched the medium carefully, hardly looking at Jeni as she spoke. "I'd like to talk to Marielle and see if anything changed," Jeni said. "I want to know if I am... altering history."

"Your idea is to change past events?" Phoebe's eyes darted to Ice and then back to Jeni.

"Tweak," Jeni muttered, not crazy about the woman's dubious inflection. "I'm not going to try to change anything major."

Phoebe rubbed a finger under her bottom lip. "Tell me again how you're accomplishing this."

Jeni explained how she was able to *come forward*—as she thought of it—and interject her will into Marielle.

"Reverse possession," the medium stated.

"It has a name?" Ice asked.

Phoebe lifted an eyebrow. "Not technically. It's just what it sounds like. I've never heard of anyone doing something like this. I'm not sure it's a great idea."

Shoulders sagging, Jeni let out an inaudible sigh. "Why?"

"My understanding is that when you *come forward*, as you put it, your mind enters the spirit world. It could explain why you didn't wake. Fortunately, Ice was able to reach you there and bring your consciousness back. This kind of thing is why I told you to always have a mooring in the living world."

"That was in relation to talking to Marielle," Jeni protested. "I had no idea it applied to dreaming about her."

"Having a dream is one thing. If you're planning to take part in the dreams, it would be wise to anchor yourself in reality." Phoebe eyed the woman she'd left in the store perusing candles. "I should go check on her. I'll be right back."

Jeni looked at Ice and crinkled her nose. "So my idea is a complete bust. I can't have you there while I dream unless I happen to fall asleep during the day like I did yesterday."

Ice had the courtesy to look sympathetic, though Jeni noticed the softening of his stance. He stepped close to her, touching her shoulder. "You should probably consider—"

"Don't." Jeni cut him off, turning away. From the store came the sound of the cash register drawer banging open.

"We can come back here," Ice offered. "When you figure out your ability, I mean. When we have a plan that will work."

"And in the meantime Marielle will continue to suffer. Who knows how long it will take to dig up my family history without her help?" Balling her fists, Jeni stabbed her fingernails into the flesh of her palms to keep away unbidden tears.

Phoebe returned, instantly sensing the tension between them. "What's going on?"

"Ice and I aren't sleeping together. We're with my parents." Jeni was surprised at how bitter she sounded and tried to neutralize her tone. "He won't be there when I dream."

"Mmm." The medium pursed her lips. "Do these dreams happen as you fall asleep?"

Jeni cocked her head. "Um… yeah. At least it seems like it."

Phoebe regarded them both for a moment. "Then I think I can help you."

"How?" Jeni asked. Ice looked unsurprised, exchanging what appeared to be a knowing look with the medium.

"Just before you fall asleep," Phoebe explained, "there's a stage of deep trance as your conscious mind winds down. It's not unlike what Ice might experience during a vision quest or a sweat."

"But we don't have that kind of time," Jeni said.

"We don't need it." Phoebe smiled. "I'm a medium. I can lead you into an altered state of consciousness that will allow the dreams."

Jeni stared at the woman, feeling a weight lift from her heart. "You can do that?"

The jingle of bells from the front of the store announced another customer and Phoebe turned, pausing in the doorway. "Why don't you go ahead and contact Marielle? You don't need me for that." She released the curtain as she left to give them privacy.

The way Ice's lips were pressed tightly together revealed that he didn't share Jeni's renewed enthusiasm, but he moved chairs to face each other and sat down. Jeni took the seat across from him, feeling awkward, as if she needed to apologize, but for what? So when he offered his open hands, she rested hers on top. Again, he adjusted his left hand so the ring didn't touch his skin.

"Is it like a shock?" Jeni asked

"No. It feels… oily. Like, unpleasantly slippery or slimy."

Jeni frowned. "It just feels like a gold ring to

me." Ice didn't wear any rings, which made Jeni wonder if the smooth metal felt odd to him.

"It's not physical. It's mental. I get a weird, elusive feeling from it."

His comment was unsettling, although she should've known Ice's aversion to the ring went deeper than what it physically felt like. "I wonder why Claude told Marielle it was in his family for longer than he knew." Jeni regarded the ring warily.

I am here.

Jeni flinched, eyes widening as the figure of Marielle materialized just behind Ice's chair. "She's here," she whispered to Ice.

With Marielle's image before her, Jeni didn't close her eyes this time, although she did communicate mentally. *I have some questions about the night Claude proposed,* she said. *Just some details that might help me.*

Do proceed.

You said Claude brought you daisies that night. Where did you put them?

*On the win—*Marielle hesitated. *No. Not the windowsill that night. I remember I did place them on the counter. I thought Papa could not miss them nearby the cash box.*

Jeni's pulse surged. *At the inn, you said you had ale while waiting for your food?*

Such information does aide in your search?

It does, Jeni assured her. *More than you know.*

Indeed, it was ale served to us. But I inquired as to wine. 'Tis not often that I partake of ale as I find it bitter.

Excitement flared in Jeni's chest. *Tell me what happened next.*

By the time Jeni finished her conversation with Marielle, Phoebe had returned.

"The changes I made are now part of Marielle's memories," she announced breathlessly, looking from Ice's diffident face to the medium's curious expression.

"It may be that that is all you're doing—changing her memories. It does not mean that you have changed the actual past," Phoebe said.

"I know." Jeni bobbed her head. "But, on the other side, what if I did modify past events in a small way? A negligible way that had no effect on the future?" She fixed first Ice, and then Phoebe, with a heartfelt look, begging them to be open-minded. "What if I could actually save Amakapa's soul this way? Isn't it worth it to find out?"

Phoebe chose not to answer, deferring to Ice.

Holding the medium's gaze, he said. "As long as it's safe."

"I will do my best to implement fail-safes where I can." Phoebe then turned to Jeni. "But understand that we are treading untested waters here. Please use caution. Err on the side of doing too little."

Jeni nodded, a crazy mix of eagerness and nerves warring in her guts. "Okay. I'll be careful."

The medium opened a drawer of the small desk and removed a tablet. Powering it on, she said, "You've probably seen how a hypnotist will use a swinging pocket watch to mesmerize his subject. Well, I've found this works much better." She touched the screen a few times and then handed the device to Jeni. "I'll tell you when to push 'play.'"

Lost in Nowhere

Dragging a chair near them, Phoebe sat, stifling a yawn. "Sounds like you had a long night of dreaming, Jeni. I bet a nap sounds good right now."

Thrown off by the abrupt change of subject, Jeni stared at the woman, perplexed. As the medium yawned again, Jeni was struck by the contagiousness of the action and sucked in a deep breath, her mouth stretching into an "O." She understood. This was the first part of the process.

"You could probably doze off right in that chair." Phoebe yawned again. "That's okay, don't fight it."

Jeni took a deep breath and exhaled from her mouth, letting her body go limp. She yawned.

"Press play," Phoebe said.

Jeni obeyed, dropping her chin to look at the screen on her lap. A black and white pattern began to swirl.

"Just keep your eyes on the center white dot," the medium said softly.

The design seemed to grow, the lines thickening, though part of Jeni's brain understood that it stayed the same, that it was an optical illusion.

"If your eyelids feel heavy, let them drift closed."

The words sifted into Jeni's consciousness and her eyelids fluttered.

From far away she heard the medium say, "That's good." Then a hand patted her shoulder. "When I tell you to wake, you'll wake immediately."

The lamp in the parlor was lit so she circumvented the room and went straight up to bed. Without a candle, she fumbled in the dark to light the lamp on her dresser, trimming the wick until the glow reached the corners of the room. The ring felt odd on her finger as she reached into a dresser drawer for her nightgown.

From the shadows in the corner of her room a figure emerged, strong arms trapping her arms by her sides, a hand quickly sealing her lips as she opened her mouth to cry out. A weak whine issued from her throat as she struggled to get away.

The size, strength and musky smell informed Marielle that the intruder was a man. The heat of his breath fluttered her hair as his lips moved close to her ear. "Marielle. 'Tis only me."

She froze, heart hammering. After a moment, the hand dropped from her mouth, arms releasing her so she could turn to face him. Lifting his hat, the man moved closer to the lamp.

His hair was closely cropped and a bushy mustache hid his upper lip, but the strong jaw and gentle eyes could not be denied. Marielle's heart leapt with joy.

Amakapa had returned for her.

Stifling her urge to shout with elation, she clamped her lips shut and threw her arms around him, squeezing tight. "Oh, how you did keep me waiting," she whispered, tears springing to her eyes.

A chuckle rumbled from his chest. "I, too, have counted the days. Too many have passed."

She pulled away, clutching his hands, refusing to let go.

He turned over her left hand, eyes doleful. "You have moved on then?"

She shook her head, digging for a handkerchief in her dress pocket to wipe her eyes. "Only the favor of a good friend. Mayhap my only friend."

Amakapa searched her face. "You would break his heart?"

"No. He knows my heart belongs to you." Her lips curled playfully. "And his heart might belong to the miller."

Amakapa's eyebrows rose, his mouth curving into a smile, yet the tuft of hair above his lip remained rigidly straight.

Marielle raised a tentative hand, touching the mustache with her fingertips.

Amusement sparkled in his eyes. "A ruse." He squeezed her hand. "I have made arrangements. We must go tonight."

Marielle nodded, reluctantly letting go of him to pull her valise from under her bed. As quietly as possible, she removed clothes from her chest of drawers and stuffed them into the bag. Last, she twisted the ring from her finger and set it on the dresser.

When they heard footsteps on the stairs, Amakapa moved to the corner behind the door and Marielle lowered the flame until the shadows swallowed him. Then she carried the lamp to her nightstand, crawling into bed.

A soft knock sounded at the door. "Good night, daughter."

"Good night, Papa." And suddenly it struck her that this was the last time she'd tell him good night. Because she'd dreamed of this day for over a year, the pang of sadness was unexpected. She'd been angry with her father for so long. "I love you." She said it out loud although he was already gone.

Swinging her feet to the floor, she padded across the room to her writing desk, bringing the lamp with her. The scratch of pen on paper in the quiet room was like a saw cutting wood in a peaceful forest.

Amakapa approached the desk. "For your father?"

She shook her head. "Claude." She glanced up, reading the question on his face. "Should the worst happen, I prefer a Christian burial."

He nodded.

"And you?" she asked, careful to keep her voice low. "What be your preference? Christian or Indian?"

His brows sank low. "Father Pierre be the only priest I did know that might bestow Christian rites on an Indian. Needs be that the Great Spirit and God the Creator be one in the same. My belief is such that a tribal ritual would bid my spirit across the river and commit my soul to Heaven."

"I shall ask that your tribe does receive your body." She finished the letter, folded it, sealed it with wax, and then tucked it into her pocket. "'Tis our one task to deliver the letter afore taking our leave."

Amakapa shifted on his feet and looked away, but didn't protest.

They sat side by side on the bed, hands clasped, waiting for Marielle's father to settle and fall into a deep sleep. Time seemed to stretch out agonizingly long, but eventually, the steady rhythm of her father's snores penetrated the wall.

Silently, they crept from the house.

"… three, four, five, awake!"

Jeni opened her eyes and raised her head, the

bright overhead lights making her blink.

The medium studied her with peaked eyebrows. "Well?"

"It worked." Jeni bobbed her head. "I dreamed. But there's more that I want to do. That I want Marielle to do, I mean."

"I'm glad it was successful." Phoebe said. "But I'm afraid we'll have to continue later when I have someone here who can watch the store."

Ice stood. "I could go for some lunch." He picked up his chair and returned it to the table.

Jeni rose from her chair slowly, smoothing her shorts where they'd bunched up from sitting. "Okay. Thanks for your help, Phoebe." She turned to move her chair but Ice had already taken it. She followed him from the store, immersed in thought.

As eager as she was to implement her plan and find out if it worked, dread was beginning to form in her gut. Even if she was able to save Amakapa's soul, this story came to the same tragic end.

And Jeni didn't relish the thought of experiencing it firsthand.

Jeni sipped her soda and then chased the ice cubes around the glass with her straw as she told Ice what she experienced while in the trance. "I had Marielle write a letter to Claude telling him that she and Amakapa were going to run away. She said she knew that once her father realized she was gone, he'd track her down. If she and Amakapa were found— if they were captured—she needed Claude to do something important for her. That her father would kill Amakapa was a foregone conclusion, so she asked Claude to claim Amakapa's body and take it to his tribe for a customary burial."

Ice stared across the diner, fingers fiddling with his straw wrapper. "Your theory is that a proper burial would keep his soul out of limbo, or wherever it currently is."

"Yes." Jeni sat very still, studying him.

"And I can buy into the thought that if that did happen—barring any complications—"

"Complications?" Jeni broke in. "Like what?"

Her outburst finally brought his attention to her. "Like Claude shows up with the body and they think he killed Amakapa, for starters."

"Oh." She deflated, slumping against the padded back of the booth.

Ice leaned forward. "That's not my point, though. I can see where your plan has the potential to not alter future events, but I'm not convinced that you're actually changing the events."

"But Marielle has confirmed the changes."

"I know." He looked pained as he ran a hand through his hair.

Jeni lowered her chin, staring at the table. "You think I'm only changing her memories."

Ice said, "I guess we'll find out."

The crease between his eyebrows seemed to have taken up permanent residence. Jeni was about to ask if there was more, if he still felt as though something was wrong, but the waiter arrived with their food. Jeni eyeballed her salad, thinking that she wasn't really hungry, despite the fact that all she'd had that day was a breakfast bar. Then the smell of warm, crispy potatoes wafted from the plate of fries in the middle of the table, and her appetite perked up.

Squeezing some ketchup onto the corner of the plate, Jeni dipped a fry and popped it into her mouth. "Uhhh... hot." She sucked in some cold soda to combat the burn.

When she looked up and caught Ice wearing a lopsided smile, she considered the brief pain totally worth it. The transformation from the tense expression he'd worn all morning was a welcome change. "How nice that my pain amuses you." She delivered the line deadpan, but he saw through her sham and chuckled.

She didn't bring up Marielle and Amakapa again until they left the restaurant. "I know things could still go wrong, but I've already set my plan in motion. I'd like to make sure that letter gets to Claude. Then I'm done, whether it works or not. I don't have any other ideas."

"But that doesn't mean you have to give up forever." Ice slipped his arm around her waist. "As you learn, you may find a way. Maybe you won't even have to come back here to do it."

Jeni thought that over. When things happened on these weeklong trips, she was constantly up against a time constraint. What would it be like to have the luxury to really think things through, to research, to make a solid plan? "Do you think that could be true?" she asked.

He looked into her upturned face. "Absolutely.

Physical location rarely matters in the spirit realm."

Jeni was still pondering that concept when they arrived back at Memories and Magic. A cluster of middle school girls gathered around the revolving display of earrings while Phoebe talked to a couple near the shelves of old board games. Jeni and Ice hovered in the vicinity until Phoebe finished with the couple.

"You two can wait in the back room, if you'd like," Phoebe said. "Hannah will be here in about twenty minutes."

Jeni checked in with her mom and then she and Ice snickered quietly at the comments from the group of girls. The tweens seemed unable—or unwilling—to speak at a conversational level. They'd made it to the Wiccan section of the store and were butchering most of the names of the roots and herbs.

Hannah breezed through the curtain, jerking to a halt when she saw Jeni and Ice. Her blue hair was twisted into two knots on top of her head. "You guys are back."

"Yeah. Phoebe's helping us again," Jeni said.

The girl let her backpack slide from her shoulder, snagging it before it touched the ground and looping it onto a coat hook near the bathroom.

"Guess I should go watch the register," she said, and retreated back into the store.

Moments later, Phoebe entered. "Okay, Hannah will keep an eye on those girls. The trance will happen quickly this time, so get comfortable."

As she and Ice again took their seats, a worm of trepidation rolled in Jeni's belly. She wished there was a way for her to wake, or cut off the dream, as soon as the note was successfully delivered to Claude.

Phoebe offered Jeni the tablet, the illusion already swirling. "Ready?"

Raising her chin, Jeni filled her lungs with courage and locked eyes with Phoebe. "Ready," she said, letting the breath go. Then she lowered her eyes to the reeling pattern, praying this would work.

"Your eyelids are growing heavy," Phoebe said. "So heavy."

The black and white whirls shrunk until they were blacked out.

She followed Amakapa as they crept from her father's mercantile—the only home she'd ever known—and dodged swiftly into the shadows of the building next door. "Where be the horses?" she asked, her voice hushed.

"The stable behind the inn." Amakapa's eyes appeared black in the dark as he scrutinized the street for movement.

"This must reach Claude." She pulled the folded paper from her pocket.

Amakapa nodded. "On your lead."

He carried her valise, which allowed her to lift her skirts and tread carefully. As they approached Claude's home, she was dismayed to see a light in the front window. They would need to be extra quiet.

Marielle had never been inside but knew from talking to Claude that the frame for growing beans was just below his bedroom window. He'd confessed that sometimes, when the beans were ready to harvest, he would lean out his window and pick a few to eat right there in his room.

Heart racing, she edged to the back of the house, pausing to examine the yard until the jutting shadows resolved into rows of vegetables. There, under a window, were the bean frames. Gingerly making her way into the garden, she reflected that although the beans served to identify Claude's room, they also restricted access to the window itself.

The window shutter was angled open to allow some of the cool night air into the room. Wedging herself between the wooden frame and the house, she rose on her toes and slid the folded paper onto the windowsill. A forceful tap with her fingertips sent the paper over the edge to fall inside the room with a soft swish as it landed on the floor. She prayed it remained visible and hadn't drifted under his bed or chest of drawers.

Satisfied, she moved to exit the garden, panic flaring when she was yanked backward. The image that immediately rose in her mind was of her father with his hands fisted in her skirt. Uttering a strangled yelp, she attempted to twist away but was held fast. When no deep-voiced protest or threat was issued, the truth of the situation dawned on her. She peered over her shoulder and found the only thing with a hold on her skirt was the rough-hewn bean frame.

The realization did little to relieve her mounting tension, and extracting the fabric from the splintered wood was more of a struggle than it should have been. When she rounded the house to where Amakapa waited, her pulse still raced from the scare.

By the time they reached the inn, fear had sunk its claws deep into her chest. The horse Amakapa acquired for her shied away from her approach, smelling her unease, so she forced herself to take a few long, calm breaths before reaching out to stroke its neck. Once her valise was secured to the back of the saddle, she hoisted herself onto the horse. They walked the mounts slowly until they were beyond the town, and then took off at a fast gallop.

When they'd put some distance between them and Kaskaskia, Amakapa slowed to a trot. Marielle followed suit, drawing up beside him. "Should we not make haste?"

"The way is long. I thought not to tire the horses."

Marielle nodded, and they continued to follow the road north.

The bone white slice of moon had traveled almost to its apex when Amakapa jerked his head to peer over his shoulder. Twisting in her saddle, Marielle searched the road behind them, a tangle of dread sitting heavy in her stomach. She saw nothing; heard nothing. But unlike Amakapa, she hadn't grown up hunting the woods, so the wrinkles in his brow as he cocked his ear toward the darkness in their wake spread terror through her veins.

That same terror was reflected in his eyes when he hissed, "Run."

They both kicked their horses, pushing them into a fast gallop. Marielle wondered if they should get off the road, but they were flanked by dense forest. Should they enter, speed was no longer an option; they would have to hide. Then a shout from behind them permeated the wind rushing in her ears. Her heart pounded wildly and her breath came in short rasps as she clung to the back of the horse and urged it to go faster.

"… four, five, awake!"

Jeni's chest heaved as she opened her eyes. Her fingers squeezed Ice's hands in a death grip and she relaxed the hold as she looked up. "Uh… sorry."

Ice leaned forward, anxious eyes examining her. "Are you okay?"

"Yeah… uh… yeah." She nodded, attempting a reassuring smile. "They were being chased. It was terrifying." Looking from Ice to Phoebe, she asked, "Why? What was I doing?"

"Aside from grasping my hands as if your life depended on it, your breathing was labored. That's why Phoebe woke you up." Ice turned to the medium. "Are you sure that's normal?"

"People—well, animals, too—often have physical reactions while they dream," she assured Ice.

"I know my cat does," Jeni commented, rolling her head to stretch the tension from her neck and shoulders.

"Did Marielle get the note to Claude?" Ice asked.

Jeni sighed. "Yeah, all that's left is finding out if it worked or not."

Phoebe clasped her hands together. "Since you don't need me for that, I should help Hannah out there." As she stepped out of the room, she added, "Let me know what happens, though."

Ice had risen to his feet, perhaps to shake off residual anxiety, perhaps because he thought they were finished. When Jeni remained seated, he looked at her and asked, "Are you up to contacting her right now?"

"I'm fine," Jeni said. "I really want to know if Claude got the note. If he was able to do anything."

"All right." Ice released a long exhale as he sat, then offered Jeni his outstretched hands.

She reached out tentatively, suddenly afraid she might discover that her last-ditch effort had failed. She met Ice's tired stare, curling her fingers around his. Then she closed her eyes.

Marielle?

*It was as though a cord had tied itself to
her and was pulling her forward
from the center of her chest. There was
nothing she could do about it.
Her fate was sealed.*

Mongette ~ Henri Pourrat

Chapter 13

*T*hat Marielle might not answer was a hope in
the corner of Jeni's mind, though she would not
allow it to become a conscious thought. Even so, when
the French girl's form materialized, despair ached in
her chest.

If you're here, Jeni said glumly. *Then I've failed.*

*In all this time, you alone did offer help. And I be
most grateful.*

*It's just so frustrating. I think I should have the abil-
ity to help you, but I'm inexperienced. I don't know how.
And I leave for home tomorrow.*

You may yet find a solution.

Jeni's heart hurt. *Marielle?*

Yes?

*From what I've seen of Amakapa in the dreams, I
think he would want you to move on without him. Have
you considered that?*

The question earned an unearthly sigh, like wind rattling through tree branches. *A century ago did I ponder such, only to find that my anchor in the living world be rutted so that the light no longer draws me. You have dreamt of my love?*

Sure, you know, the dreams about you and Amakapa in the past. I thought you were sending them to help me help you.

No. That be not my doing.

Jeni frowned. Could it be that her own imagination had filled in the blanks? That seemed unlikely. Unless… unless this was another manifestation of her spiritual ability.

Thoughts returning to their conversation, Jeni asked, *Did you leave a note for Claude the night you left with Amakapa?* She wondered where her plan had failed.

Yes. I asked that in the event of Amakapa's death, Claude might reclaim the body, that it might receive a tribal funeral. The priest at that time had a skewed notion about Christian ways; he refused to perform funeral services for an Indian.

Did Claude do what you asked?

Oh, yes, Marielle responded right away. *He did ride to the river when news of the lynching reached him. Yet his search produced nothing. Mayhap the current was too swift or drew the log down.*

Did you marry Claude? Jeni asked impulsively.

Though we were betrothed, illness claimed my life before we were wed. Be it best that Claude was not a widower.

The tragic story brought tears to her eyes that escaped her closed lids and welled on her eyelashes. *I won't forget you after I leave. If I can find a way to help you, I will.*

When Marielle faded from view, Jeni opened her wet eyes, more tears forming and spilling onto her cheeks. Eyebrows cocked sympathetically, Ice wrapped his arms around her. She let a few tears fall to his shoulder and then blinked, refusing to generate any more.

"I take it he never got the note," Ice said gently.

Jeni sniffed and pulled away, knuckling the wetness from under her eyes. "He did get the note. And he tried to do as Marielle asked. When he heard the commotion, he followed Bernard's men to the river. But he couldn't find his body. He wasn't able to bring Amakapa to his tribe."

"I'm sorry, Jeni." The compassion on Ice's face was genuine.

Jeni's gaze went distant for a few seconds and then she focused on him. "Maybe I did only alter her memories, but at least now she can remember how hard she tried to do right by Amakapa."

"That's true." Ice stood, placing a hand on her shoulder. "You can feel good about that."

Following his lead, Jeni rose and turned her chair back toward the table. "I'm gonna figure this out, Ice. And when I know what to do, I'm going to rescue Amakapa's soul."

The curtain shifted and Phoebe appeared in the gap, eyebrows peaked. "So?"

Jeni shook her head. "I tried to make it so Amakapa would get a proper funeral, but it didn't work. His body was never recovered."

"Aww, I'm sorry." She looped the curtain behind the hook and stepped back to let them through. "There are so few of us. We just can't help them all."

Jeni put on music for the ride back, choosing the more reflective, melancholy tunes in her primarily upbeat collection. As they got out of the car, Mandy appeared, asking what had developed since they'd acquired the ring. Jeni relayed a condensed version of the dreams and Marielle's reports. She didn't begrudge Mandy for wanting the update, but repeating the tragedy made her even more depressed.

Talking through everything again reminded her to tell Ice what Marielle had divulged: that she hadn't sent the dreams. "Have you ever heard of anything like that? Do you think manifesting a story while in a sleep state could be another facet of my spiritual ability?"

"I suppose it's possible," he said. "Dreams play a large role in Native American spirituality. I imagine they do in other beliefs as well."

Everyone gathered at the big cabin for their last family dinner of the trip. The camaraderie helped Jeni to swallow her melancholy mood and enjoy being with her relatives—and with Ice. They joined a card game which matched words with phrases, twisting it by choosing the worst (or funniest) answers possible, and as the evening wound down, Jeni had moved beyond the failure and set her sights on what the future might bring.

She and Ice escaped for a while to the swing on the cabin's front porch and enjoyed some alone time until they were discovered by Aunt Jessie and Neil.

Lost in Nowhere

"Oops… sorry guys. We didn't know you were out here." Aunt Jessie tried unsuccessfully to stifle a grin. "I hate to be the bearer of bad news, but your mom is wondering where you disappeared to."

Jeni sighed. "Would you tell her we're out here?"

"You got it." Jessie prodded Neil around the side of the house.

Before they were out of sight, Jeni called, "And tell her the porch light is on." She didn't try to disguise her annoyance and Ice was chuckling when she turned back to him.

"Who knows, maybe knowing the light is on will buy us some more time out here." She spoke in a pragmatic tone, but she was smiling as she snuggled back up to Ice's side. "It seems like the week went too fast. I'm sorry I spent so much time trying to help Marielle."

"Don't be sorry." His arm was behind her, fingers playing with a lock of her hair. "You were trying to do a good thing. Your spiritual connection is going to be part of your life more and more as you develop it."

"So I may end up like Phoebe. You know, helping others out." Jeni pursed her lips, contemplating the idea. "I can accept that."

"I'm just glad we didn't have to fight off some kind of creature," Ice said. "Honestly, I fully expected something like that would happen."

"I guess I got so involved with trying to save Amakapa that I didn't think about it too much. Maybe we were far enough from the river." *Maybe it's over.* The thought came up, but Jeni didn't want to jinx herself by saying it out loud. There were more family trips to the Mississippi River in her future—it would be great if she didn't have to spend them battling some otherworldly foe.

When she finally climbed into bed, Jeni looked forward to a night of dreamless sleep. Or at least, normal dreams. She settled in with her book, and then closed her eyes, thinking how awesome it had been to wake up and see Ice each morning. The sudden image of him pulling his T-shirt off in the back seat of the car shaped her lips into a curve. The sight had been little more than a silhouette in the darkness, but she hadn't missed the contours of hard muscle under his smooth skin.

Opening her eyes, she looked down at the page in front of her, doubting anything in her book could compare to that, but she began to read anyway.

Tied cruelly, the ropes bit into Marielle's wrists and ankles. She was then hauled up like a sack of flour and thrown unceremoniously across the saddle of the horse she'd been riding. Sobs tried to escape the gag shoved between her teeth and tied around her head. The horrible smack of a fist hitting flesh caused her to flinch, knowing that Amakapa was the recipient of the blows.

"Leave some life to the heathen. Bernard wished to do the killin' hisself," a gruff voice said, halting the sickening sounds.

Marielle raised her head, instantly wishing she hadn't as she saw Amakapa's bruised and bloody limp form hoisted onto his horse. His hands and feet were also bound. The party set off, the rhythm of the horse's trot causing her stomach and ribs to jolt painfully and repeatedly on the hard saddle.

The pain was a welcome punishment for what Amakapa had suffered for her. She should have let him go—should have told him to stay away. She should have married and forgotten about him so that if he did return, he'd have no choice but to move on with his own life.

Now he would die for her.

Fresh tears sprang to her eyes at the thought. She wriggled, hoping to fall from the horse, break her head open, get trampled, whatever it took. Death was preferable to what life might bring.

After a time, the pressure on her stomach caused her to wretch and gag. The group paused, someone removing the cloth from her mouth so she could throw up without choking on her own vomit.

One of the five men who'd captured them said, "Mayhap we ought to have her sit. I can take her on my saddle."

Still on hands and knees, she shook her head vehemently. "Dare not to lay a filthy hand on me," she spat. The men laughed and her gag was retied.

She considered it a mercy that they returned her to her previous position, the saddle continuing to bruise her already aching ribs.

She knew they were approaching town when a man in their party shouted, "Alert Bernard. We have the runaways."

The blood had rushed to her head and she felt faint, yet fought to remain coherent as desperate thoughts raced through her mind, searching for a way out of the situation. Someone grabbed her around the waist and she wriggled furiously until she was dropped on the ground. Nearby, Amakapa's body collapsed to the dirt like a burlap sack filled with potatoes.

"He ain't dead, is he?" a voice asked.

"Nah, just out cold."

"Untie my daughter." It was Papa's harsh command.

She refused to look his way, remaining motionless even after her bonds had been removed.

"To your feet, girl," her father ordered.

Still, she didn't move.

He grasped her arm and nearly yanked it from the socket, forcing her to sit. "Have you not a brain in your head? Running away with a savage! 'Tis not in keeping with your upbringing."

"I love him." The words rasped from her raw throat.

"Love." Papa's voice dripped with sarcasm. "Pah! I expect you to abide a man with equal stature to yourn. Git yourself up and to the house."

Her father was angrier than she'd ever witnessed, yet Marielle ignored his command. Footsteps pounded the stairs leading into the house, and moments later, the door squealed again. Something jangled as her father called, "Wilbertson, Roget, should it be necessary, drag the girl to the wash building and do lock her inside whilst we deal with the heathen."

That got Marielle on her feet. As soon as she rose, a man grasped her arms, pulling them behind her back. She jerked violently, surprising him, and twisted from his grip, running to Amakapa. Throwing both arms around him she sobbed. "Were it not that you returned for me. I am most sorry." Though his face was battered and swollen, she could see that his eyes were open. His lips twitched as if he wanted to speak.

A man grabbed her wrist, trying to pull her off Amakapa. "No!" she screamed. "Do what you will to me. I care not. But spare Amakapa. He's done no crime."

Two men were on her now, hauling her away. "I shall always love you," she cried, still thrashing. But one of the men held her fast as the other grabbed her feet, lifting her off the ground. As they dragged her, she craned her neck to see Amakapa one last time. Then they rounded a corner and he was out of sight.

The windowless structure with a barred door was called the wash building or wash house—and that's what they used it for—but she'd always known its secondary purpose was to lock up runaway slaves. Tonight, her father put it to use to lock up a runaway daughter.

She'd fallen still after they rounded the corner, catching her breath. But as they neared the building, she renewed her struggles. With only two men present, this was her best chance to break free. She would retrieve one of her father's many guns and kill anyone who meant to do harm to Amakapa. Including her father.

But her efforts were thwarted by the two men, and they thrust her into the small one-room structure, slamming the door and securing the padlock. She beat against the bars, shouting for Sally. Her quarters were right next door. Surely she could hear her.

From the street came the commotion of horses and men's voices. She sank to the ground and sobbed helplessly as the sounds moved off in the direction of the Mississippi River.

Jeni's eyes popped open, her heart thumping madly. The dream was unexpected. She'd admitted defeat. Moved on. Did her subconscious insist on finishing the story?

She sat up, checking the time. It was nearly five a.m.

Damn.

She really wanted to talk to Ice. Or Marielle.

Scrubbing her hands over her cheeks and smoothing the hair away from her face, Jeni pondered her choices.

She'd promised Ice she wouldn't contact Marielle again without him, and she intended to keep that promise. She could text him, but what was the point when it was too early for them to be up?

Frick.

Going back to sleep wasn't an option. She was not only a little freaked out, but she didn't want that dream to continue.

Pulling her legs up, Jeni wrapped her arms around her shins and rested her chin on her knees. Witnessing the capture and brutal treatment of Amakapa had been a harrowing experience. She was relieved yesterday when Phoebe woke her before the couple had been apprehended. The only thing more horrific would be to actually watch as Amakapa was tied to a log and set adrift.

No, she would not be going back to sleep.

Sighing, Jeni rose and grabbed her computer from the other bed, returning to the warmth of her covers. Stacking her pillows behind her back, she opened an online game to keep her occupied until the sun rose.

Not fifteen minutes later, her eyelids began to droop. She straightened her spine and focused on the screen in front of her. One minute she was mulling over how to decorate her virtual house… and the next minute she was shaking herself awake.

Obviously, her body was striving for more sleep. But she would not watch that terrible death scene. Especially through Marielle's eyes.

Wait a minute. If Marielle was locked in the wash building, there was no way she could see Amakapa's death. Slumping into the pillows, Jeni let her head fall back to the headboard. The only way Marielle could've seen it was if she got out. That door was padlocked shut. There was no way—

Jeni's eyes sprang all the way open and she stared at the ceiling, picturing the padlock hitched onto the belt of one of the men who'd carried Marielle away.

When Jeni researched how to pick the lock on the museum case, there'd been a ton of videos showing how to jimmy open all different kinds of locking mechanisms. She imagined once you got the idea, picking other locks probably came easily. But in order to open that padlock, Marielle would need some kind of tool. Had there been anything suitable inside the wash building? It'd been quite dark inside, and Marielle was more concerned with calling through the bars for someone to let her out.

Going back over previous dreams, Jeni reviewed the details of that night, wondering if Marielle might have something on her person that could be used as a lock pick.

A streak of excitement drove Jeni to sit up straight. She pictured Marielle getting ready for her date with Claude, standing in front of the mirror in her room. She'd slid a clip into her hair—a distinctly bobby pin type of clip.

She checked the time displayed in the corner of her computer screen: 5:42.

Minimizing her game, she Googled "18th century padlocks." Absorbed in her research, she didn't realize until a half hour later that the room was beginning to get lighter.

She spent the next fifteen minutes trying to decide how to finagle a trip to town on the day they were packing and cleaning the cabin to head home. Ice's flight wasn't until 9:10 p.m., and she knew her mom had arranged for a late check out, but she wasn't sure how her parents would feel about her and Ice taking off for a while.

She texted Ice to see if he was awake.

"I am now." Was his response. *"You OK?"*

"Yeah. But I need to talk to you."

As Jeni waited for a reply, she heard Ice folding up the sofa bed. Grabbing a pair of socks, she slipped them on and pulled a sweatshirt over her head as she opened the door.

Ice yawned, rubbing his eyes. "What's up?" He held an arm out, settling it over her shoulders as she sank into the couch next to him.

"I had another dream." Jeni described the awful capture of Marielle and Amakapa. "It was so brutal, Ice. And Marielle was heartbroken. She wouldn't do anything her father demanded so he locked her up." She drew in a breath and looked up at him. "But I think I figured out a way to help her escape."

Ice's eyes widened, eyebrows riding high on his forehead. Then, apparently reading the look on her face, he let his head fall back and sighed. "Seriously? You said you were done."

"I know. Because I didn't have any more ideas. But now I do. Why not try one more time since we're still here?" Jeni turned to look at him, but he continued to stare ahead. "Plus, I never bought anything for Carolyn. We always bring each other souvenirs from our trips."

Ice sighed again. "Well." He finally lifted his head and looked at her. "It's not my first choice of how to spend our last day together, but I know it will eat at you if we don't go."

"You're the best." She stretched up and kissed his cheek. "Thanks."

Her mom agreed to let them use the car, her dad adding the stipulation that they not be gone too long because he wanted to start packing the trunk. Then Jeni called Phoebe to let her know they were coming and asked if she was available to help.

Upon arrival at Memories and Magic, they found the store owner unloading a box of packaged crystals and hanging them on display hooks. She looked up when Jeni and Ice entered. "Good morning. I just want to get these unpacked and then I'll be right with you."

Jeni eyeballed the crystals, wondering if Carolyn would like a necklace similar to the one Mandy had purchased. Too keyed up to make a decision, she gestured to an open carton on the counter near the register. "Can we help?"

"Absolutely. Those come in their own display boxes," Phoebe replied. "There are three boxes inside the large one. Just set one up to leave out and then put the other two under the counter."

Removing one of the boxes, Jeni's mouth curved in amusement when she saw it contained mood rings. She folded the cover back and tucked it to create the display while Ice rounded the counter and found a spot to stow the other two boxes.

As she waited for him to finish, the painting of Rose caught Jeni's eye. Once again, she envied Phoebe's concrete knowledge of her ancestry. The medium knew exactly who she was and where she came from. Days ago, Jeni's wishful thinking had conjured an image of a box of genealogy records in Grandma Marie's attic; now she added a few ancient portraits to that imaginary picture.

Rolling her eyes, she shook the fantasy from her head. Things were never that easy.

"All right," Phoebe said from behind her. "Bring that empty carton in back with you."

Ice picked up the box and Jeni followed him to

the back of the store. "Thanks for helping us again," she said, turning a chair away from the table. "I truly did think we were done yesterday." The anticipation of possibly pulling this off before going home had given her the jitters, so she drew a deep breath in through her nose, expelling it slowly.

"Don't worry about it, I rarely have customers this early." Phoebe retrieved the tablet from the desk drawer and turned it on. "Besides, I'd love to see this story reach a happy ending."

Once seated, Jeni accepted the tablet from the medium. She placed it on her lap and then looked up at Ice, arms outstretched. He closed his eyes briefly. When he opened them, he gave a slight nod, and grasped her hands in a light hold.

"Okay, Jeni," Phoebe said. "It should be fairly easy for you to slip into a trance after yesterday. Just stare into the illusion."

Jeni looked down, losing herself in the swirls. If Phoebe spoke, she was unaware.

A low murmur of voices was all that was left after the pounding horse hooves and raucous shouts receded. Marielle knew none of the townsfolk would defy her father and come to her aid. But the news would spread, eventually reaching Claude. By then it would be too late to save Amakapa, but hopefully Claude would retrieve the body and bring it to Amakapa's tribe.

No. Don't leave this to chance. Don't assume Claude got the note. He may be sleeping peacefully at this moment.

The thought caused her to hitch in a breath, blinking.

Try to get out. Check the lock.

Yes. Why hadn't she done that already?

Marielle squeezed her eyes shut and then blinked to clear away the tears. Snaking a hand through the bars, she tugged on the padlock. It was secure. She shook her head, wiping the sides of her face with the heels of her hands, unable to stem the warm stream of tears.

Pick the lock.

She perked up and stood, trying to see in the darkness.

The hair clip.

Her fingers searched through her hair until she located the clip she'd put in what seemed like ages ago. By the faint light of the moon, she slipped her hands through the bars and unbent the clip until it was nearly straight. Stopping frequently to blot the wetness from her eyes, the task seemed to take forever.

Awkwardly, she took hold of the padlock and poked the clip inside, fishing around blindly.

Feel for a lever and apply pressure to it.

The idea made sense and hope dawned within her as she found an edge and pressed.

Nothing happened.

Push down, not up.

Marielle rotated her wrist in the opposite direction and heard a metallic click. For a moment, she thought the lock had opened and she yanked on it, but it remained secured to the door. With a frustrated groan, she dropped the clip into the dirt and began rummaging around the small room for something else that might work.

Go back to the clip. Try bending the end.

What was the point of that? Her jerky motions and raspy, uneven breath hinted at her crumbling composure.

Calm down. For Amakapa's sake. Deep breaths.

She paused, pulling air into her lungs.

Pick up the clip and bend the end. Hurry.

It was worth another try. Retrieving the clip, Marielle tried to bend the end, but the metal was too stiff. About to hurl it back into the dirt, she had an idea. The door was affixed to its wooden frame with large plate hinges. Making a quick examination of the mechanism—more by feel than sight—she finally found a space where the metal wasn't quite flush with the wood. Sliding the end of the clip into the slot, Marielle levered the rest upward at a right angle. Satisfied with the result, the small triumph afforded a spark of hope and she slid the bent piece of metal into the lock with renewed conviction.

She wasn't sure why, but a vague optimism was rising within her.

Intent on the task, Jeni imagined—no, she actually felt—the sensation of metal on her fingers. She could feel the resistance of the inner workings of the mechanism! Determination quickly outweighed her surprise. She found the lever and pressed on it with a quick, sure force. The round chunk of metal slipped down the arched rod and swung forward.

With a surge of elation, she twisted the lock free and cast it aside, pushing the door open. She paused for a second, contemplating her full control of Marielle's actions. Reverse possession. If there was such a thing, this was it. Phoebe had warned her not to go too far, but Ice was anchoring her this time, securing her spirit to the living world, to the present.

As soon as possible, she'd figure out how to relinquish control of Marielle. Right now, she couldn't afford to waste time pondering her new situation.

She ran to the barn for Fleur. Jeni had been horseback riding a few times, but never bareback. Yet saddling or bridling was out of the question under her time constraint. Using a stool, she climbed onto the horse, wondering if she had access to any of Marielle's knowledge or experience. Fingers curled in the thick mane, she pressed her knees to the horse's sides and Fleur walked out of the barn.

With no bridle, Jeni attempted to use the mane to steer the horse, but regardless of the direction she pulled the hair, Fleur continued straight. So Jeni bent down, releasing her right hand and pressing the horse's neck toward the left. It worked, and they were now facing the direction the men had headed with Amakapa. She kneed the horse in the ribs, hanging on for dear life.

Marielle's battered body protested every jostle. Trying to ease the discomfort, Jeni did her best to adjust to the rhythm of the horse's stride. But when she bent low and spurred Fleur to go faster, the gait changed, throwing her out of sync, and her pelvic bone slammed painfully into the horse's back. Still, she clung, trying to regain synchronous movement.

Panic surged when she saw the road ahead divided in two. Slowing Fleur, Jeni wondered if the horse would habitually head toward the river. It would be a risky gamble; she knew little of Marielle's life other than this one tragic event. The right fork split off at nearly a right angle, where the left fork appeared to continue straight, leading her to conclude that it might be the main thoroughfare. She nudged Fleur straight, praying she'd made the right choice. But a few yards later, the road hooked to the left, causing her to question her judgement.

Hoping Marielle's familiarity of the area might rise to the forefront of her brain, Jeni closed her eyes for a moment, willing a thought to form. A map image emerged in her consciousness. She would have assumed the memory was Marielle's, except Jeni realized she recognized the document. It had hung on the wall of Bernard's mercantile.

When Francoise Poule had entered the store, Marielle had been desperate not to speak to him. She'd turned her back, pretending to study the territory map. Eventually, he spoke to her, forcing her to turn and respond, but there'd been enough time for Jeni to commit some of the map's details to memory.

The road she was on led to the Mississippi River, to the Ste. Genevieve crossing. Surely it was the way Marielle's father had come.

Digging her heels into the horse, Jeni fixed her attention on the murky horizon, searching for the river. A curve to the right brought the broad expanse of water into view, looking slick like oil in the moonlight. Wary of being seen by Bernard or his posse, she leaned forward and tugged on Fleur's neck with both arms, bringing the horse to a halt.

Sliding to the ground, she walked Fleur into the

trees and picked her way along the edge of the woods cautiously. The grumble of male voices reached her and she crept onward until figures came into view. Revulsion formed a lump in her throat as the men hoisted a large, bulky object, grunting with effort.

A voice of another timbre joined the commotion. "Death be not... the end of our love." Each word was gasped with great strain. "It shall endure until we do again meet... and..." A wet cough interrupted. "...so shall we live together for eternity."

Rude laughter erupted. A man said, "I hate to tell ya, heathen, that even God don't care for the likes of you."

"Just shut yer traps and set him afloat." The gruff command sounded like Bernard.

Jeni wanted to run, screaming, stop them from pushing the log into the river, but she knew better. She could only attempt to save Amakapa's soul.

Turning away, she swore under her breath, realizing it had been a mistake to follow the lynching party. She should be downriver, waiting for Amakapa's log to appear so she could follow unseen. Rushing to Fleur, Jeni again pictured the territory map. A different road out of Kaskaskia led to the river—to a location downstream and around the bend from the Ste. Genevieve crossing. That's where she should have gone.

There was no time to return to town and take the other road. However, by cutting through the woods, she would run into that road eventually. Jeni climbed onto the horse and urged her to a brisk pace. The shortcut alone wasn't enough to assure a rendezvous with Amakapa around the corner. She needed to hurry.

Assuming his log wasn't caught up.

Or held submerged by the current.

She whispered a little prayer that the men wouldn't follow Amakapa once they'd seen the log clear the turn.

But this idea that she wasn't herself anymore
went on to make her feel weak.

The Woman Who Wasn't Herself Anymore
~ Henri Pourrat

Chapter 14

*I*ce straightened in his chair, jaw dropping. "Jeni!" Her hands still in his, he squeezed her fingers and shook her arms. Panic turned his blood cold when she didn't respond, her limbs limp and heavy. "Jeni! Wake up." Afraid to break contact with her, he bumped her knee with his, knocking the tablet to the ground while shouting for the medium.

Phoebe rushed through the curtain. "What is it? What's happened?"

"I don't know," Ice said, voice uneven and breath coming in gasps. He maintained his grip on Jeni's hands, terrified to let go. "The connection is gone. It just… cut out."

He didn't like the deep creases that appeared on Phoebe's brow as she drew in a calming breath. "Okay, Jeni." She managed to sound normal. "I'm going to count to five and then you'll wake up. One, two, three, four, five, awake!"

Jeni remained motionless, slumped in the chair, eyes closed.

Ice's pulse raced, his heartbeat thrumming in his ears. "What's going on? Why didn't she wake up?"

"I'm not sure." Phoebe's eyes darted rapidly over Jeni's still form. "Have you tried reaching her spiritually? Like you did when she didn't wake up yesterday?"

The sliver of hope wasn't enough to ease Ice's alarm. But in order to prevent Jeni from seeing visions while they held hands, he'd had to adjust his inner balance—blot out their shamanic link. "No. I'll try that now." He closed his eyes, finding it hard to rein in his free soul, which was overwhelmed with panic, and bring it into balance with his ego soul, allowing him to reason and act with forethought.

He opened his eyes. The attempt had had no effect on Jeni; however, Ice had gained clarity. He could think rationally, though it did little to diminish the hysteria building inside him. He met Phoebe's eyes and shook his head.

The medium leaned forward and laid a hand on Jeni's cheek. "I'm going to try to channel her. You can let go."

Ice reluctantly released his hold, hating the way his hands felt suddenly cold and empty. He'd been here to keep her safe, keep her grounded. How did he manage to let her slip away?

Phoebe pressed her fingers on Jeni's temples and closed her eyes. Mumbled phrases fell from her lips. An agonizing stretch of time passed before she finally dropped her hands to her sides and turned to Ice, the pallor of her face disheartening. "She's no longer in our world."

Lost in Nowhere

"What do you mean?" He thrust a hand toward Jeni. "Of course she is. She's right here." But he, more than most people, understood what the medium meant.

"I mean, I don't feel her presence," Phoebe snapped, hands clamped to the sides of her head as she began pacing. "She's an empty vessel. Her essence is no longer in her body."

"But how could... what..." So many questions and ramifications raced through his brain, Ice didn't know what to ask.

"She was visiting another place in time. Perhaps she stepped into that reality." Phoebe looked at the ceiling and shook her head. "This is out of my league."

"She was having dreams," Ice argued. "They were just dreams."

The woman shrugged. "I thought so, too. Even when Jeni said she was changing past events."

Ice stood, rubbing his hands on his shorts. "How could she be gone? I was her anchor." He dropped back into the chair, shaking his head. Then he lowered his chin, fingers digging into his hair. "Maybe I was a poor anchor."

"Ice, this isn't your fault."

He barely registered the medium's words, mind racing. The tripartite belief—that humans are made up of a body, ego soul and free soul—promoted harmony among the three parts. Ice had suppressed his ego soul so Jeni wouldn't see images when they held hands, so she could open herself to the trance. By doing so, Ice was unbalanced. He'd decreased his spiritual strength.

He *had* been a poor anchor; a flawed anchor. Balling his hand into a fist, he struck his thigh in frustration. He should've realized. He should've known better.

Reading his stricken expression, Phoebe placed a hand on his shoulder and locked eyes with him. "I can just as easily blame myself for putting her in a trance so she could dream. Before we go wasting our energy on blame, why don't we try to figure out what has actually happened. Yes?" She released him and stepped back, holding his gaze.

Ice returned a sullen nod.

"Let's start with Marielle." She focused on Jeni's right hand.

Instantly understanding what the medium wanted to do, Ice squatted next to Jeni's chair and lifted the hand with the ring. Swallowing his reluctance to touch the metal band, he grasped it, wriggling it back and forth to extract it from her finger. A shudder of revulsion gripped him at the prolonged contact, and again he chastised himself for allowing Jeni to wear it and use it. He dropped the ring into Phoebe's hand, lips curled with distaste.

The medium didn't attempt to slip the gold band on a finger, but folded her hand into a fist instead. She cocked her head, eyes narrowed slightly. "This ring has elemental magic." She looked at Ice. "That must be what you feel when you touch it."

"It doesn't feel bad to you? Wrong?"

"It feels ancient," Phoebe said. "And… yes, perhaps tainted. Your spiritual sense of touch must be very strong, Ice."

Ice shrugged. "So you're going to try and talk to

Marielle like Jeni did?"

Phoebe nodded. "I know Jeni didn't speak her side of their conversations out loud, but I will, so you can have some idea of what we're talking about. Feel free to chime in if you have a thought or question."

When Ice lowered his chin in assent, she raised her voice, calling, "Marielle Bernard, I summon you to this room." Her eyes flitted about. "Marielle Bernard, show yourself."

Ice watched anxiously, his knee jiggling up and down while he racked his brain for any clues, any questions, that might help them if Phoebe reached Marielle.

Then the medium's attention fixed on a spot across the room. "She's here," she whispered.

"Ask about the dreams," Ice said. "Marielle told Jeni she wasn't the source of the dreams. We thought maybe Jeni's spirituality was filling in the blanks, but maybe that's not it."

"Jeni dreamed of you and Amakapa," Phoebe said out loud. "What was the source of the dreams?"

Of course, Ice couldn't hear the answers, and he started pacing, trying to shake off his anxiety.

"Do you know the identity of this spirit?" Phoebe asked.

Ice halted, his attention on the medium. Icy dread swept through him and he shivered. *He should have known.*

"And Jeni?" Phoebe continued. After a brief pause, she added, "Has anything changed? Amakapa?"

"Goodbye." She released the ring to the table-top and then addressed Ice, her expression grim.

"Marielle has no idea what has happened to Jeni. Everything is the same in her existence."

"And the dreams? There's another spirit?"

The medium's brow lowered as she narrowed her eyes. "Yes. I could sense Marielle's reluctance, but she finally admitted that after the first Ouija session she was contacted by a magus."

Ice frowned. "Magus?"

"Like a magi or wise man," Phoebe explained, shaking her head. "He told Marielle that with his intervention Jeni could succeed in rescuing Amakapa's soul. However, he stipulated that Jeni must believe she was acting alone; she must rely solely on her own ability. So Marielle allowed this spirit access to the link between her and Jeni. He is most likely the source of the dreams."

Ice's anxiety transformed quickly into anger. He was familiar with malevolent spirits and knew how tricky and convincing they could be. This other force might explain his feelings of foreboding. "So the spirit might have used the dreams to coerce Jeni into a dangerous situation, one where her spirit would separate from her body."

Phoebe nodded. "That's along the lines of what I was thinking. This supposed magus spirit also claimed that once Jeni recovered Amakapa's soul, it would still need to be ushered into the afterlife so Marielle and Amakapa could be together. And guess who could help with that?"

Ice muttered a curse. "The magus, of course. He wanted to ensure that Marielle would keep him informed or involved as things progressed. And

Lost in Nowhere

Marielle was so desperate after hundreds of years that she totally fell for it." He dug his fingers into his hair. "So if Jeni's spirit is separate from her body, where could it be? How do we find it? Please tell me there's something we can do."

"The only thing I can assume is that her spirit exists somewhere in the spirit world. If that's true, we can try to contact her." Phoebe retrieved a large candle from the desk and placed it in the center of the table. "We're going to have a séance."

She must not have completely taken over Marielle because she was doing far better on the horse than her scant level of experience should have warranted. The thought was reassuring, allowing Jeni to believe that she could eventually recede back to merely an idea in the frontier girl's brain. But for now, when every second counted, it was much more efficient to do what needed to be done rather than guide Marielle into action.

Sensing a clearing ahead, she pulled on Fleur's neck until the horse stopped. A wide trail was visible through the trees. Remaining still for a moment, her ears strained to detect the sound of breaking twigs or the swish of movement through the underbrush. When leaves rustled to her left, Jeni jumped, then released a relieved breath when she spotted a squirrel scaling a tree. Deeming it safe, she clicked her tongue against the roof of her mouth, prompting the horse to continue onward warily.

Minutes later, they reached the river. Jeni slid off the horse, hurrying to the shore to peer first upriver, searching for something afloat, and then downriver, on the chance the log had already passed by. The white crescent moon cast only weak light, but it was enough to discern that the water's silently moving black surface was undisturbed in both directions. Her shoulders slumped. Had she missed him? Perhaps she'd misjudged the swiftness of the current.

Spotting a dark divide in the river downstream, Jeni coaxed Fleur along the narrow strip of muddy sand. As she suspected, the object was a small island not far from the shore. She scoured the edges of the half-sunken mound of earth for a man-sized log. There were so many fallen trees between the shore and the island, that in the darkness, it was hard to distinguish where one limb began and another ended.

She almost missed it. But one of the men who helped tie Amakapa to the log must have had rudimentary knotting skills, because the sloppy loops of rope protruding from the wood did not look like branches. The large log was butted up against a tree from the island that had fallen toward shore. Once she recognized the rope, she was able to follow its silhouette and identify the partially submerged body.

"Amakapa," she called, even her soft voice sounding loud in the silent darkness. Was there a chance he was still alive? Oh God, she hadn't thought of that. She wasn't supposed to save his life.

Nothing stirred except the water parting around the obstacle.

With no way to get to him—no boat, no rope, no tools of any kind—she paced the shoreline, assessing her options.

Lost in Nowhere

The fallen tree that had caught Amakapa's log reached toward the shore, but was short by about five feet. Jeni had not forgotten that this was the Mississippi River. Something tied to this river was seeking her out to exact vengeance. Did it matter that the time preceded her grandfather's lifetime? Was her presence masked by Marielle? She didn't want to wade into the water and discover that the answer to those questions was "no."

Approaching the tree line, Jeni wished she had brought a lantern. The feeble moonlight would allow only a limited search at the edge of the dark woods. Finding a downed tree wasn't a challenge; there were plenty. But what she needed was something sufficiently large and long, yet rotted enough that it would be lightweight. Without the ability to evaluate her options by sight, she was constantly stooping to heft the dead wood, her muscles aching with every move.

Jeni admonished herself again. If she'd thought to grab rope, she could've had Fleur help drag a large piece of wood to the river's edge.

Pushing past her aggravation, she continued her search and was eventually rewarded by a dried-out length of tree trunk. A nudge with her foot proved that it was movable. Upon closer inspection, Jeni saw she'd earned a small break. The dead tree was covered with the remains of branches, which would provide handholds, and once it was in the water, the protrusions would dig into the sand and prevent the piece of wood from floating away.

She heaved on the dead tree, cringing at the noise it made, branches cracking like gunshots as she extracted the log from the forest. Every few seconds she paused, listening for evidence that someone was approaching. When she finally reached the river's edge, she noticed the log Amakapa was tied to had shifted closer to the end of the fallen tree. It wouldn't take long for the current to work the log free and send it downstream, which explained why Claude had failed to recover the body. He'd simply been too late.

A new burst of adrenaline spurred Jeni to shove the scavenged piece of wood into the water, letting the force of the river push it against the downed tree. Then she rotated it until the stumps of branches dug into the mucky riverbed.

Running back to the woods once more, she selected a smaller branch, one she could carry and use as a walking stick for balance.

Placing a foot on her makeshift bridge and watching the water lap over top of it, Jeni hesitated. Nearly three centuries separated her reality from this one. How dangerous could it be to get her feet wet? Already nervous about the amount of time she was spending in Marielle's consciousness, Jeni rejected the notion to find another suitable piece of wood. She needed to get this done and get back to the present. Fortifying her determination with a deep inhale, she stepped onto the log.

She teetered, stabbing the stick into the muck and holding her other arm out for balance until she made it across the dead wood to the fallen tree. A few unsteady steps brought her to Amakapa.

For a moment, she froze, staring down at the young man bound to a log. The river swirled and eddied through the curve of his eye socket and across his cheek. The sight of his face beneath the surface—the thought of his airways filled with water—made her feel as if she, herself, couldn't breathe. She closed her eyes against the tragic end and forced air into her lungs.

When she opened her eyes, she avoided looking at Amakapa's head as she squatted down. Knowing it was a waste, still, she pressed her fingers to his icy wrist to check for a pulse. Nothing. A brief wave of sadness was overcome by relief (because she wasn't supposed to save him) and then guilt for feeling relieved.

Pushing down her emotions and shifting her mind to the job at hand, Jeni assessed the situation. Using her balancing stick, she measured the water beneath Amakapa's log. It was a couple of feet deep. If she untied him right there, his body would sink to the bottom and likely get caught by the current. Crouching low for stability, she nudged the large log with her stick, and prodded it toward the riverbank. She managed to drive the large piece of wood inland until it was grounded in the sand.

There'd been no alarming repercussions when her shoes got wet while standing on her makeshift bridge, but to free Amakapa's body, she'd have to wade into the edge of the water. Gathering her skirts, Jeni held her breath, and then stepped into the river.

She wasn't sure what she expected—that a rogue wave would knock her down and carry her away or the mud would suck her down—but nothing more happened than her shoes and stockings becoming soaked. Crouching, she stuffed her skirts into her lap and bent to work on the knots. Freeing Amakapa's legs first, she then caught hold of his arm while loosening the rope around his chest. The body slumped to the river bottom, and she slipped her arms under his to drag him to shore.

Feet planted in the sand, Jeni heaved, managing to get Amakapa's head and shoulders out of the water. Looking down on his still and lifeless eyes broke her emotional barrier, and a lump formed in her throat. His only crime had been loving someone. She reached down and pushed his eyes closed. Maybe it was a mercy that Marielle wasn't doing this herself, even if it did become part of her memories.

Although he wasn't a large man, Amakapa had stood a half-head taller than Marielle and was well-muscled. Doubling her efforts, Jeni tugged again, hard, falling backward into the sand. Only his feet now remained at the water's edge.

Jeni looked over her shoulder at Fleur, calmly grazing at a patch of long grass, and imagined trying to haul Amakapa's body onto the horse's back. Shaking her head, she cursed her impulsiveness, wishing again that she'd taken a few seconds to grab a coil of rope.

Instead, she took stock of the pieces of rope that were used to bind Amakapa to the log, judging if it was enough to hoist the body onto the horse. With the rope over the horse's back she could use her full body weight as leverage.

She tried. But as soon as the weight of Amakapa's body drew the rope taut across Fleur's back, Jeni could see how it burrowed into the horse's hair, ready to slice into skin next. The horse shifted on her feet, yanking the rope from Jeni's hands. She balled her fists in exasperation, lips pressed flat.

The only alternative to bringing the body herself was to convince the Native Americans to fetch it. The situation introduced a host of questions. Did they speak English? How would they react to a white girl boldly showing up at their village? Assuming she got her message across, would they believe her? Would they even care?

Groaning, Jeni retrieved the rope that had fallen to the sand and slung it over her shoulder. She let frustration fuel her as she tugged the body to the edge of the woods. Although the strip of shore was blessedly narrow, she was panting by the time she'd shoved Amakapa's body into the shadows. She gazed sadly at his lifeless form, and then bent down and removed the rope from his wrists, gently laying his arms alongside his body.

Almost reluctantly, Jeni climbed onto Fleur. With a last glance toward the shadows that concealed Amakapa, she clicked her tongue and urged the horse onto the road leading back to Kaskaskia. The map at the mercantile had shown the location of the Native American village on the Kaskaskia River, northeast of the town. She needed to find the road that led in that direction.

Her damp dress chilled her to the bone and her wet feet and legs were nearly numb from riding with her skirts bunched up. As she approached Kaskaskia, shivering, the thought of dry clothes was a heady temptation, but it was too big of a risk. Instead she gave the town a wide berth as she circled it to find the road along the Kaskaskia River.

Jeni's teeth were chattering, and she was shaking uncontrollably by the time she finally detected the smell of burning wood. To her right, the dancing orange glow of firelight appeared intermittently between the trees. She watched the edge of the woods carefully for a path, but after a time, it was evident that the flickering lights were falling behind her. Either she'd missed the trail to the camp or there wasn't one.

She slid from Fleur's back, reluctant to leave the horse's body heat. Perhaps walking would help warm her. She didn't backtrack far before giving up on finding any kind of trail. Then, using the flare of firelight as a beacon, she led Fleur into the woods.

The ride had given Jeni time to contemplate her arrival at the Native American village. She decided that once she reached her destination, she should withdraw from Marielle. The frontier girl would be far better equipped to communicate with the Kaskaskians. Because Marielle had been aware of Jeni's previous interventions—reacting with surprise at her own actions—Jeni believed the girl would remember all that had happened and would know what she'd set out to do. She hoped she was right.

Her progress through the forest was slow. It was denser—and darker—than the woods she'd passed through earlier, forcing her to constantly change course. If not for the winks of firelight, she would have easily gotten lost. As she shuffled along with one hand on Fleur's mane and the other held out in front of her, Jeni wondered if she should have left the horse behind. Navigating passage for only herself would have been far easier.

Eventually, she was able to make out the looming shapes of structures unlike anything back in town. Creeping a bit closer, Jeni saw that the buildings were long with domed roofs. She couldn't help smiling as she recognized them as longhouses. She'd actually built a small-scale model of one in fourth grade.

It was time to let Marielle take over.

Jeni stood for a moment, lips pursed, realizing she had no idea what to do.

Mind racing, she tried to remember how she'd obtained control. She'd wanted to pick that lock so badly... she'd imagined what it felt like.

Closing her eyes, Jeni called to mind the back room of Phoebe's shop: the round table, cluttered desk, shelves crowded with boxes... then she imagined the smooth surface of the wooden chair, the hard seat, slats pressed into her back, Ice's—

A rough hand covered her mouth as an iron arm wrapped across her chest, pinning her to her captor. It was a nightmarish repetition of her earlier capture and she struggled wildly. How had Bernard's men tracked her down? Terrified, Jeni bucked and kicked backward, having little luck making contact.

A second set of hands grasped her ankles, sweeping her feet from the ground and holding them fast. She could see this man, and he was not one of Bernard's cohorts. He was Native American.

She ceased her resistance, making noise from the back of her throat to try and convey that she wanted to talk, that she meant no harm, but the hand remained over her mouth. They carried her easily through the remainder of the woods, emerging into the clearing of longhouses.

When she was dropped unceremoniously in front of one of the houses and Jeni could finally speak, she said, "I come in peace. I come in peace."

Neither man would look at her. When she tried to scramble to her feet, she was pushed down, her back forced against a pole while her hands were bound behind her back. She winced as the binding scraped her bruised wrists.

"I just have a message." It took effort to speak softly, calmly, when her heart was a runaway train.

One of her captors ducked into the longhouse. "Please," Jeni said to the other, who stood nearby, arms crossed over his tattooed chest. "I just want to talk to someone."

He didn't meet her eyes or reveal any sign that he'd heard her speak. Movement caught her attention and she saw a younger man, possibly a boy, leading Fleur into the camp.

Jeni tried again. "I meant no harm." She looked from the man to the boy, who'd paused to stare at her curiously. "English? Does anyone here speak English?" she asked.

The man barked something at the boy who snapped to attention and then led Fleur out of Jeni's sight. She opened her mouth to voice another plea, but closed it immediately when the man stretched out a length of fabric between his two fists. His threatening glare required no words. Jeni shook her head, lips clamped shut. He didn't need to gag her. She'd be quiet.

*L*ost in *N*owhere

A fire was near enough that she could feel its heat, and she inched her feet forward, studying the man. He wore only some kind of leather or hide leggings with a loin cloth. His ebony hair was closely cropped on the top so it stuck straight up. The front was trimmed into bangs—although Jeni was sure the Native Americans wouldn't use that term—and the back and sides hung long. His chest was tattooed, but otherwise bare, though he seemed unaffected by the chilly night air.

Eyeing her surroundings, Jeni was impressed with how big the longhouses were. A scale model along with actual size measurements didn't have the impact of the real thing. The buildings were thirty to forty feet long and twice as tall as a man. Her close vantage allowed her to see the texture of the woven reed mats that covered the domed structures. The pole she was tied to was part of a porch-like awning roofed with green leafy foliage.

Jeni's mind was spinning with questions. Because the Native American village was so close to the town, she'd assumed the people were friendly enough. That might have been a deadly assumption. The longer she sat, the more terrifying scenarios played out in her head. She pulled against the ties binding her wrists, wriggling her hands to see if there was a chance she could free herself.

A deep voice behind her jerked Jeni's head around. A man stood under the awning. He was naked except for the loin cloth, which she could see from her sitting position was a long continuous strip that went between his legs and looped over a belt, leaving a panel hanging in front and back. He, too, was tattooed; chest, arms and legs covered in triangle and parallel zigzag patterns.

He moved to stand in front of her, feet planted and arms crossed in an authoritative stance. "You watch. In trees." His stare bore into her.

He thought she'd been spying? Jeni shook her head vehemently. "No. I wasn't watching. I have a message for you."

"What message." His stance and expression didn't change.

"Amakapa has died," Jeni said. "He needs a funeral." She was unsure of which words to use, how to make him understand.

"No Amakapa here," he stated. "Many seasons pass."

"I know, but he wanted his people to send him to the afterlife."

The man squatted, his face inches from Jeni's. "You take his life."

Again, Jeni shook her head. "No. I... I wouldn't. I couldn't. I care for him."

He searched her face. "How." The single word was a demand, not a question.

"He drowned," Jeni said, nearly choking on the words. "I can show you where his body is."

The man rose to his feet, looking skeptical. He said something sharply in his own language. The man in the leggings who'd brought her to the camp stepped forward. "You say where."

Jeni drew in a breath. How could she explain where to find Amakapa's body? "On the bank of the

Mississippi River. Take the road out of town that does not lead to Ste. Genevieve."

The man listened, his expression showing no sign of comprehension or confusion. But it must have been enough, because he stepped away and whistled. Within minutes, another man showed up with three horses. As the two men swung onto their mounts, Jeni raised her voice and said, "His body is at the edge of the woods."

The muffled sound of hooves on dirt accompanied them out of the camp. Jeni slumped against the pole. The authoritative man had disappeared. They were going to see if she was telling the truth before deciding what to do with her.

Her breathing came quick and shallow, her emotions a tangled mess. She kept thinking she should try again to withdraw from Marielle, assuming she might fare better in the situation. Perhaps she spoke the language and could offer a better explanation for her presence here, for what had happened to Amakapa. At the same time, Jeni wondered if she was telling herself this because she was a coward. She'd gotten herself into this predicament, how could she just leave Marielle to deal with it?

"Amakapa?"

Jeni raised her chin to see an old woman regarding her from across the fire. Although the word was spoken as a question, she didn't know if she was expected to answer.

Silver hair framed the woman's deeply lined russet face. She also wore leggings, but they looked to be fabric, decorated with beads. Her skirt hung past her knees and a hide, that Jeni guessed might be deer, encircled her shoulders. Multiple strings of beads hung from her neck and clattered on her wrists as she moved toward Jeni.

"You know Amakapa?" the woman asked.

Jeni nodded. "I love him."

The woman crouched down, so close that Jeni could make out the fine wrinkles at the corners of her eyes. Without words or warning, Jeni's head was clamped between the woman's hot, leathery hands. She caught a glimpse of wrinkled eyelids sliding closed before images of undulating bodies silhouetted against orange and yellow flames blotted out her vision. Drums beat incessantly in Jeni's head. Then the old woman's wrinkled face swam back into view, arms at her sides and eyes narrowed as she considered Jeni.

The images were the same things Jeni saw when she and Ice made skin to skin contact—before he'd learned how to circumvent them. They confirmed what Jeni had already suspected, this was a medicine woman. She must be a very powerful medicine woman to elicit Jeni's visions through Marielle's body.

"You are two," the woman said. "One have broken heart. One have danger."

Jeni nodded, a spark of hope flaring. "Can you help me?" Being hauled into the camp might have been lucky, in the end.

The medicine woman crossed to a nearby longhouse and disappeared inside. Jeni's eyes were glued on the opening until the woman emerged with a wide, flat basket. She set it down between Jeni and the fire, revealing its contents: an earthenware vase or bottle, a bowl, rocks of various sizes and a few mounds of dried herbs. Though she hadn't answered Jeni's question, the gathering of supplies seemed to indicate some kind of ritual.

Kneeling next to the fire, the woman picked up a stick and stirred the embers until the flames climbed higher. The additional heat was welcome and Jeni straightened her legs, soaking it in. A thousand different questions that she would like to ask the medicine woman popped into her head, but the woman was bowed over her basket, intent on her task.

Selecting a stone, she crushed some of the dried herbs in the bowl, gathering the fine pieces together in a single mound. Pinching the flakes between her fingertips, she deposited the herbs into the small opening of the clay vessel. Then she sorted through some pebbles, selected one, and reached for the stick she'd used to stir the fire.

Next, she picked up a leaf from the basket and wrapped it around the stick—no, she was wiping a glob of something onto the end of the stick which she then poked into the flames. A hiss sounded as the substance quickly became liquid and bubbly. Black smoke and an acrid smell rose from the mass. In a fast motion, the stick was applied to the lip of the jug, smearing the hot goo around the edge. The pebble was then pressed into the melted material, sealing the container.

Pinning Jeni with her gaze, the woman said, "Breath of Great Spirit." Then she brought the bottle up to her lips. Pulling it away, she said something, and then repeated the motion.

Giving the woman a quizzical look, Jeni asked, "Will this help separate me from the other?"

The woman placed the clay jug into Jeni's lap. "Only if need most. Life or death." She delivered the words in a cautionary tone.

"What do I do with it?"

But the medicine woman was on her feet, looking in the direction the three men had gone. She carried the basket back to her longhouse. Jeni studied the bottle-like container, sealed with a stone, and pondered what purpose it might serve.

Some time later, the sound of horses drew her attention to the forest where the two riders had returned. A surge of elation expanded her chest when she saw Amakapa's body strapped to the third horse.

The medicine woman emerged from her longhouse, followed by two boys. She went to Amakapa, laying a hand on his head. Then she said something to the boys and they untied the body, carrying it away.

The woman turned to Jeni, speaking in Kaskaskian. Raising her eyebrows, Jeni was about to say she didn't understand, when the deep voice behind her answered the woman. How long the man had stood there, Jeni wasn't sure.

They exchanged words over Jeni's head, and she couldn't help but feel they were discussing her fate. Then the woman marched up to Jeni and drew a knife from her belt. Jeni stared wide-eyed, terror gripping her. She shrunk away as the woman bent down and sliced the hide binding her wrists. "You go," she said, pointing to the woods.

Nearly sobbing in relief, Jeni rose to her feet, the forgotten bottle rolling to the dirt. She scooped it up and turned, surprised to see that Fleur was standing at the edge of the camp. Curling her fingers in the horse's mane, she found the trail the men had used and hustled back to the road.

When she was far enough from the camp that she could no longer smell the smoke from the fires, Jeni paused, drawing in a few gulps of air.

She had to get out of Marielle and return to her own body, her own time. Taking the clay jar from her pocket, she brought it to her lips as the woman had demonstrated; she held it in her hand, and then in both hands. Her disgruntlement grew at each failed attempt to leave Marielle.

Was she supposed to open it? Why, then, had the medicine woman sealed it? She hadn't mimed tipping the container up, so Jeni didn't think she was meant to ingest the contents.

Only if need most. Life or death.

She couldn't imagine a greater need than to separate herself from Marielle. Groaning, Jeni shoved the jar back into her skirt pocket. As she caught a handful of Fleur's mane, she stared at her hand. Marielle wasn't wearing the ring from Claude. The same ring that Jeni *was* wearing in the future. What if the ring provided some sort of connection through time?

The theory seemed plausible.

Her feelings warred between hopeful and disheartened. She knew exactly where the ring was—Marielle had left it in her room before running away with Amakapa.

But that meant returning to town. To Marielle's house.

To Marielle's father's wrath.

Yes, just that morning the gates of heaven
had stood open; and now,
that same evening, she was looking through the gates of hell.
That's the way life goes.

The Grain Merchant ~ Henri Pourrat

Chapter 15

*T*aking the ring from Marielle's dresser, Jeni slipped it onto her finger. She forced her feet to move, resisting the temptation to try and recede from Marielle's body immediately. Getting into the house had been easy because Bernard and his crew of henchmen were at the saloon, but it had taken a few minutes for her to figure out the oil lamp and find the ring. Every minute in the house amplified her panic another notch. She needed to get out while she still could.

She'd try to withdraw again when she was safely away from town.

Lamp in hand, she crept down the stairs, pausing to listen for signs of movement before hustling out to the barn. She was glad to see Fleur with her nose still in a bucket of oats. The horse had been her lifeline this night.

This time, Jeni took a moment to find a coil of rope. Tying a quick loop that she could use as reins, she tossed the rest of the rope over her shoulder and grabbed a bridle for good measure. She gently convinced Fleur to leave her oats behind and then blew out the lamp before climbing onto the horse. The faint tinkling of piano and murmur of voices came from down the street. Hearing nothing else—aside from her pounding heart—Jeni left the barn. Looking over her shoulder at the empty street, every stir of shadow seemed a potential threat of discovery.

When Kaskaskia was out of sight, she slowed, and then walked Fleur into the edge of the forest. The darkness in the trees was thick, and she didn't bother to close her eyes. Breathing deeply through her nose while clearing her mind, Jeni then pictured Phoebe's shop: the table, the curtained door, the painting of Phoebe's ancestor and even the box of mood rings she knew sat on the counter. Attempting to channel Marielle's ring, she imagined the spicy smell of incense and candles along with the earthy scent of dried herbs.

Fleur shifted underneath her.

Jeni moaned. The ring wasn't working. The medicine woman's jar didn't work.

Her heart beat against the sharp edges of panic. She was screwed. Oh God, she was so screwed. And she'd done it to herself.

Tears of frustration welled in the corners of her eyes and she brushed them away angrily. There had to be a way. Even if she had to hunt down a priest to perform an exor—

Wait.

The pressure in her chest lightened slightly as

*L*ost in *N*owhere

Jeni's thoughts ran. Phoebe said her ancestors lived in Ste. Genevieve from the time it was established. Ancestors who'd fled Salem because of the persecution of witches. Ancestors who had spiritual abilities.

Ste. Genevieve was just across the Mississippi River.

Turning back toward the road, Jeni rode into the open area to benefit from the meager moonlight. She hopped down to bridle the horse, thinking that she hadn't appreciated the simple invention of a flashlight enough in her lifetime. It was going to be a challenge to get the bridle on the horse correctly without sufficient light.

She'd put on and removed the bridle for her American Girl Doll horse enough times to have a general idea how it worked, but the toy hadn't included a bit—the piece that goes in the horse's mouth. Removing the rope, she tossed the leather reins over the horse's head and then located the opening for Fleur's ears. As she raised the bridle, it became obvious the bit needed to be inserted first. Fleur was an obedient horse, but Jeni doubted she was just going to open her mouth. As she brought the metal piece close to the horse's head, her thumb slipped into the side of Fleur's mouth and then her fingers poked the bit inside. Jeni blinked in surprise, realizing her hands had taken on a life of their own, folding down the horse's ears and lifting the leather strap over them. Marielle's muscle memory had kicked in, performing a motion she'd done hundreds of times.

Even so, it took Jeni two tries to get everything right, probably because her hands were shaking. She was unsure if the trembling was due to excitement that Phoebe's ancestor might be able to help her, or dread that if her idea didn't pan out, she was trapped in another girl's past.

Satisfied with the bridle, Jeni patted the horse. "Thank you for being so patient," she whispered. Then she hoisted herself up, kneeing Fleur gently. Earlier, she'd noticed a railed raft tied to a dock just upriver from the place where Bernard had set Amakapa afloat. She was hoping that its purpose was to ferry people across to Ste. Genevieve.

Though her skirts had begun to dry near the fire at the Kaskaskian camp, her shoes and stockings were still quite damp, and she shivered, wishing she'd thought to grab some dry clothes. She let the horse set the pace, holding the reins loosely and crossing her arms over her chest. She was thinking about how she might find Phoebe's ancestor, when she suddenly sat up straight, ears tuned to the sounds around her. Was she paranoid or was that the sound of hooves pounding the road?

She pulled back on the reins, stopping Fleur for a moment. A knot of fear gathered in her belly. Someone was coming her way. Nudging the horse into motion, she tried to remember how much farther it was to the river.

It could be anyone, she reasoned, but the hair on the back of her neck prickled ominously. "Come on, Fleur," she murmured, urging the horse to go faster. "Get me to the ferry."

The rhythmic thumps were unmistakable now. The rider was gaining on her. She recalled the shifting shadows on the street that she'd chalked up to paranoia. Had she been seen? An image of Bernard, returning from the saloon to find the wash house door open and his daughter gone made her shudder in fear.

Spying the clearing ahead where the road ended at the river, Jeni coaxed a little more speed from the horse, laying low with her fingers twisted in Fleur's mane. She turned her head and tipped her chin to peer over her shoulder, spotting a dark figure advancing quickly.

Any hope that she was wrong about the rider shattered when a masculine voice bellowed, "Marielle! Stop right there!"

It was Jean Bernard.

Terrified of being locked up again while trapped in Marielle's body, Jeni evaluated the distance to the river. "We can make it," she breathed to the horse, squeezing tightly with her thighs.

Reaching the riverbank, she guided Fleur to the right, slowing as they neared the ferry.

To her surprise—and relief—a man stood on the raft, a long pole at the ready, waiting, presumably, to ferry people across the river. The thought ran through her head that she'd lost all track of time and it must be close to dawn if a ferryman was waiting. No matter, it was to her benefit that the crossing would be much swifter with the man steering the raft.

She swung off Fleur before the horse had even come to a full stop, then paused, regretting she would have to leave her lifeline—her companion—behind. "Thank you, Fleur." She stroked the horse's nose once, and then rushed to the ferry.

The man held the raft steady as she clomped onto the dock and then stepped to the raft. "I must get to Ste. Genevieve immediately." The words rushed out with her breath.

The ferryman leaned into the pole and the raft pulled away from shore.

Bernard burst from the trees, riding hard.

"Hurry," she pleaded, fingers gripping the railing. "Please, hurry."

Marielle's father barreled onward, looking as if he intended to jump his horse onto the ferry, but the horse was neither drunk nor enraged, and it stopped short at the edge of the dock. Bernard let out a string of curse words, threatening Marielle.

"You can't do anything worse to me than you've already done tonight," Jeni yelled back at him.

"About that you be wrong, daughter," he shouted, shaking a fist. "You, poling the ferry. A reward should you bring my daughter back. I be a man of means."

"No," Jeni beseeched the man. He neither looked up, nor paused his actions.

"Then I curse you." Bernard's horse danced on the shoreline. "I curse you both," he growled. The raft was near the center of the wide river. Riding the length of the shoreline once more, Marielle's father yelled, "There be more than one way to cross this river." Then he wheeled the horse around and rode away. Fleur whinnied, bobbing her head and trotting off after them.

Jeni slumped against the rail, her thoughts

turning to how to find Phoebe's relatives. Could she ask openly for a healer? If they'd fled Salem, they might have taken up some other means to make a living here.

Suddenly she realized the raft had halted in the middle of the river. "Is something wrong, sir?" she asked the man. "Oh, do you require payment?" Jeni scrambled to think of anything she might offer the man in trade for his services.

He didn't respond, and Jeni thrust her hands into her skirt pockets on the chance that Marielle might keep a few coins there. But all she felt was the clay bottle she'd received from the medicine woman.

The man was slowly turning toward her, head tipped down so his hat hid his features.

Before Jeni could begin to explain her dire situation, he spoke. "I know who you are, spawn of the Vrillier bloodline."

Jeni's jaw dropped, fear shooting sharp spears throughout her body. The rough voice sounded like rocks shifting against each other—or like claws grating on stone. Fully opposite her now, he raised his chin. When his face became visible, the voice ceased to matter. Inky black pools filled his eye sockets, complete with ripples across the surface, which sent a shudder throughout her body. Her jaw worked uselessly.

"Those of your brood have spurned me for the last time." His image flickered, winking out of sight so quickly, Jeni wondered if it had happened or if she'd blinked. "I would have accepted your soul for that which was taken from me by your ancestor." The words were harsh, accusatory. "Instead, you have persisted in stealing yet another soul from my flock. I cannot abide any loss of strength."

Jeni looked to the shore to see if Marielle's father had perhaps returned, but the strip of sand was empty. She would've gladly gone with him over facing this specter. Desperately, she searched the opposite riverbank, but in the wee hours of the morning, the beach was void of life.

A menacing laugh bubbled up from the depths of the being. Was it a being? Was it a man possessed? It didn't matter. Jeni knew that for the first time, she stood in the presence of the vengeful entity that had targeted her since her visit to Lake Itasca last summer.

And there was no escape.

Jumping into the river would only be giving herself up. Her mind raced for a way out, but there was nothing.

Nothing.

"L-l-loss of strength?" she stuttered, doubting even a stall tactic would help her. "Wha-what are you talking about?" Her eyes lifted to the sky, wondering how long it would be until sunrise—until people would be up and about.

The ferryman flickered. This time Jeni was sure of it.

"Imagine my delight when I learned that I can devour living souls and feed on their energy."

The sensation of cold wetness on her feet drew her attention to the water pooling on the platform and seeping into her shoes. Was the raft sinking? The shudder that wracked her body was impossible to suppress. "So you just take lives to make you stronger," she spat, trying to channel fear into anger.

"Why not? Humankind is weak and foolish. Though I believe your life is more valuable to me than simply your human essence." His mouth stretched into a grin, lips parting to reveal stark white teeth guarding a black void.

His gravelly voice continued, "Besting a fae witch is no easy task. It was only then that I discovered who you really are. I should like you to join me."

Jeni's head was spinning. She knew he referred to the Korrigan—the shapeshifting, siren-like predator that had kidnapped Ice last fall. But asking her to *join* him? She couldn't wrap her head around the suggestion. Nor could she comprehend how the river was rising over the sides of the raft to gather at her feet. "I will not help you kill people and take their souls."

"Lucky for you, that is not what I require. With your abilities, I cannot fail. Your debt will be paid. Your entire bloodline will be safe for all time. I shall even return you to your place and time until I desire your services."

"I don't understand." Her heart thrummed like a bird pinned down by a cat as she realized she was unable to lift her feet from the water.

"I deign to take control of all earth's waters. You are a conduit to my foe. A formidable weapon in his vanquishment. "

The water was a living mass that had risen above Jeni's knees. Terror coursed through her as it shifted her entire body toward the end of the platform. "F-foe?" she stammered. "I don't know what you're talking about. Who is your foe?"

"It matters not! Will you promise your abilities to me and save your bloodline? Or perish here, leaving me to exact my revenge on your people?"

"I don't even understand what you're asking!" Jeni shouted, her voice rife with desperation. In truth, she understood enough. What this being wanted was to control all the waters across the globe. He would take countless lives, becoming more and more powerful. Perhaps powerful enough to bring the waters on land: tsunamis, hurricanes, cyclones... there'd be no stopping the devastation.

Tears leaked from the corners of her eyes. She couldn't be a part of it.

"What is your decision?" The voice boomed like thunder.

Now encased in a static wave halfway up her thighs, the ramifications of a negative answer were obvious: she would drown—whether in the Mississippi River or by the rising water, she would die here. "No," she hissed. "It's a trick, a lie. My family will still die. Everyone will die."

With a swish, she was swept into the river and sucked down as if her feet were weighted. Her descent stopped when her chin touched the water.

The ferryman creature stared down at her with empty eyes. "Last chance, blood of the Vrillier line."

She was trembling. Cold, fear, despair, all contributors. Drowning was right at the top of Jeni's list of worse ways to die, and dread squeezed her chest so she could hardly breathe. Parting her lips, she drew in a lungful of air. "No," she whispered, hot tears streaming over her cheeks.

Her body plunged underwater. Although her arms were free, no amount of flapping could propel her to the surface. Still, she continued to struggle, her lungs feeling as if they would burst. A message from her brain screamed at her to open her mouth. To inhale.

Clamping her lips tight, she fought the instinct to breathe, knowing she'd fill her lungs with water. Bubbles from her nose rushed to the surface as she released some of her breath and eased the strain on her chest.

She was terrified, panic driving her to claw for the surface. But eventually, Jeni stopped fighting the downward pull. Her brain seemed to be working only in fits and starts and she needed to concentrate to… to…

She prepared herself for death. The vague question of what would happen to her body in Phoebe's shop drifted into, and then out of, her head. Impeding her reasoning was the need to breathe… to draw in a breath…

Breath.

Breath of Great Spirit.

Life or death.

Snapping out of her complacency, Jeni's fingers worked feverishly to find the opening to her skirt pocket and dig out the clay vessel.

Frantically, she prodded the rock sealed on the top, rushing the container to her mouth as soon as she felt it give. Lips secured around the opening, she let the rock fall onto her tongue and sucked the air into her lungs.

For a second, she did nothing but revel in the relief. As her faculties began to return, she realized the air in the jug should not have been enough to fill her lungs. And what about the herbs the medicine woman had sprinkled inside? Shouldn't she have sucked those in as well?

Her body was no longer being drawn down. As she floated toward the surface, Jeni wondered if she would be able to play dead, yet manage to roll face up, so when she did emerge, she could breathe.

Then she heard something, a type of commotion under the water. She stiffened. Should she stay still? Make a break for shore? Already her lungs were aching again.

Then a beefy arm encircled her waist and hauled her to the surface.

She gulped in air and sputtered, instinctively pushing against the arm.

"If you'd not struggle, Miss. I might get you to land."

Jeni blinked, startled. Was she being rescued?

"She alive?" The shout came from shore.

"She be breathin' all right." The reply rumbled from the chest of the man moving her swiftly through the water.

With her back to the shore, Jeni scanned the waters. The ferry had drifted downriver, but she could see it clearly.

It was empty.

Lost in Nowhere

"The ferryman." The words rasped from her strained throat.

"Ferryman?" His feet hit the river bottom and moments later so did hers. He steadied her, and then helped her from the water. "There ain't no ferryman, Miss."

Jeni lifted the sodden fabric of her dress and trudged down the wooded path. The sun was finally rising, making it easier for her to find her way. She filled her lungs with air, the action still feeling miraculous after nearly drowning. The thought sent a tremor through her and she took another breath, just to prove that she could.

The boy—she'd realized as she spoke to him that he was only a boy—who saved her had looked at her incredulously when she'd insisted she didn't need a doctor.

"Doc Emmet's place be just there." He pointed at the town that was taking on more detail as the sun inched over the horizon.

"I'm just wet, I assure you. By healer, I meant more of a… wise woman," Jeni hedged, still unsure what term would keep her out of trouble.

The boy's brother stepped forward. "Mayhap she talkin' 'bout the herb lady."

She turned to that boy with a broad smile. "Yes, right. The herb lady. Where might I find her?"

The boy wrinkled his nose at her request, but proceeded to give her directions. "Out t'other side of town. There be a trail in the wood, opposite direction of the river." He peered at her. "You want that we take you by Doc Emmet on the way? It's no trouble, Miss."

"No. I'll be fine." She offered what she hoped was a reassuring smile, meeting each boy's eyes. "Thank you for rescuing me. I wish I could repay you."

Her rescuer's neck turned red. "'Tweren't nothin', Miss." As she turned toward town, he said, "And Miss?" When she looked over her shoulder he lowered his voice. "Ain't a good idea, yer askin' folks 'bout a wise woman. You might as not get thrown in jail for frattinizin' with witches. Folks be touchy 'bout that."

"Thank you," Jeni said, grateful for the warning.

She hurried through town, managing to go mostly unnoticed due to the early hour, and found the path leading away from the river. Cold and exhausted, Jeni's first order of business—once the forest provided a sufficient barrier from prying eyes—was to rid herself of her saturated underskirts. Gathering the soggy mass, she stuffed it into some leafy brush at the bottom of a tree. Although she was no warmer, omitting the layers of water-logged cloth made walking easier, and she reasoned that the dress would dry faster without the skirts.

Finding only trees and woodland animals for what felt like a long time, Jeni began to wonder if she was on the right path, though she'd seen no other. Then the scent of woodsmoke wafted past her nose. Picking up the pace, the smell became stronger and constant. Soon, flashes of a cabin appeared between the trees and, after the next bend, she could see the entire small structure. The chimney belched white smoke and leafy bundles hung from the porch ceiling.

It had to be the right place. Jeni paused to take a deep inhale and exhale. This woman was likely her only chance of getting out of this body and back to her own.

She hadn't taken very many steps when a voice shouted, "Hold up!" The door inched open and a rifle muzzle extended through the skinny space. "Your business?"

Jeni staggered backward a step and raised her hands. "I... I need help," she stuttered, attention fixed on the barrel of the gun. What more could she say? If she announced she was from the future or stuck in Marielle's body, she'd probably be shot on sight.

"What might be the problem?"

She fought the urge to flee, forcing herself to respond. This was her last chance. "It's... uh... delicate." She peered over each shoulder in turn, reluctant to shout out her business. "It's spiritual in nature."

"I grow herbs for medicine. Don't want your kind of trouble." The gun was withdrawn, and the door started to close.

"Please," Jeni said. "I came here because someone in your family sent me."

"Who might that be?"

Jeni shook her head. "I don't know her name." She'd been tempted to blurt out "Phoebe" in hopes that it was a family name, but decided ignorance might be the best course of action.

"Please," she pleaded, her voice breaking. "I don't know who else can help." She allowed her despair to bubble up and tears pricked her eyes. "I just want to go home." The last came out as half-whisper, half-sob, and must have done the trick.

A pale face appeared in the slice of open door. "Have you a weapon?"

"No." Jeni held her arms out in a T.

"All right, then." The door swung inward, and a thin woman with a severe face appeared. She was not the person in the portrait—even taking into account the age difference—yet she shared a similar nose and mouth. "I shall check on those weapons meself." She reached her hands out as Jeni stepped onto the porch.

Jeni accommodated, again stretching out her arms.

"Fine, then." The woman stepped back so Jeni could enter, and then surveyed the forest outside before closing the door and securing the piece of wood that held it in place.

Although the walk from the river, through town and then through the woods had given her time to think about what she might say, Jeni still hadn't come to a conclusion. Everything she said was going to sound crazy to this woman.

"You be soaked to the bone." The woman pulled a three-legged stool to the fire and beckoned Jeni to sit. She took a cloth and pressed it to Jeni's head to help dry her hair. "Do tell the nature of help you be seeking."

Jeni sucked in a breath. "I'll tell you the entire story from the beginning to this moment. I swear that it is all true, but I know it will sound unbelievable."

"I shall be the judge," the woman said, hanging the damp towel on the back of a chair and then sinking into a rocker opposite Jeni.

*L*ost in *N*owhere

After the hours she'd spent damp and cold, the heat of the fire was like a tonic, renewing Jeni's optimism. She stretched her legs out, spreading the skirt of the dress so it could dry. Eyes on the dancing flames, she began her narrative with the apparitions of Marielle. She didn't bother with dates, as it made the story that much more outlandish, but if the woman asked, she would tell the truth.

The crackling fire seemed overloud in the silence after Jeni finished speaking. She could feel the weight of the woman's scrutiny. Her first question wasn't what Jeni had expected. "What be the name of the woman in the portrait you speak of?"

"Rose..." Jeni thought back to the conversation with Phoebe. "Rose..." What was the last name? It had made her think of poetry. Something from her English class... something amusing. A faint smile curved her lips. *Where's Waldo?* "Rose Emerson," she said triumphantly, recalling the trick she'd used to remember Ralph Waldo Emerson for her English exam.

The woman narrowed her eyes at Jeni. "Rose Emerson be the name of my niece. Her mama—my sister—and her papa live in nearby Bourbon. That my family did flee Salem be a secret none in these parts are privy to."

Jeni released the breath she'd been holding in a slow, steady stream.

"I be called Lydia." The woman rose from her chair. "For all of my life have I known and felt things others do not. Believing the unbelievable be my right state of mind." She opened a chest and squatted down, rummaging through it. Removing a bundle wrapped in cloth, she moved to the small table. "Join me." She gestured to the chair across from her.

Jeni moved to the table, already missing the warmth of the fire. Lydia untied the cloth to reveal a dark bowl filled with oddly shaped items with a yellow cast—the kind of yellow that comes with age. She swirled the bowl, jumbling the contents, and then cast them onto the tabletop.

Scattered across the wood surface, it was obvious the items were bones. Jeni straightened, pulling away, although she could tell the small bones were from an animal.

"A raven," the woman said, noticing Jeni's reaction. "It did not die by my hand. I found it." She spoke absently, her attention on the bones. "The bones do tell of duality, and hint of future events." Then Lydia looked up at Jeni, staring into her eyes for a moment. "I should like to know more of this battle."

Jeni furrowed her brow. "Battle?"

"This ferryman, did he not speak of it?"

Scrubbing her hands over her face, Jeni shook her head. "That was the first I heard of this struggle. I don't even know who the river spirit wants to fight."

Lydia studied the bones. "Yet somehow yours is a pivotal role."

"How can that be true? I don't even know the source of my ability, or how to use it properly." Tears threatened to spill and Jeni blinked them away. She'd reached the end of her rope. "I can't even help myself," she said miserably. "How can I possibly be of use to anyone or anything else?"

"Many mysteries do make this world. Rarely be

it our privilege to know what the future holds." The woman's eyes rose to Jeni's. "Mayhap you should think yourself fortunate that even this warning has come to you."

"Can… can you see if I am destined to remain as I am? Here? In this body?" The questions came out as a whisper. She almost didn't want to ask; didn't want to know.

Yet she had to know.

Lydia's lips curved in a gentle smile that softened her stern features. "Nature's laws have been set on end. You being the reason for it. I make no doubt the powers of the universe will be at my aid as I cast you out."

Jeni slumped as air rushed from her lungs. A fresh batch of tears stung her eyes, but for a different reason. This time, she was smiling.

*"By my unpardonable disobedience," she
said to herself, "I have caused
the most terrible misfortunes, which it
is not in my power to repair."*

Blondine ~ Comtesse de Ségur

Chapter 16

"Ice, go flip the sign to 'closed' and bolt the front
door," Phoebe said, spurring him into action as
she surrounded the large candle on the table with
three smaller ones.

Passing into the store, Ice moved mechanically,
only a fraction of his brain on the task at hand. He
swore under his breath. When he woke up this morning, his biggest concern had been making his flight
back to Minneapolis. Now he was frantic, wondering if Jeni's body was doomed to remain an empty
shell. An ache swelled in the back of his throat, and he
blinked back the sting of threatening tears.

Then a new thought settled like a stone in his
gut. It would be his responsibility to offer her parents
an explanation. What could he possibly say?

When Ice returned to the back room, Phoebe had
her phone on her ear. "As soon as you can get here.
Great. Thanks, Cecelia." Turning to him, her soft expression offered sympathetic understanding, but she

simply said, "We're going to need more energy than just the two of us."

"I should be able to get one, maybe two, more people." Ice took out his phone, realizing he had only Tyler's number. He shook his head, unable to imagine the turbulent reaction from Jeni's cousin. Instead, he rummaged in Jeni's purse and found her phone. Entering her passcode, he located Mandy in the contact list and dialed the number.

"Hi, Jeni."

"Mandy, it's Ice. Listen, I don't have time to explain. Jeni's in trouble and we're going to have a séance. We need more people. Will you come?"

She mumbled something to someone in the room with her. "Are you serious?"

"Deadly," he responded.

"Are you at your cabin?"

Ice pressed his fingers on his temple. "Memories and Magic. Please hurry." He ended the call. His throat felt thick, like he couldn't swallow. Seconds later, his phone buzzed. The message said it was from Tyler but the text read: *"Hey Ice, it's Mandy. We're on our way."*

So Tyler was with her—probably not because he wanted to take part in the séance, but because he was too pissed off to stay behind. "They're on their way," he told Phoebe. "I'll watch for them out front." He glanced at Jeni's slumped form before leaving the room. It would work, he told himself, trying to shift to a positive frame of mind. Phoebe would contact Jeni and bring her back from wherever she was.

As he peered out the front window, Ice

whispered the phrase over and over like a prayer. *This is going to work.*

What felt like an eternity passed before he saw Tyler's hatchback go by the store and around the corner. Ice tapped his thumb on the lock, looking in both directions for people on the sidewalk. Then Mandy came into view, Tyler trotting behind her.

Ice twisted the lock, pushing the door open as they approached.

"What's happened?" Mandy asked.

"And where's Jeni?" Tyler demanded, nostrils flared.

Resetting the bolt, Ice said, "She's back here." He strode toward the back room without meeting Tyler's eyes.

"Take a seat," Phoebe said as they entered. "My friend should be here any minute." She released the curtain in the doorway to block the light coming from the store windows.

Tyler ignored the chairs, advancing to where Jeni sat. "What's wrong with her?" He shook her shoulder.

"She's in a trance," Ice said. "She was altering things in her dreams about Marielle, trying to save Amakapa's soul." He half-expected Tyler to ask who and what he was talking about, but Mandy must have been keeping him up to date because he seemed to comprehend what Ice said.

"And? What happened?" Jeni's cousin demanded.

Ice looked to Phoebe, thinking Tyler might best accept the explanation if it came from her.

"We're not quite sure. It seems she's left her

body," Phoebe said. "Perhaps she went too far into the spirit world."

Tyler crossed his arms over his chest. "And what, exactly, do you plan to do about it?"

"Find her spirit," Mandy spoke up, hand sweeping toward the round table with candles in the center. "That's why we're having a séance."

A knock sounded from farther back in the store and Phoebe disappeared for a moment, returning with another woman who regarded Jeni curiously.

"This is Cecelia. She knows her way around a séance. Let's get started, shall we?" Phoebe nodded to Ice. "Help me with this." She reached for the seat of Jeni's chair.

Ice bent and lifted the other side of the chair, turning Jeni to face the table. When he stood, he saw Tyler and Mandy near the curtained doorway. Mandy had a hand on Tyler's arm, whispering insistently. Finally, they both approached the table, Jeni's cousin wearing a scowl.

"I need positive energy." Phoebe looked directly at Tyler. "If you're a non-believer or have a negative attitude, it would be best if you leave the room and wait in the store."

Tyler looked sideways at Mandy. "I told you," he muttered, pushing through the curtain.

Phoebe lit the candles and turned off the lights. "Okay, join hands and channel your energy toward me."

Ice tried to clear his mind of the fears running through his thoughts and project his spiritual force toward the medium, praying she would find Jeni and bring her back.

Lost in Nowhere

After some words that sounded Latin, Phoebe called Jeni's name. "Jeni Stonewall. We seek your spirit." A moment of silence stretched long. "Spirits, help me find Jeni Stonewall." She continued the mantra at least a half dozen times.

Everyone at the table started when a small clink sounded nearby.

"What was that?" Mandy whispered.

Ice searched the shadowy tabletop, eyes landing on the gold ring Phoebe had set there earlier. "I think it was Marielle's ring."

The ring lifted and dropped.

"Perhaps she has a message for us." Phoebe looked at Ice. "I'm going to allow her to speak through me. You can ask her questions if you wish."

Ice nodded, swallowing hard.

Moments later, the medium spoke. The voice was hers, but the quality had changed from mature to girlish. "I must express my gratitude to Jeni."

"What is your name?" Ice wasn't taking this contact at face value.

"Marielle Bernard. Jeni did save Amakapa's soul."

Ice shook his head. Fifteen or twenty minutes ago, Marielle had said everything was the same. They must be dealing with an impostor. He searched his memory of the dreams Jeni had told him about for something that only Marielle could know. "Uh... what was your horse's name?"

"Fleur."

Ice nodded to Mandy and Cecelia while considering what else he could ask. If he was speaking to the spirit who had sent the dreams, it would've known the horse's name. Instead, he tried something Jeni had changed. "Where did you place the tulips Claude brought the night you went to dinner?"

"No. Not tulips, daisies. The windowsill be the usual spot. Only the night of Claude's proposal, I did display them on the counter just above the space occupied by the cash box. There, Papa could not help but see them. What be the reason for asking such questions?"

"Because Marielle told us nothing had changed."

"Yes. I spoke true when no change occurred. Yet Amakapa's soul be on the other side now. The light appeared as it has not for centuries and in it, my love awaits. I wished only to extend my thanks to Jeni. I cannot see her spirit gathered with you. Is she not there?"

"Her body is here, but her spirit is not. We were trying to reach her when we reached you," Ice responded, his voice clipped. "If Amakapa's soul is saved, how did Jeni do it?"

"That, I do not know."

"The night Amakapa died, what happened after your father locked you up?" Ice knew it was the point in the past that Jeni had returned to.

"I did holler for the slaves to come, to release me. Mayhap they did not hear my cries, but no one came so did I try to pick the lock."

"Did you pick the lock?" Ice was feeling confident that the spirit was Marielle after all.

"I couldn't… I don't think… I'm not sure. My memories be most befuddled after that."

Ice met Mandy's eyes, answering her raised eyebrows with a shrug. "What's the next thing you remember from that night?"

"Not a thing. I… I must have fled to Ste. Genevieve. It was there that I awoke the next day."

Ice closed his eyes for a moment. This was a dead end. Then he flicked his gaze from Mandy to Cecelia, wondering if they had further questions.

Mandy spoke up. "Marielle?"

"Yes."

"Will you look for Jeni? And if you find her on the other side, ask her to contact us?"

"'Twas never my intention that her spirit be lost in the search for Amakapa. Be assured that I will do my best."

"Goodbye, Marielle," Ice said.

Phoebe's chin fell to her chest and Cecelia rose to turn on the light. A moment later, the medium raised her head. "What did you find out?"

"Assuming that was Marielle—and I'm pretty convinced that it was her—she has no memories of what happened after her father locked her up," Ice replied, his voice lacking energy. "I wonder if that means Jeni took control of her body."

A crease deepened on Phoebe's brow as she regarded him. "Unfortunately, that makes sense."

"That can really happen?" Ice asked.

"I honestly don't know." She sighed. "The spirit realm is shrouded in mystery."

Cecelia cleared her throat. "If Marielle remembers waking the next morning, wouldn't that mean Jeni's spirit no longer resided within her?"

The medium's eyes tightened as she stared at her friend. Then she nodded slowly. "Presumably."

Ice glanced at Jeni, still slumped in her chair. "If her spirit isn't in the past, or in the present, or on the other side, where else could it be?"

His eyes searched the faces around the table.

They all wore blank looks.

Jeni woke to find Lydia bustling about the cabin. A lit oil lamp cast the thin woman's shadow on the walls, and Jeni was surprised to see that it was dark outside. "Did I sleep all day?" she asked, sitting up.

"Right past sunset." Lydia gathered Marielle's clothes and draped them at the end of the bed.

After their conversation earlier, Lydia had warmed some soup for Jeni and then gave her a shift to wear while her clothes dried. "Take rest," she'd said, indicating the bed. "My preparations do take some time."

Jeni hadn't realized how bone weary she really was until she stretched out on the bed and pulled up the quilt. Her intention to observe Lydia had melted away as the comfort of dry warmth overcame her impatience to go back to her own body.

Now, a streak of alarm brought Jeni fully awake and she swung her legs over the side of the mattress. "Why didn't you wake me?"

"You were all but exhausted. And be assured, nighttime be best for this spell."

Jeni's stomach burned with worry, wondering what had transpired in present time while she'd slept all day. She'd been in this time for nearly a full twenty-four hours. Had as much time passed in the present? What did her parents do? Was her body in a hospital? Did they hold Ice responsible? The last question spurred a sharp ache in her chest and she pressed her hand to her heart.

Closing her eyes, Jeni took a deep breath. Worrying wasn't going to change anything. Reaching for Marielle's clothes, she changed from the borrowed nightdress and did her best to neaten the bed. Then she approached the table where Lydia sat.

The bones, bowl and cloth the woman used earlier had been put away. A bundle of dried herbs and a small cameo pin lay near the oil lamp. Jeni lifted the pin to examine it. "This is pretty."

"And be it familiar to you?" Lydia regarded her curiously.

Jeni shook her head. "I don't—" She broke off, looking up. "You're wondering if Phoebe has it. I don't know." She thought for a moment, something itching her brain. "However, I'm pretty sure Rose is wearing it in the portrait."

The woman's eyes shone. "My grandmother passed it to me. As I will die a spinster, be it my intention that Rose have it. Even though this pin may not be in my family in your time, 'tis my hope that it remain with my kin a while. Foregoing a personal item of yours, I shall direct the spell by channeling my own bloodline through this cameo."

"What do I need to do?" Jeni pulled out a chair and sat down at the table.

Turning up the lamp, Lydia touched the bundle of dried herbs to the flame. Jeni recognized the homey scent immediately: sage. "In your mind should you strip away this physical body and all of its sensations: thoughts, emotions and sentiment. Be it that you lay your consciousness bare." She waved the smoldering bundle of sage as she circuited the room.

Unnerved by the prospect of failure, Jeni reminded herself of the seemingly impossible things she'd achieved during the riverboat cruise, when Ice's friend Dale had taught her Druid magic to combat the mythic Celtic witch.

"I shall call out Marielle," the woman explained, snuffing the sage at the edge of the hearth. "You might not be so much cast out as crowded out. It be by your leave to withdraw your essence and return to your physical self."

"Sure. No big deal." Jeni's attempt at a laugh sounded more like a whimper.

Lydia lifted a shawl from the back of the rocker and handed it to Jeni. "We shall employ the doorway." She pointed to the front door of the cabin, then picked up a pan sitting near the hearth and continued, "When you be in place, shall I transfer a hot coal to these herbs and move the pan to your lap. With your face above, draw the shawl over your head to touch your knees, capturing the smoke. Breathe the smoke into your lungs. The effect be helpful in peeling your spirit from this physical body."

Jeni understood Lydia's use of the cabin doorway—it was a *between* place, neither inside nor out. It should aid her journey back to her body. She wondered what kind of herbs were in the pot, but it didn't matter much, as long as it worked. "What about Marielle?"

"I shall see to her. By employing this method, likely as not there will be no memory of the time you possessed her."

Jeni frowned. "Remember, her father is a horrible man. I wouldn't want him to take his wrath out on you for helping her."

Lydia smiled. "Rest assured I will give that consideration. My privacy here be necessity. Mayhap Marielle will not remember myself or this place." The woman faced Jeni. "Would you be ready, then?"

Sucking in a breath, Jeni met Lydia's eyes and said, "Yes."

Taking the rifle from where it leaned against the doorframe, the woman slung it under her arm and then unbarred the door. Moving the weapon to her shoulder and her finger to the trigger, she stepped out onto the porch and surveyed the darkness. Once she was satisfied, she returned to the cottage and motioned Jeni toward the doorway.

Jeni drew the shawl around her shoulders and dropped to a cross-legged position on the threshold. She watched as Lydia picked up a pair of iron tongs and thrust them deep into the red-hot coals of the fire, stirring them about. Selecting a chunk that was probably equal to two of the briquettes Jeni's dad used in the barbecue grill, the woman dropped it into the pan. She placed a cloth under the pan and passed it to Jeni, who lowered it into her lap.

Smoke had already begun to rise as Jeni hunched forward, pulling the shawl completely over her head and down to her knees. The fumes smelled similar to marijuana, but she also detected a bitter, less green smell. The tissue inside her nose stung as she breathed in the smoke, so she inhaled through her mouth, finding the burn in the back of her throat preferable.

Her head began to swim and she heard Lydia chanting. Jeni turned her consciousness inward, blocking out the sore limbs, watery eyes and aching throat. Then she employed a meditation technique she'd learned, letting thoughts that entered her head drift through without contemplation. She had no name, no standing in life—she just *was*.

And then all of her senses were nullified. She floated, weightless, in infinite blackness. After a second—or a millennium, there was no way of knowing—shapes began to take on dimension, and she realized the shawl and pot of herbs had disappeared. Her surroundings appeared *thin*.

Able to make out the murky shape of trees and the flat surface on which she sat, Jeni recognized where she was. She was in the *between*. The space between the living world and the other world. Dale had taught her to shift to the *between* at dusk or dawn, or in a mist. Lydia had employed the doorway to make the transition.

Excitement flared. Jeni had been here before and knew exactly what to do. She should be able to simply shift back into her body. Closing her eyes, she called to mind where she'd left her physical self. Just as she'd peeled the layers away from her consciousness, she now added them back on. The feel of the wooden chair beneath her, the smell of herbs and incense… She fleshed it all out and then opened her eyes.

Nothing had changed. She was still in the hazy *between*.

Lost in Nowhere

Staring at the wood planks in front of her, Jeni tried to remember what she'd learned from Dale nine months ago. It had been a crash course in order to defeat the Korrigan and she hadn't used or practiced what she'd learned since then. There'd been something about a feeling — Jeni had thought of it like the way her stomach dropped when a roller coaster plunged down a steep hill. Dale had told her not to resist that feeling, but to go with it.

Jeni closed her eyes again, opening herself to possibility and expanding her senses for something magical about to happen. The roller coaster was cresting the rise, tipping forward… until momentum propelled the train down the tracks. She evoked that feeling: the lurch of her stomach, the burst of adrenaline.

Her mind thought it, but her body didn't feel it. Jeni was crestfallen, yet not surprised, when she opened her eyes to find herself in the same spot on Lydia's porch, in the misty *between*.

Except a glance over her shoulder revealed that the cabin was gone. She rose and stepped to the grass, watching in alarm as the forest started to melt — or maybe the better word was dissolve. Trees, bushes and grass dissipated until there was only gray fog.

She'd never experienced the *between* fading away. Frantic, Jeni spun in a circle. She was wrong. The gray murkiness wasn't fog, because she could see the moon clearly. The giant orb seemed to be sitting at ground level, the way a huge orange harvest moon hung low in the sky in the fall. A single tree remained, starkly silhouetted against the moon's golden glow. She waited for this tree, too, to dissolve, but it stood firm.

Jeni moved toward the tree, noticing how black, how two-dimensional it seemed, like a cardboard cut-out or a stage prop.

And then a shape separated from it.

A human shape.

Jeni stopped in her tracks, relief warring with alarm.

"*Bonjou*, child," a male voice beckoned. "Come. I am da way home."

After the appearance of the ferryman—the river spirit—she should have been suspicious of this being, but instead she felt an odd kinship. The way she imagined an emigrant felt when visiting their homeland.

Cautiously, Jeni advanced.

The man wore a formal black suit, complete with top hat. A red flower—a carnation, perhaps—was tucked into the hat band, complementing his ruby tie as well as his blood-red cloak. He radiated exuberance and power. When he spread his arms out wide, the cloak flowed over heavily muscled shoulders.

"You are wise to show care, girl." His voice was rich and bold with an accent that Jeni couldn't place, although it conjured visions of tropical islands. "Daemons of da night bring danger. I am refuge."

Peering nervously over both shoulders at the void around her, Jeni asked, "Where am I?"

"You are *nowhere*." His narrowed eyes challenged her.

"Am I stuck here?"

"Your choice, child. I offer da way back."

He made it sound like a trap, or some kind of

puzzle she needed to solve. "Who... who are you?"

"Call me Lord of the Moon." He lifted his top hat and bent into a small bow.

It hadn't escaped her notice that the man had shown no surprise at her presence. "My name is Jeni. Although I have a feeling you already know that."

"What I know," he said, pointing directly at her face, "Your *maji* be lost, Priestess. You must regain da *maji*. To be *mambo*."

Jeni frowned, blinking. "I don't understand. *Maji*? *Mambo*?"

"Magick, child. What you once were." His eyes shifted from side to side. "Da daemons grow restless."

Hugging her arms to her chest, Jeni peered over her shoulder, seeing only the eerie grayness. Enough riddles, she wanted to get out of here. "Is that how... how I get back to my body? Back to the present?"

He crooked a finger, bidding her to come closer. With no other recourse, Jeni shuffled forward, noticing the whites of his eyes had a yellow cast, even contrasted against the burnt umber of his skin and irises. He reached out and Jeni stiffened, flinching as he cupped the base of her head in his large hand. There was a moment of discomfort when his hot fingers splayed against her skin, and then the images rushed in.

Flames leaped for the dark sky, licking up oxygen and consuming the wood heaped on the dirt surface. A circle of figures undulated to the rhythmic beat of a drum. She, too, moved her body to the beat, arms in the air and hips swinging. Her chest vibrated with the chant that fell from her lips and a heavy weight around her neck shifted in a sinuous motion.

All at once, the vision winked out and the man in the top hat was before her. "What you see be your destiny, child. I have claimed you for a guay. When da mark complete, a guay will call, and you best be *mambo*."

Jeni wanted to ask what a guay was and about the mark he spoke of, but she was just so tired— physically, mentally and emotionally exhausted. She wanted to go back to her own reality. So she nodded.

"You choose to leave, a promise be made. Your return be the reward for your calling. A debt you will pay to a guay in the battle to come."

Her head reeling with confusion, Jeni watched as the man grabbed the edge of his cloak with the hand closest to the tree. When he furled the material outward, the cloak and the tree seemed to blend together, forming an opening of utter blackness.

"Allons," he said, motioning with his free hand. "Go."

All Jeni understood at that moment was that her choices were to go back to her own time or remain *nowhere*. It wasn't much of a decision, really. She ducked under the man's arm and stepped into the inky dark.

*It often happens that one needs only to determine a person's
weak points to win their trust and do
with them what you will.*

The Blue Bird ~ Madame d'Aulnoy

Chapter 17

*W*hen Jeni opened her eyes to the round table in Phoebe's back room, she was shocked. She blinked rapidly, taking in the tense atmosphere and hushed conversation.

Ice was first to notice that she was conscious and swooped in, bending to wrap his arms around her. "Oh, God." The words were muffled against her neck. "Don't ever do that to me again. Don't leave me like that."

Then everyone was speaking at once and Jeni let go of the determined facade that she'd fought to keep in place throughout her ordeal. Tears welled and spilled over, rolling down her cheeks and into Ice's hair. When he pulled away, she dropped her face into her hands and sobbed.

"It's okay," Ice soothed, rubbing her back. "Everything's okay now."

Phoebe brought her a bottle of water and a box of tissue. Pulling out a tissue, Jeni uttered a wry laugh as she wiped her eyes. "That's just it, everything *is* okay now." Her breath hitched, interrupting her. "But I was nearly convinced I'd never get back here."

Ice sank into the chair next to her and scooted it close, laying a hand on her shoulder.

Sniffling, Jeni raised her face to see who was in the room. A woman she didn't recognize whispered something to Phoebe, squeezing her hand. Then she offered Jeni a gentle smile before exiting through the back door. Mandy sat down in a chair across the table, eyeing her curiously while Tyler stood just inside the curtained doorway. Oddly, he didn't look angry; a line of concern marked his brow.

Staring at the clock on the desk behind Phoebe, Jeni asked, "11:35? Is it... is it still Saturday?"

"All day," Tyler stated.

"Morning?" Jeni looked at Phoebe.

The medium nodded. "Yes, it's Saturday morning."

"Wow. I thought I was gone an entire day." Jeni's mind raced to reconcile her perception of the passage of time.

Mandy spoke up. "Where were you?"

"Uh... it seemed like I was in the past. In Marielle." Jeni's eyes slid to Ice and then back to Phoebe. "Can you...?"

Phoebe's lips curved upward. "We've already heard from Marielle. Whatever you did, or whatever happened, was successful. Amakapa's soul moved into the afterlife and Marielle has joined him there."

Jeni's heart skipped a beat and her eyes stretched round. "You mean, it worked?"

Phoebe nodded and asked, "What happened?"

$\mathcal{L}$ost in $\mathcal{N}$owhere

Recounting her experience, Jeni admitted where she'd gone wrong. "I wanted her to get out of that wash building so bad…" Eyes closed, she shook her head. "I should've immediately pulled back. Although I have no idea if I could have. But I was caught up in the urgency of the moment. I…" Jeni dropped her chin and turned slightly toward Ice, meeting his gaze. "I'm sorry," she whispered.

Silence filled the room as he filled his chest with air. "It's over now," he said, his voice tight.

"So once they had his body, Amakapa's tribe must have performed a funeral ceremony," Phoebe mused. "And his soul made it to the otherworld."

Ice nodded, then turned to Jeni. "How were you able to separate from Marielle, then? Did the Native Americans help you?"

"Um, they helped, but not with that. I decided to seek out Phoebe's ancestor in Ste. Genevieve."

Phoebe straightened. "Did you meet Rose?"

"Actually, no. I met her aunt, Lydia."

"What was she like?"

"Very cautious," Jeni said, glad that she'd skipped over the confrontation with the ferryman. She was anxious to talk to Ice alone, so she quickly explained how Lydia had placed her in a doorway to cast her out of Marielle's body. Her throat was dry when she finished, and Jeni twisted the lid off the water bottle, taking a long drink.

A muffled alert chimed and Tyler pulled his phone from his jacket. "It's Jake. We gotta get going if we want to be part of the caravan back to Wisconsin," he said to Mandy.

"All right." Mandy stepped forward and touched Jeni's shoulder. "I'm glad you're okay. That was pretty scary."

"Thanks," Jeni said. "And thanks for coming to help."

Unexpectedly, when Mandy moved away, Tyler stood there. "Do me a favor, Cuz." His voice was soft. "Don't ever pull this crap again." There was no mockery in his tone, only sincerity. A corner of his mouth curled slightly, and then he turned away.

Jeni looked at Ice and they exchanged a surprised glance. She patted his knee. "We've been gone a while. I should text my mom and let her know we're heading back."

Finished sending the message, Jeni looked up to see Phoebe bent over her desk. She straightened, a slip of paper in her hand. "Congratulations on your success," she said. "Although I'm going to side with your cousin and recommend you not try something like this again."

Jeni nodded, uttering a sheepish chuckle as she hugged the medium. "Thank you for helping us. Thank you for everything."

As they pulled apart, Phoebe handed Jeni the slip of paper. "This is my cell number. Please call or text if you need anything."

"Thanks," Jeni said, pleased. "I really appreciate it."

The proprietor smiled. "It's the most activity I've had in my spiritual life in quite a while. I'm just glad you're back in one piece, so to speak."

Ice said nothing when Jeni handed him the car

keys. He opened her door and then slid into the driver's seat.

Jeni waited until Ice had navigated through town, and then said, "I left some stuff out."

"I know." He sounded wary and kept his eyes on the road. "You never said how the Native Americans helped you."

Jeni told Ice about the medicine woman and the *Breath of Great Spirit,* how she'd returned for the ring, and then fled from Jean Bernard. "I was so frightened of him that I ran onto the ferry without paying any attention. And then…" Her throat seemed to close up.

Ice glanced at her. "What?" he encouraged softly.

"I was face to face with the river spirit." Her voice faltered as she forced the words out. The skin on Ice's face grew taut as she recounted the conversation with the ferryman and the way the water enveloped her.

"That's why we didn't encounter some kind of supernatural minion this time." Ice's tone was bitter, the words clipped. "The spirit itself was behind this."

"Do you think he sent Marielle?"

"No. He used Marielle. Remember when Phoebe asked if there were two spirits?"

Jeni nodded.

"Well, there were. The river spirit convinced Marielle to give him contact to your link, telling her that he would usher Amakapa's soul to the other side once you found him."

"He sent the dreams," Jeni concluded. "But why lure me into the past to confront me?"

Ice shook his head as he clicked the turn signal

and slowed. "Did he want you to join him for something that happened in the past?"

"I don't think so. That wasn't the only mention of a coming battle. Getting back here wasn't as simple as Lydia sitting me in a doorway." They were climbing the hill to the row of cabins lining the ridge. "I thought I went into the *between*. You know, what Dale taught me about."

Ice nodded as he rolled to a stop and turned the engine off. "Why do I get the feeling you weren't able to shift out of there?"

"You're right. I couldn't." She described how things in the *between* seemed to melt away and then she saw the moon and the tree, and the man with the top hat. "He told me I was *nowhere*. Everything he said to me was cryptic. But he did mention a battle."

The screen door on the cabin squealed and Jeni's dad emerged, moving toward them purposefully. Heaving a sigh, Jeni opened her door and Ice followed suit.

"Glad you're back," her dad said. "I've got my fishing gear packed and I'm ready to load it into the car." He took the keys from Ice.

It was bizarre, adjusting to normal and acting as if she hadn't just spent nearly a day in another time, in another person. The sound of her parents talking as they gathered their things helped her feel more grounded, as did packing her own suitcase.

She swept the kitchen and dining area while Ice vacuumed the rug in the living room. When they were finished, Jeni sought out her mom. "Is there anything else we should do?"

£ost in ℵowhere

"Not really." Her mom finished zipping a suit-case and set it upright. "We've got a little time to kill."

"Then we're going for a walk," Jeni said.

She'd just reached the living room where Ice was waiting when her mom's voice came from the bedroom. "Hey, what did you end up getting for Carolyn?"

Jeni locked eyes with Ice, her jaw dropping. She'd completely forgotten about getting Carolyn a gift! Ice's focus darted to her bedroom doorway, back to her and then to the doorway again. Unsure what he was hinting at, Jeni backed toward her bedroom as her mom entered the room. The only thing Jeni could think of was the ring. She'd dropped it into her change purse before they left Phoebe's shop. "I... uh... hang on a sec." Jeni shot Ice a questioning look.

"She'll get a kick out of it." Ice's stare attempted to convey a message.

Pausing inside the bedroom, Jeni wondered what Ice meant by "a kick out of it." He couldn't mean the ring; there wasn't anything amusing about it. Stumped, she reached for her purse on the dresser, when it suddenly stuck her. Ice was brilliant!

This not only solved the problem of Carolyn's gift, but also provided an explanation for her pur-chase. As she revealed the Ouija board to her mom, she said, "After listening to you and Aunt Jessie, when I saw this, I couldn't resist."

Her mom laughed, stepping closer to look at the box. "Wow, it's old. It could be a collector's item. I don't know what Carolyn's mother is going to think about it, though." She raised her eyebrows at Jeni.

Pursing her lips, Jeni responded, "Well, at least she can blame it on me." She exchanged a knowing glance with her mom. Carolyn's mother was exasperatingly strict. Who knew what her views on a Ouija board might be?

With the box returned to her room, Jeni and Ice left for their walk. "Thanks for saving me back there," Jeni said. "Have I told you lately that you're amazing?"

"Not today," he replied.

She caught his grin and returned it. "You're amazing." She bumped her shoulder on his.

"So tell me what this man in a top hat said to you," Ice prompted.

"I asked him who he was, and he said he was the Lord of the Moon." She chewed her bottom lip, thinking. "He said he was the way home. And he called me a priestess."

"Isn't that what Princess Itasca called you? A priestess?"

Jeni nodded. "Yeah, she did. But this guy said I'd lost my maji, or magic, I guess. And I had to get it back to be... uh... All I can remember is it sounded like a Latin dance."

Ice cast her a sidelong glance. "A Latin dance?"

Jeni shrugged. "A lot of what he said didn't seem to make sense."

Ice stopped when they approached the path to the overlook. "You want to go down here?"

Jeni nodded, finally struck by the significance of what she'd accomplished. "Why not? I won't see Marielle. She's gone." As she followed Ice down the narrow path, her lips curved. She'd done it. She'd saved Amakapa's soul and helped Marielle to cross to the other side. Of course she'd done it all wrong and had a great deal to learn, but she had used her ability for good. The feeling inside her was like a bite of her grandma's warm apple pie.

In the small clearing at the end of the path, they sat with their backs against a boulder, looking out over the flood plains. Ice settled his arm across Jeni's shoulders and she wriggled a little closer. "I'm sorry, Ice. I didn't mean to do that to you. I know how awful it was when you were kidnapped. I never would have wanted you to be in the same position."

"I should have stopped you as soon as I felt like something was wrong."

Jeni snorted. "Yeah, 'cause that would've worked." She shook her head. "No. This is on me. I went too far. I let my emotions get the better of me. I need to learn control."

They sat in silence for a few minutes and then Jeni said, "I hate when we have to separate."

"Me too."

Jeni looked up at him and he leaned down and kissed her slowly, almost reverently. She responded readily, hungry to experience something real, something she thought she'd lost. "Wow," she whispered when they broke apart. "You are getting good at avoiding the images."

"I hadn't even thought of it," Ice said. He interlaced his fingers with hers and his soft expression transformed to a troubled frown.

"What is it?" Jeni asked, feeling her chest tighten

uncomfortably.

"I don't feel your spirituality."

Straightening her back, Jeni stared at him. "What do you mean?"

"I didn't think about changing my inner balance because it usually happens naturally now, and you only see a few visions at first. But you didn't see anything." He took both of her hands in his, staring into her eyes intently. "I can't feel the connection. The shamanic connection."

Jeni felt the blood drain from her face. "Oh, no. No." She scrubbed her cheeks with her hands as the gibberish spoken by the Lord of the Moon began to make sense. "My maji. He said I lost it. Was he referring to my spiritual ability?"

"But how —"

Jeni cut Ice off, the synapses of her brain firing rapidly as pieces of the puzzle fell into place. "That's why I couldn't get back. Why I couldn't withdraw from Marielle. Even when Lydia cast me out and I landed in the *between,* I couldn't shift back to my reality. I couldn't do anything because I'd lost my ability." Her heart beat hollowly.

"How?" Ice furrowed his brow. "When?"

Jeni thought back over everything she now knew. "*He* sent the dreams," she said with surety. "The river spirit. He must have sent the dreams to lure me in and push me too far. And when I took control of Marielle, I lost my ability."

Ice nodded slowly. "I could buy that. As if you burnt it out," he stated. "Or stripped it away." Then he turned to her. "Except why strip your ability if he wanted you to join him?"

Jeni shook her head, puzzled. "He said I'm a conduit to his greatest foe. Maybe he only needed to go through me to reach his enemy."

They were both quiet for a time, lost in thought.

"Or maybe," Jeni said. "Maybe he could restore my ability. Because the man in the top hat said I must get my maji back. That makes me think there must be a way to restore it."

Ice locked eyes with Jeni. "So maybe, ultimately, the river spirit did you a favor. If you don't have your ability, you can't be used as a pawn in some other-worldly battle."

The ramifications of her situation were beginning to sink in. "But if I can't communicate with the spirit world, how will I know if Marielle is able to find my ancestors?"

"You don't need a special ability to use a Ouija board," Ice said. "And Phoebe gave you her number. Maybe she knows of authentic mediums you can meet with once you get home. I can even try to contact Marielle during a vision quest."

"Okay, sure... but I also made a promise." As Jeni explained that the top hat man had made her see a vision similar to those Ice caused when they made skin to skin contact, her hand slid to the back of her neck, remembering the heat of the man's hand there. She stopped talking abruptly when the pad of her finger brushed over a bump. Pushing her other fingers into the hair at the base of her head, Jeni gaped at Ice, goosebumps tingling across her shoulders.

"What?" he asked, reading the alarm in her eyes.

"He said he marked me." She lifted her hair with one hand and turned her head. "What does this look like?" She ran her fingers over the series of bumps.

Ice parted her hair with his fingers. There was an uncomfortable long pause before he answered. "It looks like raised scars."

"He claimed me for something called a guay." Jeni's voice was quiet, resolute. "He said when the mark is complete, a guay would call on me." She dropped her hair and turned to face him. "He said I'd better be ready for the coming battle."

"You promised to fight in the battle?" Ice asked.

Jeni mentally replayed the last of her conversation with the Lord of the Moon. "I kinda did. My return was the reward for my calling." She searched his eyes. "I couldn't stay there. In… in *nowhere*. So I willingly ducked under his cape to return here."

Feeling the weight of the decision she'd made, Jeni hesitated, finding it hard to admit out loud what she knew in her gut to be true. "I'm indebted, Ice. I have no choice but to regain my ability and be ready for the battle."

A *few things before you go...*

If you're wondering what Jeni's going to do now that she's lost her spiritual ability, don't worry, the next book in the *Legacy in Legend* Series is well underway! Here's a little teaser:

Jeni arrives in Memphis desperate to mend her spiritual ability. But a bargain with a crossroads demon lands her in a dangerous battle of wits with a vengeful entity that draws power from the consumption of human souls. With her family slated as the next victims, Jeni must rely on intelligence and sheer cleverness to thwart this deadly foe.

If you'd like an occasional email update about my books, you can join my Reader Group at www.barbarapietron.com. (I promise I don't send a lot of email.) There's a bunch of free stuff on my website for Reader Group members: a *Legacy in Legend* series prequel, short stories and some other fun things. I also post updates on Instagram or Facebook along with book reviews and recommendations.

Can I ask you a favor? Would you leave a review for this book on Amazon or Goodreads? Aside from buying my books, this is the single best thing you could do for me. You don't need to write anything fancy, or outline the story, or anything like that. Just say if you liked the book and maybe what you liked about it. Reviews do more than help others decide what to read next, they also encourage booksellers to promote my books to potential readers. A review is a priceless gift that keeps on giving.

I love to build my stories around real places

and historical events. When I found The Curse of Kaskaskia legend online, I was fascinated by the tragic fate of this once booming town. Perhaps Marielle and Amakapa are merely fictional characters of legend, who knows? But the Mississippi River did change course due to a flood in 1881, joining the Kaskaskia River and separating the town of Kaskaskia from the state of Illinois. Likewise, a disastrous flood in 1785 prompted the gradual relocation of Ste. Genevieve to its present site. I visited both places, and if you ever find yourself in the area, Ste. Genevieve—the oldest town west of the Mississippi River—is worth a stop. Full of historic buildings and colonial charm, it's like a step back in time. There's not a lot to see in Kaskaskia, but crossing the bridge over the creek that was once the mighty Mississippi River is impactful, bringing past events into stark reality. Check it out if you're into that kind of thing. I thought it was cool.

Until we meet again, happy reading!

Barb

Thanks

My husband took vacation time to travel with me to Ste. Genevieve, Missouri and Kaskaskia, Illinois, so I could see the actual setting of my story. That's first-rate support and I love and appreciate him for that. Aside from the historic sites, we found an excellent doughnut shop, a cool old-fashioned diner and ate some delicious schnitzel and spaetzle. Good trip!

My beta readers, Nikki Pietron, Donna LaTour Thompson and Judy Skemp, deserve special acknowledgement for reading imperfect drafts and giving invaluable feedback. I could not do this without them.

During the production of this book I started a writer's group. Having a group of writers that know your work, brainstorm with you, and listen to your writing woes is a wonderful thing. Being able to support the others in your group the same way is good for the soul. I owe them all a debt of gratitude.

This book would not be in your hands without the hard work of Scribe Publishing Company. To Jennifer Baum, Allison Janicki, and especially, Mel Corrigan—who has put so much time and effort into this book—I offer my sincere thanks. I love collaborating with all of you.

For artwork, we had the good fortune to work with Maria Petrenko, who produced yet another beautiful cover for the *Legacy in Legend* series. And for

Lost in Nowhere

the first time, my book includes interior illustrations! I have Allison Janicki to thank for creating the super cool family tree and the historic map of Kaskaskia. She made this new and exciting element a lot of fun.

For those of you who read my books, write a review, offer opinions on cover art, ask how my writing is going, read my emails, follow me on Facebook and/or Instagram or any of the many other things you do to support me, please know that I appreciate you. Writing can be a lonely occupation; you make all the difference. Thanks for that.

About the author

Photo Credit: Cassie Pietron

Barbara Pietron is author of the Legacy in Legend series, *Heart of Ice* (prequel to the series) and stand-alone novel, *Soulshifter. Thunderstone*, Pietron's debut novel and Book One of the *Legacy in Legend* series, was awarded Indiefab's 2013 Book of the Year Finalist by Foreword Reviews, and was a quarter-finalist in the 2012 Amazon Breakthrough Novel Award contest. She has been a contributing writer for *AAA Living* and *FamilyFun.*

After years in the corporate world, Pietron now pursues her passion for books and the written word, balancing her time between writing and working in two libraries. She lives in Michigan with her husband and sassy cat. Find out more at www.barbarapietron. com.